c

Kusanagi

By the same author

The Armageddon Trade

The Twain Maxim

CLEM
CHAMBERS

Kusanagi

NO EXIT PRESS

First published in 2011 by
No Exit Press, an imprint of Oldcastle Books Ltd,
P.O.Box 394, Harpenden, Herts, AL5 1XJ
www.noexit.co.uk

A CIP catalogue record for this book is available from the British Library

ISBN
978-1-84243-342-3 (hardcover)
978-84243-367-6 (paperback)
978-1-84243-424-6 (epub)
978-1-84243-453-6 (mobi)
978-1-84243-451-2 (pdf)

2 4 6 8 10 9 7 5 3 1

Typeset by SunTec, Web Services Pvt. Ltd. India
Type size 11/13.5 pt in Minion Pro

Printed and bound in Great Britain
by CPI Antony Rowe, Chippenham and Eastbourne

To
Barney and Oscar

1

London, March 2013

The sun had only just risen over the rooftops and had not penetrated the low, sullen cloud that threatened to drizzle on him. The tide was coming up quickly with a sound of trickling ripples, the rising water driving him further up the Thames foreshore and away from the low tidal points that invariably held the most interesting flotsam. He had found a rather nice George IV farthing to add to his collection. The little orange-red copper disc had lain below the cold grey water of the river Thames for two hundred years. Each find was a little redemption, an inanimate resurrection.

Jim climbed in carefully through the lounge window of his home. It was a large part of an old converted warehouse, now transformed into a riverside townhouse that retained an eighteenth-century feel and a faintly nautical character. He loved his personal ladder onto the tidal Thames; it was a portal to another world. As he clambered in, he tried not to catch his muddy boots on anything along the route from the rungs to the thick bristle mat on the lounge floor. He never seemed to manage re-entry without leaving some slightly smelly dob behind. Getting up to his home from the Wapping foreshore without leaving a trace was a challenge he always set himself.

His lead foot set safely on the mat, he leant forwards and turned nimbly in a pirouette to bring the other through the window. He didn't clip his foot on the frame, so he might have pulled off a flawless entry. He looked back. There wasn't a mark. He scanned for signs of mud that might have flicked off his boots and splashed out on random trajectories. He couldn't see any evidence of it. He smiled with satisfaction. At last he had managed it.

Stafford, his butler, entered with a tray of breakfast. There was a newspaper on the side. 'Apparently you are the most eligible bachelor in Britain.' Stafford put the tray on the coffee-table by the sofa. 'According to the headlines, "Hot Billionaire Gives".' He opened the tabloid at the centre spread and laid it, too, on the coffee-table with a snap.

'What?' Jim stepped forwards to grab the paper. He stopped mid-stride, his muddy boot on the carpet. He stepped back hastily onto the mat.

'No good deed goes unpunished,' remarked Stafford, glancing quickly at the muddy bootprint. He looked quite amused as he turned and left the room.

Jim slipped his boots off and went to his breakfast tray. He grabbed the paper. Someone had blown the whistle about him and his money. If he hadn't started giving it away, no one would have known he had so much, except the taxman. Now it looked like the press were going to make a big thing of it. He felt a little flattered, but the article had a nasty edge: it seemed to suggest there was something mysterious about him, something sinister about 'the richest man under thirty in Britain'. He snorted. 'No one seems to know where his £2 billion fortune comes from.' He wondered what they would write if they knew it was actually £10 billion.

2

Tokyo, *March 1970*

Akira Nakabashi was looking up at the cherry tree, trying to stare at the blossoms with the same blank concentration as his father. The pink flowers were pretty but uninteresting. To the six-year-old, any more than a few seconds was long enough for him to get bored with the tree.

The white pink petals peeled off the twigs in clouds as the wind gusted down the hill. His father stood perfectly still, gazing up at the blooms. They seemed, to the child's eye, like bunches of torn paper stuck at the ends of knobbly brown sticks. 'Father, what do you see that is so interesting?' he asked.

'The cherry blossom is an ideal beauty,' said his father, still staring up at the tree. 'The flowers show us perfection. Their life is such a beautiful joyous moment.'

'But they fall so quickly.'

'Is that not also beautiful?'

Akira looked down at the petals on the pavement. The crushed flowers seemed to be melting into the black surface. He waved his right hand inside the sleeve of his coat, flapping the empty cloth tube from side to side. 'I'm glad I'm not a cherry blossom.'

His father closed his eyes and sighed.

A passer-by noticed his empty sleeve and Akira caught his gaze. He held out his hand from his armpit and let the sleeve hang down at a seemingly impossibly angle. The man's mouth fell open and he looked away, shocked and embarrassed.

His father glanced down at him, right eyebrow raised.

Akira dropped his hand back into his armpit and the sleeve hung limp. He had embarrassed his father as well as the passer-by. He felt shame. He knew his father was angry.

Now the cold spring wind blew straight into his father's face. His brown hat lifted from his slick black hair and took off behind him. He twisted around to catch it, took two steps and grabbed it. Another gust sent a dense cloud of blossom tumbling about Akira. He swiped at them with his left arm, as if they were a swarm of bees. He was laughing as they fluttered around, beating against his face.

His father was crouching, his hand pinning his hat to the ground. He was watching Akira thrash at the petals in the same way that he had gazed at the blossom on the tree. The petals fell to the ground, eddied and rolled. His father got up. He walked over to Akira and picked him up. 'So, young samurai,' he said, pulling at the empty sleeve, 'shall we cut these off all your clothes, so your little arm can be free?'

'Yes,' said Akira, happy in his father's embrace.

'Fate has a purpose,' his father said, and Akira nodded, not understanding what he meant. Then his demeanour changed. 'Let's go for some *takoyaki*.'

'Oh, yes please, Father!' Akira loved octopus balls.

The walk was long, but Akira didn't mind. To be with his father and walk to the palace with him was a great event. His father was a member of the royal bodyguard, as Akira's grandfather and great-grandfather had been. He imagined himself marching like a soldier alongside his father, two steps for every one of his. 'Just around this corner,' came the answer to his query as to how far they had still to go.

The palace was set in grounds surrounded by a giant moat with castle-like ramparts. The walls were made of giant flat-sided grey-green boulders set together like a huge vertical jigsaw, above which Akira could see the trees of a mysterious garden, the delights of which were shielded from view. His father stopped and lifted him onto a crude fence made of what appeared to be scaffolding posts so that he could see better. Akira looked down the sloping face of the wall into the dark waters below, then across to the walls that sloped up to the palace gardens. It was an impregnable structure that would hold back an army.

'Let me tell you about your great-grandfather.'

Akira leant forward in his father's grasp, craning his neck. He felt as if he was hovering over the water.

'It is 1900...'

3

James Dean Yamamoto was driving as fast as his Harley Davidson would go. He was heading for the race meeting point. His bike was far too slow to win, but winning wasn't the purpose of the Saturday night event or, for that matter, any other that he took part in around Tokyo. The purpose was ritual and spectacle.

Outlaws had their place in society, the same as politicians and businessmen, and the racing was part of it. The competitors made as much noise as they could, as they tore along the intercity freeways and roads of Tokyo. Rebellion and crime served social functions, like sewers and rubbish tips, and Saturday was the night the garbage drove through the city and reminded the sleeping citizens that it was there and, in a strange way, kind of friendly. The bikers, the junkies, the crazy rebels, the mobsters, all were represented on their bikes, whether on home-grown tricked-out racers or fat unreliable Harley hogs from America.

James Dean Yamamoto's Harley couldn't have been fatter or louder, its black paint spotless, its chrome shining even in the late-night sodium-yellow city lights. The local-made bikes, the Hondas, Kawasakis, Yamahas and Suzukis, had seats, but his machine had a saddle. His black leathers and peaked cap were a tribute to his other hero, Marlon Brando in *The Wild One*, but when he took his cap off he would comb his greaser quiff back, like James Dean or yet another of his American heroes, Elvis.

To a Western eye he was a crazy, ironic figure, a small Japanese guy who pranced and aped an American pose that, even ten years before, had seemed dated. Yet to the citizens of

Tokyo, he looked dangerous – and, as a member of the Yakuza, however peripheral, he actually was.

The engine of the hog suddenly misfired in a series of bangs and clunks. He tried to nurse it with the throttle but it rattled and clattered out of life. He cruised into the kerb on a hill to the side of the Imperial Palace. He grimaced, resigned to resuscitating his machine and missing the race. He tried turning the engine over with a series of kick starts, but the hog wasn't having it. The Harley was dead.

He climbed off and took out a soft pack of Lucky Strike cigarettes from his jacket pocket. The Harley would probably start up again if he tightened the plugs. He would wait for the engine to cool. He lit up with his Zippo, staring at the inert bike in what a spectator, if there had been one, would have taken for a pose. Something caught his eye by the fence separating the pavement from the palace moat: a pile of clothes, neatly folded.

He took the cigarette from his mouth and walked over to it. Had someone jumped into the moat? He looked over the rusty barrier down the sloping side of the wall. A few feet below, a child was clinging to the side. James Dean looked away and took a drag of his cigarette, then looked back. The child, eleven or twelve, was peering up at him.

'What are you doing there?' James Dean asked.

The boy said nothing.

There was something funny about him. 'Do you need help?'

'I don't know,' said the boy.

James Dean noticed the child's right shoulder. His hand seemed to be coming straight out of his armpit as if he had no arm. His wrist looked like it was plugged straight into his torso. 'What are you doing there?' he asked again.

'I was planning to swim the moat, but I'm stuck.'

James Dean Yamamoto gave a short laugh. 'That's brave,' he took a puff of the cigarette, 'but pretty stupid.' The boy's arm really did come out of his shoulder. He must be one of those drug-crippled kids. 'If you fall you'll die.'

'Yes,' said the boy.

'Do you want that?'

'It might be best.'

'Let me pull you up,' said James Dean. 'You can always throw yourself in the moat another time. It's an option that will always be available to you.' He flicked his cigarette over the boy's head and into the moat below. He lay on the pavement, wriggled on his elbows under the barrier and leant forward. His prized twelve-inch flick-knife slipped out of his top pocket and fell towards the boy, who caught it in his flipper-like right hand. He stared at the illicit weapon.

'Can I have that back?' asked James Dean, reaching down for it.

The boy lifted it the couple of inches he could and James Dean grasped it. He stuffed it into his back pocket. Then he gripped the kid's flipper hand. 'Let go of the wall and take my arm.'

He did so.

'Now I'm going to pull you up and you have to do the best you can not to fall. Ready?'

He nodded.

'Ichi, ni, san.' The boy's feet scrabbled and slipped on the wall as James Dean pulled. It was an awkward lift, lying under the barrier, heaving the kid upwards without being able to move back freely. James Dean's back hit the barrier, which hurt. The kid was above the lip of the wall and, with a lunge, he rolled forwards and caught the pole of the barrier with his good hand.

The kid's face was right by his and James Dean looked into

his eyes. 'Have you got a good grip on the fence?' he asked.

'Yes.'

'I'm going to let you go, OK?'

'Yes.'

He let go and the kid grabbed the barrier with his other hand.

James Dean crawled out from under the fence and stood up. He brushed himself down and glanced at the kid, naked but for his underpants. 'You OK?' he asked.

'Yes.' The boy walked to his clothes, picked up his shorts and put them on.

With a clink of his Zippo, James Dean lit another Lucky Strike.

The boy picked up his vest.

'A vest!' exclaimed James Dean. 'What do you need that for? Men who scale the walls of the Emperor's Palace don't wear vests.'

The boy looked at him in silence. He dropped the vest, picked up his socks and sat down to put them on. 'They do wear shirts and jumpers, though, don't they?' he asked.

'Sure,' said James Dean. He walked to his bike and began to examine the engine. He took a tool-kit from a saddle bag and tightened the plugs. He looked up and saw the child staring at him.

'I owe you my life,' he said. 'My name is Akira.'

'James Dean.' He offered his hand.

Akira shook it. 'How can I repay you?'

'That's a good question,' said James Dean. He didn't want to embarrass the kid by laughing at the idea. 'I'll tell you what. I'll run you home. When I need you, I can come by and call in my marker.'

Akira made a little bow of agreement.

James Dean combed his quiff carefully, put on his cap and

mounted the Harley. He wrestled the bike upright and kicked it into life. 'Jump on, kid.'

Akira thought he must be asleep: racing through the lit streets of Tokyo on the back of a black noisy beast seemed too dreamlike for him to be awake. James Dean didn't seem to obey the lights at junctions or the speed limits. He simply flew along, with heroic skill and determination. They wove in and out of the late-night drivers and past police booths as if they weren't there. The minutes seemed like a lifetime to Akira, a lifetime that encompassed the fragile seconds it took a butterfly to climb from its chrysalis or a fish to be bitten in half by another.

James Dean stopped at the end of Akira's street and the boy got off. 'Thank you,' he said.

James Dean pushed his cap back and, with a grumble of rolling consonants, said, 'Remember, kid, don't be a little prick.'

Akira bowed.

4

Akira's father looked into his son's room. It was empty. There was a piece of paper on his pillow. He switched on the light and unfolded it.

Father, I have gone to swim the moat like your grandfather. Then perhaps I will be worthy. If you read this tonight please do not come for me. If you read this in the morning do not be sad.

Your loving Akira

He stood up, his mouth screwed tight. He was angry and he was proud. A host of conflicting emotions boiled in his heart. He left the room and headed for the door. His wife was standing in the narrow corridor by their bedroom. 'I'll deal with this,' he said quietly.

She looked shaken, her eyes pleading with him, as if he had some say in matters of Fate.

He got into the car and drove towards the Imperial Palace. Before long, he was parking on the road that led up round the east ramparts to the spot he had taken his son all those years ago to see where his grandfather had swum the moat and scaled the walls. He had been a street urchin, whose father was dead and whose mother was bedridden. He had invaded the gardens in search of trinkets, like the gold bells that hung in the trees, to bring back and sell. No one saw him, except the Meji Emperor, who watched him from behind the shutters, flitting from bush to bush like a racoon. It was a small daily delight for the melancholy old man.

Then one day the child was discovered. The Emperor intervened and ordered that he be placed under the protection of the royal household. In time he had become part of the royal retinue, a bodyguard to the Imperial Family. His son, Akira's grandfather, had followed him, and then he himself had followed the family tradition into Imperial service. They had enjoyed the honour of three generations as royal retainers, but his crippled only son could not follow in his father's footsteps.

Now the boy had sought to prove himself or perish in the attempt. It was right and proper that he should be proud but that was not how he felt. He felt as if his guts were being wrenched out.

A white flash by the barrier caught his eye. He walked to it. It was a small string vest. He clenched it in his fist and looked down into the black water below. 'Akira,' he called. He waited. 'Akira!' The road behind him was empty and the buildings looked down blankly on his desolation. 'Akira!' he called, a third time. He would not call again.

He returned to his car and drove home in the lowest of spirits. When he arrived, he turned off the engine and sat for a few moments, thinking of his son. How would he explain what must have happened to Akira's mother? Reluctantly, he climbed out of the car, locked it and began to walk up the path to his house. As he neared the front door, it opened. His wife stood there, smiling. His heart jumped.

'Our son is back,' she whispered.

He went straight to Akira's bedroom and slid open the door. 'Are you awake, son?' he asked.

Akira sat up. 'Yes, Father.'

'Where have you been?'

'I went to swim across the moat.'

He knelt by the bedroll. 'And how was it?'

'I could not climb far enough down the wall.'

'What did your adventure teach you?'

'Not to be a little prick.'

Where had his son picked up that word and such coarse pronunciation? He stood up and looked down at his child. 'I'm very glad you came back,' was all he said.

Akira trudged towards home, his satchel on his back. His face was grazed and his blazer dirty down the right side. The bullies had roughed him up yet again as he left for home. It was a daily humiliation. His eyes widened. A black Harley stood at the end of the street and James Dean sat astride it, smoking. He ran towards him.

'Hey, kid,' said James Dean. 'I've got a job for you.'

'Great,' said Akira. 'Anything. What is it?'

'I need you to take a package to someone. Now.'

'Yes.'

'It will be dangerous.'

'I don't mind.'

James Dean reached into one of the saddle bags and pulled out a small brown-paper parcel. 'Take it to this address.' He pulled out a piece of paper. Akira put the parcel in his satchel and examined the directions. Getting there would be an adventure.

Then James Dean took out five thousand yen notes from his pocket and gave them to him. 'This is for you. I'll run you close, then you make the drop and find your own way home.'

'Yes.'

'Hey, kid, don't say "yes",' he waved his cigarette, 'say "sure".'

'Sure,' said Akira.

Akira waited nervously at the wooden door. It slid open and a pretty woman in a dressing-gown was looking down at him.

'Are you Miss Mai?'

'Yes,' she said, smiling.

'I have something for you.' He swung his satchel off his shoulder and took out the package.

'Thank you,' she said. She ruffled his hair, went inside and closed the door.

He put his satchel on again and ran down the steps to the street.

Akira took his favourite *manga* from its position at the end of the bookshelf and put the four thousand yen notes between the pages. The change from the taxi ride was in his pockets and he would think about spending some of it tomorrow on his way home. He might buy his mother some flowers, perhaps some candies for his sisters. He wondered whether he would see James Dean again. Surely he had not repaid his debt so easily. He hoped not.

'Are you John Wayne?' he asked the tall, fat American who stood on the corner of the street.

The man practically jumped into the air. 'I am,' he said, flushing red.

'Do you have something for James Dean?' read Akira, awkwardly, from the note he had been given.

John Wayne looked around. 'Yes.'

Akira took a heavy package from his satchel and handed it to him. The American pulled a fat envelope from his back pocket and gave it to Akira. 'You're a bit young for this kind of caper, aren't you?' he said uneasily, looking at the kid's deformed arm. While Akira didn't understand a word of English, he understood the look. It expressed horror. He was used to it.

As he put the envelope into his satchel and bowed, the American was walking away.

James Dean was on his Harley at the end of the road. He gave Akira a ten thousand yen note on receipt of his envelope.

'Why so much?' asked Akira, putting the money into his pocket.

'It was a heavy package,' said James Dean. He pulled out a piece of paper and gave it to Akira. 'Come round my place tomorrow. I need to talk with you about some stuff.'

'Sure,' said Akira.

5

___

His mother was waiting in the hallway. 'Why are you coming home so late these days,' she asked gently, 'and always so scratched and battered?'

'I fall over a lot.'

She knelt in front of him and examined the scuffed arm of his blazer. It had a new tear. She peered at the fresh cuts on his knees. 'You need to be more careful.'

'Sure,' he said.

She looked at him sternly, then vigorously brushed the dust off his arm.

'Don't just stand there,' said James Dean, 'come in.' Akira walked into the small flat. The curtains were pulled and the den was in deep shadow. 'Into the kitchen,' said James Dean.

Akira sat down by a low breakfast table as James Dean got a beer from the fridge. 'Want one?' he asked, a cigarette hanging precariously from his mouth.

'No, thank you,' Akira replied.

James Dean sat down at the table, the chair back to front. 'You know, Akira, what you've been doing for me is kind of illegal.'

'How can delivering a package be illegal?' said Akira.

'Well,' said James Dean, 'it depends what's in the package.' He stubbed out his cigarette and lit another.

'Can I have one?' asked Akira.

James Dean studied his cigarette.

Akira waited.

James Dean tipped one out of the packet and offered it to him. Akira took it and James Dean lit it for him. Akira sucked the smoke into his mouth and puffed it out in a long jet. 'Well, I don't care,' he said. 'I want to work for you.'

'That's fine,' said James Dean, 'but I want you to know you can stop any time you like.'

'You're my only friend.' said Akira.

'Surely not.'

'Yes.' Akira sampled the smoke again. 'Every day, after school, three little pricks trip me up and roll me on the ground and every day nobody does anything.' He held the smoking cigarette in his armless hand and turned his head to drag on it. 'If I had friends at school they would help me.'

'Wait a second.' James Dean got up and went out of the room.

Akira tried to flick ash like an experienced smoker. He failed.

James Dean returned. He set his chair the right way around and put a roll of coins on the table. 'Hold these coins in your fist.'

Akira stubbed out his first cigarette and took the bar-like object. It was a stack of hundred yen coins held together by nut and bolt. The bar poked out at either side of his fist. It felt heavy.

'If you're going to work for me, you've got to be able to handle yourself.'

Akira looked at the bar in his fist, then at James Dean.

James Dean held up his palm. 'See my hand? Imagine it's the face of your worst enemy. You need to punch that face straight on the nose.'

Akira pushed his fist out slowly to James Dean's palm and touched it where the imaginary nose would be.

'Next time you see one of those arseholes, just walk up to

him and punch his nose, then walk away. Never walk with your knees when you can talk with your fists.'

'Sure,' said Akira.

Akira walked through the gate into the playground. His three torturers stood near the front door, talking. He felt his heartbeat quicken as he looked at them. Then he remembered standing naked against the wall, high above the black moat water, shivering in the warm summer air. In time his legs would have given out and he would have fallen down the wall into the water below. Only the miracle appearance of James Dean Yamamoto had saved him from a horrid death. Yet he hadn't been scared of that and he was proud to know it. If he could brave death, he could brave attacking his enemies.

He gripped the coins tightly in his sweating hand and walked up to the boys. Yasuda, the chief bully, watched him approach. 'What do you want, Flapper?'

Akira waved his shoulder hand by way of decoy and struck Yasuda with a blow he aimed, as instructed, at his nose. Yasuda bent double, blood suddenly pouring out of him in long red drips. Akira turned and walked away, the sound of his breath and his pounding heart drowning the cries of the injured boy.

A bell rang, the school door opened and the children walked towards it obediently, surprised and shocked to see Yasuda bent and bleeding on the threshold.

Akira filed past as a teacher ran to Yasuda's aid.

Yasuda wasn't in class that morning, or in the afternoon, and the usual reception committee was not there to greet Akira after school. His hand hurt, but it was a good pain.

The next morning he arrived just as the school door was unlocked. Across the playground the three bullies stood together, Yasuda with plasters over his nose. Should he go over and punch him again?

That seemed too much. He stood on the other side of the playground and waited, his face blank. They were throwing evil looks in his direction but they were not coming his way. The bell went and they filed in.

All day long he could sense the venomous cloud emanating from his three enemies. As the day drew on their menacing stares became more regular.

Then classes were over. Akira made straight for the door. He could tell they were after him – he could feel their presence looming behind him, as he had so many times before. Blows would soon follow. They would catch him by the school gate, or soon thereafter, rough him up and roll him in the dirt. They would surely hurt him badly.

As he saw the playground gate and the road beyond, he imagined James Dean on his Harley by the kerb, challenging him to act. He pulled the coin bar from his pocket and turned. They were only a few feet behind him. Akira punched Yasuda's nose, and almost laughed.

Yasuda folded in half and let out a howl of pain. Akira turned to his right to punch Umebayashi, but the boy jumped back, his hands protecting his face. Akira walked to the gate.

There was the roar of a loud engine and James Dean pulled up. 'Jump on kid,' he said, surveying the scene. The other children looked on with awe as Akira straddled the back of the Yakuza man's motorbike before it grunted away.

James Dean noticed Akira's bloody knuckles as the boy gripped his shoulder for balance.

Akira's father sat down at the low dinner table. His mother and sisters got up and left the room. His father took a mouthful of tea. 'Show me your hand.'

Akira held out his arm across the table. His father examined his hand. It was bruised and swollen, the knuckles heavily grazed. He moved the fingers. 'Nothing broken,' he said, letting go. 'The school has complained that you struck someone. Is this how you injured your hand?'

Akira remembered James Dean's words. 'I was tired of falling on my knees, so I spoke with my fist,' he replied.

His father stiffened. He gave Akira a long look. Then he smiled. 'Let me see that hand again.'

Akira held it out. His father examined the swollen knuckles. 'No wonder the child is not returning to your school.' He called to his wife and the family returned to the table.

Akira wondered whether the huge fat guy in his dressing-gown was a Sumo wrestler. The man gave him a thick envelope in exchange for the package he had handed over and slammed the door in his face.

That didn't seem right. When he met people at their addresses they were normally happy to see him and treated him kindly. He looked carefully about the street as he made his way along it. There were a couple of men across the road in the sort of raincoats his father wore. His stomach lurched and his heart began to pound. He walked quickly along the pavement, trying to keep his eye on the men. He could feel them coming after him just as he had felt the bullies behind him at school.

He went down into the subway and began to run as soon as he thought he was out of sight. He followed the signs for the platforms and picked up another route to another exit. He emerged on the other side of the road, and, as he did so, another man in a raincoat fifty yards away stared at him. Akira ducked into a department store a few paces ahead.

He ran through the rows of merchandise and came out on the cross street. He raced in front of a cab, waving frantically.

As soon as it stopped he jumped in. He gave the driver James Dean's address and slumped in the back seat as low as he could. The cab pulled away.

He couldn't see out of the window for fear of being spotted. He counted the seconds as they moved slowly with the traffic. He would sit up once he had counted to three hundred.

'Policemen, huh?' said James Dean. 'Well done for giving them the slip.' He slapped a ten thousand yen note onto the kitchen table. 'That's for you. For surviving your first chase.'

Akira flicked the ash from the cigarette in his short hand into the ashtray a foot away. He took the note and pushed it into the top pocket of his blazer. 'What does it mean?'

'I don't know,' said James Dean. 'Time for you to lie low, maybe.'

Akira's heart dropped. 'How long?'

James Dean took a swig of beer. 'We have to be careful. You're too good to waste on a stupid deal.'

Akira smiled. 'OK.'

6

Akira sat by the concrete flyover pillar and looked down into the green canal water. It had become a daily ritual to go there on his way home, sit down and smoke two cigarettes. It was a lonesome private place to linger and think. His empty days without a mission passed slowly. He longed for James Dean to be parked at the end of the road, waiting for him, engine running. Yet the days had rolled into weeks and he felt that the gates to his magical world of excitement and adventure had slammed shut.

He heard someone approaching and looked up. It was a grey-brown raincoat-clad figure. His father.

Akira stood up smartly.

'Quiet smoke?' his father enquired.

Akira relaxed a little: his father was not furious with him, it seemed.

His father took his own pack out. A moment later Akira had pulled out his Zippo and was offering to light his father's cigarette.

'I thought I should seek you out,' said his father, after the first puff. 'Your mother is worried about you.'

'Worried?'

'Yes.'

'She didn't worry when I came home every day beaten.'

'Certain hardships she expects. She wonders why you often come home so late.'

Akira swapped his cigarette into his short hand, took a drag and said nothing.

'So this is where you come?'

'Sometimes.'

'What of your friends?'

'I do not have friends. Other kids think they will catch something.'

'That is their loss.'

Akira flicked his cigarette into the canal. 'Shall we go home?'

'Yes. Your mother is waiting.'

As the bell rang, Akira glanced out of the classroom window and across the playground. James Dean was parked on the road beyond. He jumped up from his desk.

The other children were heading for the next class, but he ran through the empty hallways down to the floor below and outside. He sprinted into the street and stepped in front of a tree that covered him from view. As he did so, James Dean rolled his bike to him. His face was cut and bruised. 'Jump on kid.'

Akira leapt onto the back of the Harley. James Dean revved the engine and sped off, in a cloud of blue smoke. Soon they had reached one of Akira's favourite haunts. He loved the little coffee shop. The owner welcomed him and James Dean like brothers and didn't blanch at the sight of a crippled child in school uniform. He ordered coffee like an adult and was served as one. They sat in the wooden shack like the real outlaws of his comic books.

'What happened?' he asked eventually.

'Trouble,' said James Dean.

'No kidding,' said Akira, using one of James Dean's favourite American expressions.

'I need to ask you a big favour.'

'Sure.'

'I need you to go to my place and get some things for me.'

'Sure.'

'It'll be dangerous.'

'OK.'

James Dean gripped Akira's right hand and squeezed it. 'Very dangerous.'

No one ever touched his short hand. No one dared to. He squeezed James Dean's as hard as he could. 'OK. What do you need?'

'My gun. My money. A black book.' He showed the latter's size with a forefinger and thumb. 'In the kitchen in the top drawer by the sink.'

'You in big trouble?'

'Nothing I can't fix with my money, my gun and my little black book.'

'Easy,' said Akira.

'But people might be waiting for me outside my home. They can't get the book.'

'OK.'

'I'll drop you two streets away. Go in, get the stuff. Come straight out and back to me.'

'OK.'

The street outside the rundown apartment building was empty. Akira's heart began to race, as it always did when he was with James Dean. He entered and went up the stairs to James Dean's flat on the second floor. Nothing stirred. He put the key into the lock and turned it slowly, then pushed the door open. He looked into the den. The light was out and, through the gloom, he could see that the room was empty. He went in and closed the door.

He felt safer now that he was inside and his heart slowed. He moved across the blacked-out den to the kitchen. It, too, was empty. The air smelt stale. The table was covered with beer bottles and the ashtray was full. It looked as though James Dean had been entertaining friends.

Akira moved to the sink and opened the drawer immediately to the right. There was a pile of dishcloths but he saw no gun or money. He lifted the folded linen and saw a lot of money. He pulled out the dishcloths. As James Dean had described, there were bundles of cash on the right side of the drawer and a pistol on the left. There was also a black book, held closed with an elastic band.

Akira picked up the weapon. It was a shiny, stubby chrome revolver with a black rubber handle and no hammer. It was heavy and felt large in his hand. He stuffed it into his outer pocket. He put the book inside his blazer. He swung off his satchel and filled it with the cash. James Dean's stash amounted to many millions of yen. To Akira it was a fortune of neatly bundled ten thousand yen notes, perhaps twenty thousand dollars, a good proportion of the proceeds of James Dean Yamamoto's life's work.

The satchel was heavy on Akira's back. He went to the den window and tried to look out. There was nothing to be seen from this restricted vantage-point. He put his ear to the front door and listened. He heard nothing. He opened the door slowly and looked out. The corridor was empty. He closed the door behind him and walked down the stairs.

On the ground floor, two figures were slouched in the hallway, dressed in leathers. They were smoking and talking gangster-style. The hallway by the front door was a tight space with mailboxes and barely enough room for two people to pass. Akira put his hand into his jacket pocket and gripped the pistol handle.

One of the figures cast a glance at him, but he kept walking, hurrying as he normally would. He scuttled past them to the door and trotted out into the street. He ran up the lane and back through the alleys to James Dean, who kick-started his engine as soon as he saw him.

'Did you get the stuff?'

'Yes.'

'All of it?'

'Yes.'

'Was the coast clear?'

'No.'

The bike surged off.

Akira was taking notes in the history class. No one had noticed he had been gone for nearly three hours. The school simply didn't have truancy and was not equipped to spot it. If he wasn't there, it must be for a good reason, like a trip to the optician. There were no guards in this prison camp, no tripwires to snare transgressors. He had slipped between the sunlit world of children to his dark adventure playground unnoticed, like a student between a lecture and a daydream.

On the first Wednesday of every month, he would travel to the coffee shop in Roppongi where, from five until six, he would drink and smoke and wait. He had visited James Dean's flat on several occasions but it had been empty. The last time a woman had answered, and through the gap between her and the door, he had glimpsed new furniture and family life, which had to mean that this was no longer James Dean Yamamoto's home.

His fourteenth birthday had come and gone.

He passed the cigarette from his short hand to the good one and stubbed it out. He would leave soon and not return for another month.

Perhaps James Dean was in prison – or dead, even.

A figure came through the door, a salary man in from the

rain of a dark, blustery Tokyo evening. Akira started. With a quiff, sideburns and a little less weight, he could almost have been James Dean.

The figure was coming towards him. Akira tried to focus in the dim brown light of the coffee-shop shack. He found himself standing up.

'Sit down, kid,' said James Dean, plonking himself on the bench across from him.

'James Dean! It's you – at last.'

'I've been busy,' he said, lighting a Lucky Strike. A pot of coffee and a refined cup and saucer were delivered to the table without reference to an order. James Dean acknowledged the café owner with a nod. 'I've been busy lying low.'

'I'm glad you came. Have you a job for me?'

'Yes,' said James Dean, 'but first I have to tell you I'm going to disappear. Maybe for good.'

'Why?'

'It's right for me and it will be right for you.' James Dean looked around as someone came into the café. He looked back to Akira. 'I've got an idea and it could be big. I've got to cut myself free of the past and take a shot at the moon. This town is going to go crazy and I'm going to ride the madness. But first the old James Dean has to die so the new one can be born.' He pushed his little black book across the table. 'I want you to keep this safe for me.'

Akira took it. 'Sure.'

'And I've got you a present.' James Dean took out his flick-knife and pushed it across the table. 'This is for you.'

Akira picked it up and passed it to his short hand. He pressed the silver button halfway down the handle and the blade clicked open. 'Thank you,' he said. He twisted the blade lock with his thumb and folded the blade shut.

'Well, this is it kid.' James Dean stood up. 'Remember, don't be a little prick.'

'Will I ever see you again?'

James Dean smiled and patted his own hair, as if the quiff was still there. 'You never know, kid.'

7

Tokyo March 2013

Akira looked from the palace rampart to the far wall of the moat. He squinted. If he could focus his eyes just so, he thought, he would see himself thirty years before, clinging to the far wall.

'And what of the mirror, Sensei Nakabashi?'

Akira snapped out of his dream. 'The mirror? Oh, that's very difficult. Not even the Emperor can see the sacred mirror.'

'So does it – or for that matter does any of the Imperial Regalia – actually exist? After all, as curator of the royal treasure you must be one of the few to know for sure.'

'Yes, yes,' he said. 'Of course it exists. Every piece has been at every coronation, as you surely know, since the beginning of history.'

The two American professors were looking smugly at him.

The tall stork-like woman from the New York Metropolitan Museum tilted forwards as if she was going to peck the top of his head. 'Do you think you might be able to arrange for me to see the sword Kusanagi no Tsurugi?'

'Very difficult,' said Akira. 'The priests at Atsuta allow access to it only for a coronation.'

'And what of the Yasakani no Magatama?' asked the relaxed, informally dressed young man from the Getty in California.

'It is very beautiful and also very difficult to examine. The priests at Kashikodokoro guard it with their every sinew. But I can tell you a secret about it. It is not a jewel, but many jewels of the most exquisite jade, a necklace held together by a golden chain.'

'And you've seen it,' said the improperly dressed curator from California.

Professor Akira Nakabashi, keeper of the Sacred Imperial Treasures, waved his short hand at the honoured guests. 'Please, let me show you the view further along.'

The two Americans smirked at each other.

'I am very sorry to disappoint you,' said Akira. 'The Imperial Regalia are sacred items, drawn from the dawn of our history. They represent the very soul of the Japanese nation. They encapsulate the Imperial rights and status, its authority, continuity and legitimacy. They are not items to be examined and tested. Not even by the Emperor himself.' He smiled cheerily. 'Please, come this way – there is much else to see.'

8

Brandon hated heights so today's exercise was going to be a misery. Dropping down the line from the chopper was bad enough, but after the four kilometre swim there would be a cliff to climb and he would hate every second of it. Not that the sickness or the fear was going to slow him down, let alone stop him. His face stayed as set and determined as it always did. His doubt and fear were locked inside him and throbbed deep below his impassive exterior.

In a few seconds he would hit the water, detach and form up with the three other SEALs in their squad. Danny, Reece and Casey were his spiritual brothers. The exercise was simple. They would be injected offshore from the chopper, swim in formation to the beach, scale the cliffs, quick march ten K to the RV and return to base.

It was the climb that spoilt his day. He simply didn't feel comfortable scaling things. He could be deep under water, totally reliant on his equipment for life, and yet be as relaxed as if he was in his childhood bed. Climbing up a wall, fixed by even the sturdiest of lines, set all his senses on fire. There was something overwhelmingly hostile about a vertical drop. A fall from even thirty feet up was likely to bust you up for life. It didn't matter that the stats were bad, it was just something visceral for him. There was no rescue if you fell.

The water enveloped him as he penetrated the other-worldliness of the sea. The movement and muffled sound soothed the churning inside him. The sea was his friend, the blue water a comforting blanket. The sea off Okinawa was dazzlingly clear. He could see down thousands of feet through the azure ether of the world's clearest waters. Shafts of light twisted and turned, sparkling like the facets of a sapphire. The tension of the descent melted away as he fell in at the rear of the four-swimmer formation.

Reece led the squad. He was an experienced petty officer who always seemed to know the right thing to do. He would be going up the wall first. Casey and Danny were as solid as they came. Brandon was proud and happy to be part of such a first-rate squad. He often felt he was struggling to keep up with their incredibly high standards. He copied their stone-cold courage and taciturn demeanour, but felt somehow junior to them. He wished everything could be as easy for him as it seemed to them. Nothing fazed his comrades, and while to the outside world nothing seemed to sway him either, he knew that his blood would boil and fizz like that of a diver explosively decompressing.

There were no streams of bubbles trailing behind the others. The re-breathing aqualungs they carried did not exhaust air into the water but recycled it, scrubbing the carbon dioxide from the exhaled gas and reusing the oxygen. A diver only took 25 per cent of the oxygen with each breath, and re-breather technology allowed for longer, deeper dives. It also gave them a stealthy advantage when bubbles floating to the surface would have given them away. Not that bubbles mattered on this trip.

Some SEALs liked the skydiving, others the sheer physicality of long marches on land; some liked the equipment, be it transport or munitions, but Brandon loved the sea, whether he was diving, swimming or operating out of boats. At some point he was going to leave the military and had determined to get into the sports fishing business. When he was swimming he had those kinds of dreams. Floating in the friendly blue void, he would make plans between the cross-talk of the radio, which crackled intermittently with chatter.

They were coming up on the shore.

'That's one hell of a lot of hammerheads,' he found himself reporting into his mic, as he watched a swarm of sharks far below cruising in long lazy loops.

'It's the season,' replied Reece.

'Is it shark humping season?' asked Danny, rhetorically.

The reef reared up from the abyssal plain, a sealife-encrusted face rising vertically out of the void. They would be no more than half a kilometre from the beach and the dreaded climb up the 150-foot cliff.

The seabed appeared below him, covered with coral and flecked with fish. When he had first gone diving he had seen everything around him as either a trophy to be taken or prey to be speared, but it hadn't been long before he'd realised that a reef was like a jewel, a fabulous opal you could swim through rather than look into from the outside.

Something glistened on the white sand forty feet below. On the sand a thousand golden coins winked up at him. He did a double take. He checked his tanks, everything was fine: he wasn't narked up. He didn't say anything into his mic, but flipped down and swam hard for the bottom. As he approached, the glinting coins didn't fade away or resolve into a different object. They got clearer. They were oval, like golden fingernails, and in the instant it took him to scoop up a handful, he saw they had writing on them.

Brandon wasn't going to admit to breaking formation or go on record by saying anything. He pushed the sandy handful into the rubberised pocket on his right thigh. He recorded the position and swam back to the group.

Casey's head flicked round as he caught up but nothing was said over the radio link.

The climb was only minutes away and trepidation suddenly

overwhelmed him. He was biting hard on the mouthpiece of the regulator.

Brandon climbed out of the water and put his mask up. The wall looked awfully sheer. How the hell were they going to get up that?

Reece looked around at them grinning. 'Aha,' he drawled. 'What a tiny rock – it's hardly worth the journey.'

Brandon smiled confidently like the others. 'Want me to lead us up?'

'Danny's turn,' said Reece.

Danny grinned.

'The fast way,' said Casey, wading forwards. 'I want to get back early.'

'Ah, hell, Casey, you're no fun,' joked Danny.

'Just this one time, brother,' said Casey.

Inside Brandon sighed with relief. Danny just loved a gnarly route and this time he would be spared it. Though he trusted Danny with his life, as he trusted Casey and Reece, he was glad that today the need to do so was minimised.

9

Brandon put the beer bottles down with a clunk. The boys were looking at him questioningly. They would have seemed huge around any bar table but in a cramped Japanese watering-hole, they were outlandish. He was smiling. He had kept the lid on his discovery against all his impulses to come right out with it.

The team were holding their beers and waiting, twitching with anticipation. Why was Brandon acting up? Why was the meet off base? What had got into him?

Brandon put his hand into his shirt pocket, like he was reaching for a pack of smokes. 'Well, guys, I want to show you something.' He put a coin in front of each of his comrades and two in front of himself. 'These are for you.'

'What's this?' Casey picked up the shiny oval.

'Gold coins,' said Brandon, watching their faces as they studied his gifts.

'You found these today?' said Reece.

'When we were coming onshore,' said Brandon.

'Don't bite that,' said Reece, as Danny was about to put his coin between his teeth. 'It's gold all right. You can tell by the weight. You don't want to spoil the piece or, for that matter, your teeth.'

'There's a whole hill of these down there,' said Brandon. 'Hundreds, maybe even thousands of them.'

'I saw you,' said Casey. 'Saw you come back up.'

'You're too sharp for me,' said Brandon, acknowledging him. 'We've got to go back – we could clean up.'

Reece was holding his to the light. 'Brandon, I want you to

41

think for a minute, then tell me how many you saw.'

'Buddy, they were all over the bottom – so many I could see them from forty feet up.'

'And for every one you can see, there might be ten more buried,' added Casey.

They looked at each other.

Brandon was sucking at his beer as he watched Danny compare his coin with the others.

'We're going to need a boat and we are going to need to sync up our furlough. I got plenty,' Reece went on.

'Me too,' said Brandon.

'Copy,' said Casey.

'In two weeks I get mine,' said Danny.

'Two weeks!' sighed Brandon.

'Don't sweat it,' said Reece. 'It'll take a bit of arranging to get us a boat we can crew ourselves and it'll cost plenty.'

'How much?' asked Danny.

'Fifteen to twenty thousand for a week. That's five thousand each,' said Reece.

'I'm in,' said Brandon.

'Jesus,' said Danny, 'my fucking Visa's already maxed.'

'Who cares? I'm in,' said Casey.

'Of course I'm in too,' added Danny. 'Jesus!' he exclaimed. 'I'm fucked.' He laughed into the neck of his beer bottle.

'Brandon,' said Reece, 'I'll go to Tokyo this weekend and see if I can pawn the coins. Get an idea what they're worth. No good finding out they'll only fetch a hundred yen.'

'Do you think that's likely?' Casey enquired.

'No,' said Reece, 'but let's do this properly.'

'Yes, sir.' Casey clinked his bottle with Reece's.

Reece collected all the coins. He looked suddenly very serious, and his cheek muscles flared. 'Now, guys, there's to be no mention of this. One leak and I'll turn it in to the CO and let it go through the channels. If it gets out we're up to party games, they'll drum us out.' His colleagues knew he was right – and their faces reflected their horror at the idea. Then they relaxed: a grin had crept up the right side of Reece's face.

Reece's Japanese was pretty much non-existent, and travelling through Tokyo taxed him more than any day of physical effort. He had spent the previous night researching the best place to take the coins for valuation and what they might be worth. The coins, if they were coins, seemed like Tokugawa currency, the first Japanese system to replace the Chinese coins that until the 1600s had been used in that part of Asia. However, he could find nothing like them on the Internet.

There was a store near the Tokyo Tower that seemed like a good place to start. He told the middle-aged taxi driver where to go: 'Tokyo Tower, *kudasi.*' He suspected it meant 'Give me the Tokyo Tower.' It seemed to do the trick because about twenty-five minutes later he could see the massive orange and white structure in the distance.

Reece squinted up at the Japanese equivalent of France's Eiffel Tower and chuckled to himself. The tower was typical Japanese thinking. Copy a great European idea but make it with superior technology and expertise, in this case steel rather than iron. Then show the Frenchies how to make a tower that weighs only 25 per cent of their cast-iron monster but is thirty feet higher.

He marched up the hill, then down an anonymous main road filled with modern offices, and stopped in his tracks: between two looming grey office blocks there were three low wooden buildings, grimy and worn. The middle structure was spotlessly clean, but to his eyes broken and old, like a shack in the country that needed tearing down for something, new and painted, to be put in its place.

He checked his Google printout. It was the same door. There was a warm light coming from inside and it looked open. There were two plates on the stoop, loaded with salt. Apparently that was for good luck. Reece kind of understood that salt was pure and that pure was good, but it still struck him as odd to keep plates of salt on your front doorstep.

He went in, and found himself surrounded by cabinets of swords and armour. Towards the back of the shop he saw an old man and approached him – the proprietor, he thought. The old man's desk had a case on it, filled with little white and brown carvings. Reece walked up to him and smiled. The old man smiled back.

Reece bowed a little and moved towards a chair in front of the desk. The old guy held out his hand, inviting him to sit.

Reece sat down, and immediately noticed that someone was moving behind a beaded screen. She popped her head out – a little old lady dressed in classic Japanese style. The proprietor's wife, he thought. He put his hand into his pocket and pulled out his wallet. He flipped it open and took out a coin, stuck between two five thousand yen bills. 'I want to sell this,' he said slowly. He put it on the velvet cloth that lay in front of the old man.

The old man looked at him gravely, then picked up the coin. He cocked his head from side to side and sucked his front teeth. A moment later, he pursed his lips, produced a jeweller's loupe and began to scrutinise it. He put the loupe down, pulled out a large magnifying glass from beneath the desk and moved the coin backwards and forwards under the lens, flipping it over from one side to the other.

He sighed and laid the coin on the cloth. 'Sell?'

'Yes,' said Reece.

The old man pulled out a pad and a long thin gold pen. '3,000,000 Y', he wrote.

Reece looked at the old man. Thirty thousand dollars? The Japanese didn't rip people off, or so they said – and so he had experienced. They also didn't negotiate, haggle or expect tips. 'Yes,' he said. He bowed again. 'OK.'

The old man got up and went through the bead curtain.

While he was gone, Reece turned to inspect the room. It was full of ancient stuff and it struck him that he must be sitting in the middle of a fortune. He had another four gold coins in his pocket, and forced away the thought of what they were worth. It didn't seem sensible to push his luck here. He'd try another store.

The old man came back and laid three bundles of cash on the velvet. Reece didn't count it: he knew he didn't need to. He stood up, pushing the money deep into his inside jacket pocket.

The old man was bowing.

'*Domo*,' said Reece.

Reece walked across the bar towards his unit, his face deadpan. Danny got up and headed to the bar to get them all another round. Reece took Danny's place against the wall, sliding his briefcase behind his knees.

'How did it go?' asked Brandon.

'Let's wait till Danny gets back.'

'We weren't expecting you till tomorrow. Didn't go good, then?' fished Casey.

Reece turned to see what progress Danny was making – he was on his way back, bringing the beers. For a Saturday night the place was dead but, even when they were busy, Japanese bar staff did not fuck around. You needed a drink, you got one quick time.

Reece took his bottle from his colleague and had a long draught.

'Well?' said Brandon.

'I only got to sell two coins.'

'Oh, shit,' said Danny. 'That's why you came back early.'

'What did you get for them?' asked Casey. 'I mean, if there are thousands of them it might still be worth it.'

'Well,' said Reece, 'I got thirty thousand for one and twenty-five thousand for the other.'

'Thirty thousand yen's pretty cool,' said Casey.

'Dollars.'

Casey, Brandon and Danny froze. There were no whoops of joy. Reece grinned up the right side of his face. 'Gentlemen, that's the correct response.'

'Jesus,' said Danny, 'we're going to get busted.'

'Not necessarily,' said Reece.

Brandon was chuckling to himself; he nudged Casey, whose bottle holding hand was covering his mouth. Casey threw him a look that seemed to say, 'At some point this is all going to be your fault.'

'So what are we going to do?' said Danny.

'Well, it can't do any harm to go back to that reef and take a look, can it?' Reece gazed around the table, allowing himself a smirk.

'We can't get busted for a bit of sports diving,' said Casey.

'Let's see what we find,' said Reece, 'then work out what to do. So far we've done nothing we can't explain away.'

Danny's eyes twinkled in the subdued light of the bar. He raised his bottle. 'Here's to sports diving.'

10

Jim sat forlornly at the end of the examination couch. The doctor had been gone for thirty minutes and he had put his shirt back on. What the hell was keeping him? He was pretty surprised that, considering the stupendous amounts of money the clinic charged, he could be left alone for so long, semi-naked.

Being rich and seeing doctors seemed to go hand in hand. Before he had made any money his life had been a bit of squalor and a lot of health. When wealth had entered his life through the front door, mayhem and destruction had come in at the back, he reflected. He got off the couch and put his shoes on, then sat on a high leather armchair by the doctor's desk.

At last the door opened and the old doctor walked in. He didn't look very happy. He sat down by his desk, a folder in his hand, and seemed to avoid Jim's eyes. 'I'm really sorry, but I can't help you.'

The colour drained from Jim's face. 'What is it?'

The doctor looked very unhappy indeed. He opened the folder and took out a sheet of paper. 'This is not something I can deal with.' He pointed at an image it showed.

'Is that me?' said Jim, looking at the ribcage with what seemed to be a large battery pack embedded into it.

'Yes.'

'What is it?' he asked.

'Well, Mr Evans, you tell me.'

'I don't know,' he said, rubbing his face with both hands.

'Whatever it is, I'm not qualified to deal with it, and whoever put it there clearly has a mandate.'

'A mandate?' said Jim.

The doctor didn't reply.

'Why can't you take it out?'

'It would mean replacing a large part of your ribcage,' said the doctor. 'Moreover, whatever it is, it probably does a better job than anything I could replace it with.'

Jim touched the spot on his ribs where he felt a periodic twinge and the scan showed a plate across three ribs. His fingertips couldn't detect it.

'I'm sorry I can't help you,' said the doctor, standing up. 'I won't charge you for this consultation.'

'Why?' said Jim, also getting to his feet.

The doctor seemed suddenly fearful. 'I'd prefer it if you didn't mention you'd seen me,' he said. He was pleading.

'You don't need to worry,' said Jim, as the penny dropped. 'My friends did this to me.'

'Really?' said the doctor.

'Not the grenade injuries, the other thing.' He shrugged apologetically.

'Just don't tell me any more.' The doctor hurried to open the door.

The Thames was rushing by Jim's windows as the spring tide raced up at full bore. The water was grey, like the heavy rainclouds above. All manner of flotsam rode the tide downstream to the sea, mysterious drowned shapes riding the surging currents. The innocent and the obscene churned together in the cold, turbulent waters. He was staring at his phone. He wanted to call Jane and shout, 'What did you put in me?' But one of the nagging questions at the back of his mind had been answered. How had they found him so quickly in the Congo? Well, now he had seen the picture it was obvious: they had chipped him like a pedigree puppy.

If it wasn't for the fact that smashing his phone against the wall would create days of inconvenience, he would have lobbed it across the room – or, better still, opened the window and consigned it to the bottom of the river.

Stafford came in with a tray. 'Tea and crumpets, sir?'

Jim couldn't help but laugh. The fucking Americans had stuck a transponder in his ribcage, and the British had sent an agent disguised as a butler to spy on him – and all because he could read the future of foreign exchange and stock charts like others read words on a page. Predicting the future performance of financial instruments seemed to many like something they could learn, a puzzle to crack and get good at, like a crossword. Predicting the market from charts was just another great way of making money, if you could master it. In reality, it was impossible – just as you couldn't know for certain the winner of tomorrow's three thirty at Doncaster until horse and jockey passed the post.

While hundreds of books every year professed to teach you how to predict the future of markets, the reality was that, if you could, you'd be able to suck the financial world dry. A savant who could predict the movement of markets from charts could grow their wealth exponentially, for ever increasing the size of their bets. Pretty soon no one would be prepared to play against him and the market would die. It would be a skill as powerful and as dangerous as a time machine. The ability to see even seconds into the future of the dollar would ensure that the viewer made fortunes beyond even the avarice of billionaires. So, it was fortunate that these books did not unlock the secrets of trading the market, and that it was impossible to stare at the chart of Microsoft and see how it was going to trade. The consequences of being able to do so would be disastrous.

Until one day, in a bank in London's Docklands, a trainee

who brought the coffee and fruit to the noisy traders had pointed out that the German Bund was about to go up. It had done so. His name was Jim Evans. For Jim, it had been the start of a crazy ride that, as he sat now, watching the tide roll up the Thames, seemed never-ending.

'Professor Nakabashi, I'm honoured you could see me so quickly.'

Akira smiled. 'Sit down, old friend, and show me what you have found. I am most excited.'

Shinjitai-san sat down slowly. While some men in their eighties seemed agile and untroubled by age, his advanced years had taken their toll. 'I can hardly believe it myself,' he said, pulling a handkerchief from the top pocket of his suit jacket. 'But here it is.' He unfolded the woollen cloth, a subtle tartan pattern made of finest thread.

A gold lozenge twinkled.

'Oooh,' groaned Akira. He picked it up. 'It is a treasure,' he said, placing it under a lens, a cross between a magnifying glass and a microscope. The coin grew to the size of a chicken's egg. 'This is unrecorded. It is from the fourteenth century, an almost unprecedented find. It is pristine.' He looked at Shinjitai-san. 'How much did you pay for it?'

'Sensei, I paid only three hundred *mahn* for it, but it was from an American and I could hardly believe that it was genuine. Three million yen was all I had to hand and I feared it was not genuine and that I would lose the money.'

Akira nodded. 'I understand. What would you have me pay for it?'

Shinjitai-san bowed his head. 'Ten million yen.'

'That is not enough, but I will accept your offer.'

'Thank you, Sensei. I am grateful that you will accept it into the Imperial Collection.'

'See here,' said Akira, opening a drawer. He put down a small velvet tray in front of Shinjitai-san.

The old man gasped: it was another exquisite rarity. He looked at Akira. 'Can it be?'

Akira flexed the fingers on his short hand. 'Of course not, Shinjitai-san, but it is delightful to imagine.'

'Surely?'

'We should not torture ourselves, my friend.'

11

Brandon could not relax till they had cleared the harbour. When the gentle swell lifted the boat as they left the protection of the walls, he felt a surge of relief. The Japanese had fussed over the craft and gone to excessive lengths to explain everything in minute detail. It had taken an infuriating two hours to get them on their way. Now that the wind was blowing in his face and Reece had opened up the engine, he felt like a gull flying across the tips of the waves. By the afternoon they would be on site.

'It looks like it could get rough,' shouted Reece to him, as the boat ploughed ahead at full speed. 'There's a storm front out to the east, and if it comes this way it could get nasty.'

'What's the plan?'

'We get to the target, and if the storm moves in, we'll head back out to sea. If there's no let-up, we'll have to scrub the mission.'

Brandon nodded. He loved the sea, but not enough to go sailing in a typhoon.

The other guys were below, catching some sleep. Last night had been a long one of beers that only Reece had resisted. Brandon certainly could have used some shuteye himself, but the sea braced him like breaths of pure oxygen. He looked across the horizon at the perfect blue skies, punctuated by fluffy white cumulus clouds. It seemed impossible that a storm could suddenly sweep over the horizon, but he knew that the ocean was the most fickle of landscapes. Now as they drove through the waters, a large pod of dolphins broke the surface around them; they were hunting tuna. He watched, mesmerised, for a few happy moments. When he looked up, a wall of black stormclouds had darkened the heavens.

Around the boat, the dolphins were leaping, arcing and diving in their chase. The graceful mammals filled the sea for hundreds of yards in every direction, shimmering against the black backdrop.

'No wonder the old sailors were such a superstitious crew,' shouted Reece, over the pounding roar of the engines. 'The ocean's full of omens.'

'Omens?' queried Brandon, as he was jolted by a wave. 'Dolphins are a good one, right?'

'I should think so,' shouted Reece. 'Unless you're a fish.'

Brandon was in his wet suit already and Casey and Danny were kitting up below. The wind was blowing hard and purple-black clouds made an ugly contusion in the sky. The calm swell was now a rolling frenzy. Small fizzing crests broke at the tip of each wave. They were about an hour away from the bay and its cove of gold. The barometer was falling fast.

Reece was listening to the radio. He was scowling.

Casey came up from below and looked around. 'Crap,' he stated.

'We're going to go in and see if we have time for a quick dive,' said Brandon, his voice raised enough for Casey to hear him.

Reece had heard too. 'If it gets much worse we're going to high-tail it back. Looks like we're heading for a force eight and I don't think the bay can give us enough protection once we get into the sevens.'

Brandon loved the spray as it blew on his face. He would have been looking forward to the storm if it hadn't been about to screw up the dive.

Danny came up. 'Are we sailing into a freakin' hurricane here?' he said, his eyes on the far horizon. 'It's like fourteen hundred hours, right, not sunset?'

Reece grinned. 'Let's just say it isn't looking pretty.'

'All right,' said Danny. 'Bring it on.'

The boat was riding the waves, rearing up and slamming down again in a rollercoaster fashion. Brandon looked towards the faraway headland. This wasn't going to be some leisurely sports dive. This was shaping up to be a real dangerous mission. It was going to be a race against the clock.

Soon enough they were in the bay, heading straight for the cove. Reece weighed anchor and ran back to the cockpit. 'You got about an hour, boys. I'll keep you posted on the weather. Get going.'

They rolled off the boat's shallow side into the sea.

'Look!' said Danny, over the radio. 'What the fuck do you call *that*?'

Brandon peered down to the seabed below. His eyes widened.

'Welcome to Sharkopolis,' crackled Casey.

Hundreds of hammerheads were patrolling the seabed, their flat, elongated heads sweeping the sand, like a metal detector searches for landmines.

'Wow,' said Danny. 'This could make one crazy YouTube video.'

'Didn't you bring your Android phone?' quipped Brandon. 'The fucking fish are everywhere,' he added redundantly. If dolphins were good luck, what were hammerhead sharks? The animals were right on top of where they wanted to be. 'Can you guys see anything?' he radioed.

'Sharks.' That was Danny.

'Nothing on the bottom,' called Casey. 'Just sand and coral.'

'We're right over the spot,' Brandon told them.

'Casey,' radioed Danny, 'want to accompany me down to the bottom? You can be my shark buddy.'

'Sure,' said Casey.

Brandon stared down at the hammerheads sweeping back and forth. His heart sank. Last time the gold had been lying on the sand, twinkling up at him. This time there was nothing but sand and sealife. He had been dreaming of filling the green GI duffel he was carrying with coins but now that seemed like a foolish dream. Instead a storm was brewing upstairs and a *National Geographic* shark cluster-fuck was going on below.

Closer to shore, at the edge of his vision, a dozen hammerheads seemed to be swimming in a giant figure of eight. He propelled himself towards the formation simply because he had no other point of focus.

The hammerhead had a fierce reputation but the facts were different. It wasn't like a tiger, bull or great white shark that would eat you as soon as look at you, it was a more specialised and finicky predator. The purpose of its flat head was to sweep over the sand and sense creatures hiding just below. If you were a ray or some other hidden flat fish, it would feel you with its flattened forehead and snap you up.

That information wasn't too comforting because scalloped hammerheads were dangerous, and whatever the reason they were in that cove today, it was unlikely to make them chilled out. He was pretty sure sharks got grumpy when they were breeding – and why else would they be there in such profusion?

'These fucking fish,' interjected Danny. 'Good job there ain't no piles of coins to see down there – it'd be gnarly getting them up.'

'At least we know it's the right co-ordinates,' commented Casey. 'There were quite a few hammers around last time, as I recall.'

Brandon's face did its best to smile around the mouthpiece of the regulator. The crazy shark conga was pivoting over a lump of something, and that something had just flashed a dull golden light. He didn't say anything – he wanted to be sure. He swam on. Sure enough, a gold lump was sticking up from the sand, like a Starbucks pound cake. He dived down and slowly approached it from above, hoping the hammerheads would amend their circuit to accommodate him.

They didn't.

He swam lower, side on to the sharks as they soared by on their fixed path, sailing around or over the shiny golden chunk. He thought he saw the corner of a gold bar poking out of the sand.

Brandon took out his diver's knife, waited for a gap in the shark train and swam down to the gold. He was banking on the sharks turning away from him, as sharks normally did if confronted in the right way, and the theory that the hammerhead was not a natural man-eater. A shark was coming right at him and he held out the knife to jab its nose. Then another was gliding towards him from the other lap of the figure of eight. He was going to be the jack in a shark sandwich.

He couldn't fight two sharks with one knife.

The closest animal suddenly veered away, with a violent swish of its tail, and swung off backwards. He turned to the other fast-approaching beast and motioned at it with the knife, which flashed in the flickering light from above. It was practically in his face. It opened its mouth wide and jerked away, just inches from the tip of his blade.

Brandon glanced down at the pyramid sticking up out of the sand. It was definitely gold. The metal under the sand must be giving the sharks some kind of orgasm, he thought. He swam down and pulled at the gold bar, but it didn't come free. Two more sharks were headed his way, intent on swimming over the gold. He pulled at the ingot again, but it held fast.

He pushed up from the bottom and let the sharks glide under him. He needed help. He started to transmit, but Reece came into his earpiece. 'Getting a bit wild up here, guys. You'd better start thinking about coming back up.'

'Got something,' Brandon said. 'Get over here, guys, and keep these fish off me while I dig it up. Just need five, Reece.'

'You got it, but don't be ten.'

Danny and Casey were swimming to him.

Brandon briefed them as they came. 'Got a gold bar down there, end on.' The two men were at his side now.

'Let's go,' said Casey

Danny waved a shark away. 'I don't like to think of myself as bait.'

Brandon was excavating the soft sand around the gold bar. It was narrow but long and deep. It looked like a big slab of gold.

'These fish don't like me,' said Casey. 'Can you work faster?'

Brandon said nothing, but dug into the sand like a dog scrabbling in a groundhog burrow.

'Sheeeeit!' squealed Danny, as he fended off a giant hammerhead.

Brandon was still digging. He tried to move the slab but there was no give. He had uncovered about a foot of it.

'Guys,' came Reece's voice, 'you've gotta start coming up or you'll be climbing that cliff again. We're force eight up here now and there's a nine coming in fast.'

'Brandon?' came Casey's voice.

'Just give me one minute.' He dug and yanked at the slab, dug some more and yanked again.

'We gotta go!' said Reece.

'Coming,' said Danny.

Brandon yanked once more, and felt the slab move in his hand. 'Got it,' he said, lifting it. 'Jesus – I'll need help with this.'

Casey was suddenly at his side, and as the gold glittered in the sea-light, he engulfed it in his own GI duffel bag.

'Jesus,' cried Danny, stabbing at the nose of a hammerhead.

'Fucking shark.' He swam over to Casey and Brandon. 'She tried to fucking bite me!' he gasped, as they hauled the bag upwards.

'No fooling now, fellas,' crackled Reece.

'We're coming up the anchor as the load is real heavy. Get ready with a boat hook to haul in a heavy package.'

'Roger that.'

'What the fuck?' said Danny. The hammerheads were swimming up from the bottom. They seemed to be forming a wall around them, ten metres out. A menacing grey circuit of graceful but deadly shapes was circling them.

Brandon broke the surface first and Reece was leaning over with the hook, right on cue. The chop was harsh, throwing the bow of the boat up and down in irregular lunges. Casey was supporting him on his shoulder, helping him out of the water, while Brandon struggled to hook the bag's strap over the boathook. Reece leant out as far as he could, the rigging cutting painfully into his midriff as he stretched for the bag. The strap was just an inch out of reach. The prow lurched up, but dipped quickly.

Brandon pulled on the anchor chain and lifted himself as high as he could. The weight of the bag was almost too much for him.

'These fucking sharks are creeping me out,' he heard Danny say, as the prow dipped to its limit. As his arm went out to full extension, his biceps cramped and a wave washed over him.

Shit! He had dropped the bag. The sea fell again, and as the water streamed from his mask, he saw the green bag on the end of the boathook.

Reece gritted his teeth. The bag was almost too heavy to hold on the end of the pole at the full stretch of his right arm. The rigging dug deep into his flesh. He caught the pole with his other hand and let the duffel swing down the side of the boat as the hull bucked under the swell. With a focused effort he applied himself to a giant heave – and the bag was on the deck. He groaned and rubbed his burning belly. The bag's contents had better be worth it.

'Let's get dry,' said Brandon, letting go of the anchor.

'Fuck these sharks,' said Danny again. 'They're closing in.' He was making for the dive deck at the back, which was lurching in and out of the water.

'I'll cover you,' said Casey, eyeing the predators circling the boat.

Brandon grabbed the lip of the dive platform as he saw Danny's flippers disappear from the water. A hammerhead was coming right for him. He glanced to Casey. Another shark was heading for him. He pulled out his knife. He wasn't about to let the sharks hit his friend from both sides.

Casey and Brandon were treading water back to back.

'Where are you?' yelled Reece.

'Shark attack,' Brandon snapped.

Casey jabbed the hammerhead on the nose and the shark swam off as Brandon waved away the other. Now Brandon could see three more sharks making for him. He grabbed the lip of the dive deck, grasped Casey's arm and hauled them both in line with the long edge of the deck.

A boathook plunged into the water from the side as he hauled himself up and he felt something grip him. It started to shake his right leg violently. A shark had him in its jaws. He fought to pull himself on board. Danny grabbed him under one arm and Casey pulled the other. A hammerhead had him yet he felt no pain, he thought dimly. This was how it felt to be eaten alive. The dive platform bucked in the swell and Reece was before him, clasping his chest and heaving him forwards against the pull of the shark.

His three buddies were fighting a tug of war with the

hammerhead and Brandon was the rope.

He spat out his regulators. Why wasn't he in agony? *'Pull, for fuck's sake!'* he screamed. He shot forwards and they all fell backwards. There was a crash inside the boat as Reece bounced off the bait tank. Danny threw himself into the boat and Casey rolled after him.

Brandon jumped up. The tip of his right flipper had been bitten clean off. The boat rose steeply as a giant wave washed under them and he was pitched forwards, looking down into the sea, about to fall in. He caught the side of the boat with his right hand, face angled down to the grey water. The hammerhead rose out of the water, its mouth agape. Brandon found himself staring into its red throat at the wicked white teeth. As the boat rose, tilting him ever forwards, he knew he was going to fall into those jaws.

Danny yanked him back. 'Don't fucking feed the fish, man,' he said.

The boat slumped, a wall of water shooting up at its prow. Brandon jumped into the stern. He was laughing crazily. The engines were on and the anchor was on its way up. A great storm was rising.

'About time,' shouted Reece, at no one in particular. 'This is going to get very ugly real fast. Got to clear the cove damn quick or we'll be on the rocks in no time.'

The anchor locked in, and Reece set the engines. It rolled heavily as it got underway.

They took their tanks off quickly as the boat shook them about. Casey looked at Brandon's ripped flipper. 'That's a keeper,' he shouted, above the noise of the gale.

'Mighty windy,' said Danny. He picked up the duffel bag and put it on the table next to the helm, where on a calm day anglers might have a lazy beer and watch others fish or dive.

'Want to open the bag?' said Danny to Brandon. 'You found it.'

'No,' said Brandon, his hands shaking under the table. 'You go ahead.'

'OK,' said Danny. He unzipped the duffel. The gold flashed like a torch's beam and they gasped. Reece glanced at them, then back at the mountainous seas ahead. Danny slid the slab out and turned it over.

'Boy,' said Casey.

On the reverse there was a picture.

Danny whistled, 'Holy cow.'

'Let me see that,' said Brandon, forgetting his nerves. He took it from Danny. A giant golden sun was rising over a mountainous coastline. Engraved golden birds flew above an ancient boat, fishing by the golden shore. The sea glittered. He passed it to Casey, who marvelled at the scene.

'What have we got?' called Reece, his eyes fixed on the horizon.

'Some kind of crazy carved-gold slab,' said Danny. 'You want to see?'

'Later,' said Reece. 'Let me fight this battle first. This boat wasn't built for a force nine. Not many are.'

Brandon took the slab back. It was heavy like only gold could be. It must weigh at least fifteen pounds, he marvelled. That was a lot of gold. 'How much is gold an ounce?' he asked, transfixed by the carving.

'Fifteen hundred dollars,' said Casey. 'It was two thousand a while back.'

Brandon stared at him. 'This is, like, two or three hundred ounces.'

'Yep,' said Casey. 'And even if it's nine carat that's a fairly large amount of money just in gold.'

'Nine carat?' Danny laughed. 'No way! That's pure twenty-four-carat gold.'

'You sure?' said Brandon.

'No,' said Danny, taking the slab, 'but this is an artwork, not a freakin' ingot. That means it's worth multiples of any gold price. Sheesh! Look at it! Man, it's like the fashizzle.'

The boat jinked and slammed into a wave. They jolted in their seats.

'Unbelievable,' said Reece. They were riding straight into a hurricane.

Brandon took the slab back into his hands. As he did so, he looked up and through the windscreen. They were riding up the face of a gigantic wave. Unconsciously he gripped the slab tighter.

Danny and Casey followed his gaze. They looked back at each other in silence, then at Reece.

'Hold tight!' Reece howled – and the boat corkscrewed over the crest.

12

The doctor had a gleam in his eyes. He seemed to be enjoying his patient's predicament a little too much. 'You see these?' he said. 'I think they're screws.'

Jim nodded.

'Well, I suggest they're holding a plate on – see this shadow?'

Jim nodded again.

'I think I should take the plate out and remove what's inside, then screw it back on again.'

Jim was wondering how Stafford had known of Dr Eric. It certainly hadn't been Dr Eric's plastic surgery skills that had won him the introduction. He was a small, grey-haired man in a white coat, with an excitable, enthusiastic manner. He didn't show the shock or fear of the previous doctor. He seemed almost familiar with the idea of some guy having a GPS tracker embedded in his torso.

'I can make an incision here and pull down the muscle and, without much disruption, get at the device. Your downtime will be minimal – a few aches and that'll be about it. I can do it now, if you like.'

Jim sat up. 'Now?'

'Certainly,' said Dr Eric, eagerly, his staring blue eyes drilling into him.

Jim fidgeted.

'I can do it under a local, if you're up for it.'

'Local?'

'A local anaesthetic. It's not much of a procedure.' He held out his fingers about two inches. 'It's a small cut and the whole thing should take no more than ten or fifteen minutes.'

'Oh,' said Jim, surprised that things were developing so fast. He thought about the tracking device. He really hated the idea of it, ticking away or whatever it did, inside him. All he had to do was lie down for a few minutes, still conscious, and he would be free of it. That didn't seem so bad. 'OK,' he said, 'let's do it.'

'Right you are.'

'We're heading to Higashi harbour. Over,' shouted Reece, into the mouthpiece.

The noise blotted out the first words of the response. '… do you require assistance? Over.'

'No assistance required. Over.' He repeated the message: 'No assistance required.'

Casey stood, braced, by his side.

Reece shook his head. 'Yet,' he said.

Casey had never been in such heavy seas – or not unless he was in the belly of a giant warship. A battleship could brave any seas and would barely notice a normal storm. But for them, the six miles to the nearest safe harbour would mean twenty miles of steaming because they could not travel across the giant waves. Instead they had to head into them or run with them and that meant they had to set out to sea first before they could come back to land.

They sailed into the storm, climbing up and down the mountainous rollers, blown with thick foam. It was a journey into the depths of hell.

Finally Reece shouted, 'I'm going to turn her now and surf us into port.'

'Let's go,' Casey agreed. He flicked the piece of gum he was chewing out of a gap in his teeth on the right side of his mouth.

He was smiling to himself again. Even though they were nothing but a piece of floating crap adrift in the tempest, he didn't doubt they would make the harbour. They just would. That was how it was with the team. If you were going to navigate in a typhoon then Reece was about the only guy you'd want at the helm.

Down below, Danny and Brandon were sleeping, Brandon hugging the gold slab as if it was some kind of teddy bear. Giant waves rose and fell, the wind howling like some demonic monster, its maw slathered with froth. Yet Reece was going to use the fishing boat like a surfboard and carve his way to shore. Not even the towering grey face of the wave that loomed beside them as they turned made him doubt his colleague's ability to pull it off. The boat bucked, shook, fell and rose again.

They slid down the smooth back slope of the giant wave, the crest marbled with foam. Reece brought the boat around as hard as it would go, slowing down and around into the trough of the swell. The boat heaved heavily to starboard and rode up, its stern facing the rising wave behind it, which gathered itself into a vertical wall. Reece let the wave catch up with him, then applied the power to face down the wave. 'Check,' he said.

'OK,' said Casey, looking back at the wave, a stationary wall above.

Reece's hand was on the throttle. He glanced forwards and to the side to make sure he had matched the speed of the wave. He would have to keep his heading and speed exact for perhaps two hours. 'Check.'

'Check,' said Casey, watching the steel wall rising behind them, poised and frozen above.

Reece grinned up the right side of his face. The next hour or two were going to be very real.

13

They were all in the wheelhouse as they approached land. The waves were gigantic, blown up into mountains by the force eleven gale. The sea was as white as if its steely cliffs were covered with snow. With their backs to the wind and the protection of the water wall behind them, they were sheltered from the worst of the hurricane.

Reece was nudging the boat to keep it in line with the harbour entrance. Behind the lip of the next wave, he was navigating on instruments alone. They would have to surf towards the shore past the edge of the harbour wall, then jink hard to starboard to get behind the breakwater. The closer to the outer edge of the concrete barrier they came, the better for the manoeuvre. The closer to the sea wall they were, the more chance there was that the boat would be driven onto it. He was going to try to thread it through the eye of a needle in the midst of the typhoon.

Brandon looked at the radar and its map overlay. Reece was cutting it close. He might come in too tight on starboard and wreck, or be driven off to port and get dashed onto the shore ahead. In his mind, they were in the hands of the Almighty.

Casey was calling, 'Check,' every few moments, as Reece kept the boat on the slope of the wave, continually trimming the engine to keep it in the notch.

Danny was looking out of the windscreen through the water that the wipers struggled to clear. He was grinning painfully, like someone thinking of a hurtful but funny joke.

Brandon could hear the thunder of waves breaking on the harbour wall. The white explosions were erupting into sight now, above the crest of the forward wave.

'Hold on, guys,' said Reece. He accelerated, turning the boat, dived down the wave and across its trough.

The wave was rising, a giant black jaw that was heading forwards to engulf them and smash the boat to pieces.

Jesus, thought Brandon. Reece was going to drive them along the wave and into the tube like some boat-sized surfer dude.

There was a monstrous explosion of water to starboard as the wave struck the edge of the harbour wall, forward of them. The rear of the fishing boat rolled, but its bow was dipping into the broken ocean. It sank and rose into the suddenly calm waters of the harbour.

Brandon and Danny high-fived and whooped. They turned and Casey joined them.

'Just let me get into harbour proper,' said Reece, unmoved. 'You can all buy me a drink later.'

Brandon watched the waves roll in behind them as they entered the outer ring of the harbour. To starboard, wave after wave erupted against the high sea defences. He marvelled at how a few feet made the difference between misery and bliss.

At the quayside, a small crowd had formed to watch them dock. Brandon sprang onto the quay from the gently rolling deck, as the Japanese harbour men quickly tied up the boat. The look of relief on their faces was palpable. It wasn't their boat, of course, but it had sailed in on the wing of a typhoon and they had watched it on the radar as it made its dash for their safe harbour. The boat had navigated a remarkable escape and the harbour men were proud to be part of it. They bowed a lot at the crew and the SEALs bowed back and said, '*Domo*,' several times.

Brandon sauntered along at the head of the team. He was

boiling over with adrenalin and relief, but he knew he had to hold it in so his buddies didn't see. He glanced back at the serious little Japanese guys and smiled.

They wandered down the jetty as if they had come back from an unremarkable day's fishing. On one shoulder they carried their diving kit in big nylon holdalls; Brandon had strapped his GI duffel and its golden load to his back.

14

Jim felt as if he had been slammed in the ribs with a sledgehammer. He sat turned to one side in the back of the Mercedes black cab. It wasn't like the old-style London cabs. It was much bigger, which he had appreciated when he had struggled to climb in, bent in half. The painkillers weren't helping.

The surgery had taken longer than promised but it had been worth it. He was holding the innards of the gadget that Dr Eric had removed. It was an entire device, about the size of a box of matches. The case looked like it might be platinum or some other non-corroding metal. It had a green LED that flashed every minute. He imagined it flashing in the closed container attached to his rib. It had a functional but sinister appearance, smooth and cold to the touch.

The green light flashed again. Was it sending information, or had it merely reassured its owners before it was fitted that it was functioning? He was going to put it on the shelf at home and then they would think he was sitting there permanently. It would tell them he had become a hermit, forever housebound. Now he could go as he pleased and no one would know where he was. In the Congo that would have been fatal, but he wasn't aiming to get into any more scrapes. He had had enough adventure for a lifetime already.

The black cab felt like a limo, heading back to Wapping and his riverside mini-palace. It wasn't like one of Davas's mansions, historic and huge. It was a modern sanctuary fashioned out of an old warehouse that had once stored produce from all over the world in a pre-modern chaos that would be seen now as quaint and inefficient. In the block, there was an aura of two hundred years' ground-in sweat and blood lurking below the brick. It gave off an atmosphere of a reality that was just waiting its chance to burst to the surface.

He pressed his side, which ached. He imagined himself opened up, Dr Eric working away with his scalpel and screwdriver. He was amazed that, after a few stitches, a shot of antibiotic, bandages and a dose of painkiller, he could be on his way home. It seemed mildly barbaric.

Still a little dazed, he wondered how he would feel if a limb had been blasted off in some battle. Would he drag himself along, trying to reach safety, or would he just lie there? He felt like a clock, set going at the watchmaker's behest. To Jim, it seemed that if you could just keep moving, nothing could stop you. His head was spinning. He could do with a lie down.

He gave the cabbie forty pounds. 'Keep the change.' The meter looked like it said twenty-eight, but he wasn't going to hang around to juggle change. He was hunting for keys.

'You all right, boss?' said the cabbie, but Jim didn't hear him as he lunged for his front door.

If he had been thinking, he would have rung the bell and Stafford would have answered, but instead he was trying to extract his keys from his pocket and select the right one without looking. He failed and, leaning against the door, he went through all four before he had the one he needed. He plunged it towards the lock, which admitted it. He turned it and toppled into the hallway, pulling the key out as he went. He tilted back, slamming the door. His side felt heavy. He steadied himself and moved forward. The way ahead was blurred.

There was the shriek of the alarm.

'Bloody hell.' He staggered and the floor sagged. There was a loud grinding sound and a metal grille shot up in front of him.

Jim spun round.

There was another prison grille behind him. He was penned in.

He fell to his knees.

Stafford dashed into the hallway. 'I'm so sorry,' he said, typing something into a small white panel in the wall.

Jim wanted to lie down on the carpet – it felt so friendly and warm. The cage ground back into its place.

'Are you all right?' asked his butler.

'Fine.'

'Let me help you up.'

'No, I'm OK.' He concentrated and forced himself to his feet. He smiled unconvincingly at Stafford. 'I think I need to go to bed.'

'Please let me help you, sir.'

'No, I'm fine.'

15

They looked at each other silently over their beers. There was a furious amount of telepathy going down.

'I can read you like a book,' said Danny finally, to Reece, 'but there are so many words I don't understand.'

Reece produced his lopsided smirk. He let out a groan. 'So, you want to hear what I think?'

They agreed that they did – silently.

Reece scratched the back of his head, where his right trapezium met the short hair covering his shaven cranium. 'OK, I think I should take this back to Tokyo and see what reaction I get. Thoughts?'

Brandon didn't want to cast any doubt but he asked anyway: 'Do you think a store can pay like hundreds of thousands of dollars for the slab?'

Reece nodded approval. 'Good question. I don't know. Those guys paid over fifty Gs like it was small change, but I have no idea about more.'

'Take it abroad?' said Casey.

'Cowboy!' said Danny. 'Nice idea, but we might be trafficking, like, antiquities. That would be serious.'

Casey's head sank into his thick shoulders.

'That's a good point, Danny,' said Reece. 'The slab is either a nice piece of junk or a super artefact. Either way, we need to act innocent. I reckon I take it to the old man in the first place I went and see what he says.' Reece was imagining him writing a number. The offer was big, but somehow not so big as to bring the roof crashing in.

'Maybe we should just hand it over,' said Brandon.

The three looked at him. 'What if it's worth a million dollars?' said Danny. 'Would you hand it over then?'

'It might be the right thing to do.'

'Yup,' said Reece, 'but let me go to Tokyo and see first.'

'OK.'

Reece stood at the antiques shop door. Nothing had changed since he was there a few weeks back, except that a cigarette stub had blown into the corner of the step. It seemed wrong, so he bent down, picked it up and put it into his pocket. He would throw it away later.

He pulled the door open and went in, ducking under the flagged lintel.

The old man came out from behind the beaded curtain and smiled in recognition.

This time Reece paid more attention to the cabinets as he passed them. There were swords and armour of every era, and he realised that many of the artefacts on display must be far more ancient and precious than he had previously thought. Some items were centuries older than the United States. They had belonged to generations long lost and forgotten, atoms from the past that had somehow survived while everything else had perished. When he was gone, in a few short years, no one would remember him; nothing would be left. He would be absorbed into the dirt. Yet here there were fragments of a momentous past, preserved like chicken legs in a freezer.

He felt his stomach flutter and the GI duffel sag on his shoulder. He took a deep breath. He felt like a kid on his first date. 'Hi,' he said.

'Hi,' said the shopkeeper, smiling and bowing.

Reece sat down in the little chair before the desk and dropped the bag gently to the floor. He unzipped it and lifted the heavy slab onto the counter. 'Please,' he said.

The shopkeeper gasped, in an unsettling way, at the sight of it. The old man's mouth was open. He began to nod fast. 'May I?' he said, opening his palms to Reece.

'Sure,' said Reece.

The old man ran his right hand over the decorated face. He looked up at Reece in what seemed to be shock. He traced the carving, then ran his index finger around the circumference of the sun. He looked up at Reece again, a tear escaping from his left eye. He was smiling. He was shaking.

'Would you like to buy?' said Reece, clumsily.

The old shopkeeper lifted the top of the slab and, magnifying glass in hand, began to study the face. He laid it down carefully and looked at Reece again. He dropped the magnifying glass and stared up at the ceiling as if in thought. He made a throaty gurgling sound. His forehead was suddenly covered with sweat. The colour drained from his face, which faded from pink to white to grey to green. He turned in his seat and pitched stiffly from his stool onto the floor.

'Jeez!' said Reece, jumping up. He vaulted the counter. He pressed his finger into the old man's neck. There was a pulse. The bead curtain moved. The little old lady hobbled over as fast as she could and looked anxiously down at them.

'*Ambaransu,*' he said. '*Hyu, kuyu, dayo.*'

The old man was breathing OK. Reece loosened his belt and put the embroidered cushion from the chair under his head. The old lady was still gazing mournfully at her husband.

'Ambulance – *ambaransu?*' he asked.

She nodded.

'*Asupirin?*' he said. '*Mizu!*'

She disappeared and came back with a glass of fizzing water. He sipped it quickly – it tasted of Disprin. He fed it to the old man, who was mumbling as he drank it, his eyes closed, his lips quivering. Aspirin would help a little.

Reece monitored the old man's pulse as he fed him the last of the drink. He seemed to be stable. He looked up at the old lady. 'He's going to be OK,' he said. '*Yoroshii.*' There were sirens.

He stood up, vaulted the counter and put the slab back into the duffel bag. He ran to the door and let the paramedics in, then led them to the old man behind the counter. He put his hand over his own heart. 'Heart attack,' he said. '*Tokkan.*'

The paramedics smiled in acknowledgement and went to work.

Reece grabbed the duffel bag. Time to scoot.

16

Jim looked at his email. He was waiting for a message from Jane. It didn't matter how much he hoped or waited, it never arrived early enough to keep him happy. It was like food to a starving man. She doled out scraps to just below the required calorie count needed to keep him healthy. Didn't she know he was waiting on every little word from her? Did she do it on purpose? Was she just too busy for him? Was some hunky super-agent lavishing attention on her?

When he got seriously frustrated by it, he would beat up on a stock or currency. He could spot the weak ones, like a lion could spot a calf separated from the herd. He would dive at it and drag it down. A few hundred million thrown against a weak financial instrument would cave it in under his claws. Flawed currencies, bonds or stocks were too lame to survive, and he would push them fast to the edge of extinction. Yet he would pull back from his attacks just before he drove them beyond the point of no return. While he could pile up yet greater profit if he traded them to their logical destruction, he couldn't help but imagine the faces behind the numbers.

A company might be doomed to bankruptcy from bad management but there were real people behind the stock chart of the dying company, normal folk who had to make their mortgage payment or cover their next credit card bill, thousands of them, perhaps tens of thousands, and, like the company, they, too, were clinging on. When he reached the point at which he knew he could tilt the lot of them off the cliff, a point they were doomed to reach some time anyway, he would stop and sigh.

Then he would buy back his stock to cover and consequentially push the price up again. He would make a few millions and roll a few numbers up at the end of his trading account and maybe, just maybe, there would be an email from Jane by the time he had finished.

If he could go back a few years, he would be energised by the fear of failure, motivated by the fight to hold onto his tenuous position. Now that was gone and he was floating in a void of wealth, a shallow but dense pool of anaesthetic.

Stafford brought him a round of toasted Marmite slices and a cup of sugary tea. Why couldn't she just SMS him 'Hello'?

17

The little Japanese bar had become their personal haunt. Reece looked at his men. 'There's no way we can fence this in Tokyo. This slab is worth way more than the coins, and those antiques stores can't write that sort of cheque.' He could see the old man's eyes rolling back in his head and his complexion turning from healthy red to a deathly pallor. 'On top of that, we don't know the laws here, and fishing up a valuable antiquity might just get us sunk. We've got to take this thing abroad.'

They all nodded.

'So, Danny, you look like the one to go,' he continued.

'Hey-hey,' said Danny. He grinned nervously. 'But where?'

'Home is too hot,' said Casey. 'We don't want to shit in our own backyard.'

'Right,' said Reece. 'NY would be cool, but if we got busted, it would be game over. That leaves London, as far as I can see. Anyone got a better idea?'

'Hong Kong?' Brandon suggested.

No one responded, which meant they thought no.

'So we'll go to London, England,' said Reece.

'Londonshire,' said Danny. 'I like it!'

'Good job I got our furlough reassigned,' said Reece, 'cause meanwhile we'll go back and keep looking for more of those coins while Danny's out in England.'

'Agreed,' said Casey.

'You've drawn up a plan of attack?' said Danny.

'Sure,' said Reece.

'So what's the thing worth?' asked Danny, for the

hundredth time.

Reece gestured at Brandon. 'What do you think?'

'A million dollars,' said Brandon.

'More,' said Danny.

'How much more?' said Casey.

'A hell of a lot more,' said Danny.

'A million or more,' said Reece, smiling.

Danny tittered. 'Reece, you sure you don't want to go yourself?'

'Wish I could,' he said, 'but after that typhoon I want to be behind the wheel again on our next trip.'

'OK,' said Danny, 'but don't blame me if I get more than a million for it.'

'We don't do blame,' said Reece.

Danny was happy to stretch his legs. Getting a jump seat on a military transport was not a luxury experience. The seats were made for skinny airmen, not bulky marines like him. Mildenhall was some kind of field in England, and outside it looked like a normal day in Maine. He wasn't a fan of green and rainy, he liked it hot and brown, like his home town, Austin, Texas. He was going to have to get some freakin' train to London, but for now he was nervous about clearing the base with a duffel full of ancient gold.

He didn't have much to worry about. As a SEAL he was pretty much royalty and there was a lot of smiling and nodding as they stamped his papers. For Danny, respect was about the best thing in the world. It was why he had qualified as a doctor. He hadn't expected to be a medic, but that was what it had taken for him to become a SEAL, so he had forced himself through the training. It was so much harder than the running and lifting, but to get the respect he craved he'd had to heave his brain through that course in the same way that he'd had to haul his body up and down hills and through water.

It hurt his brain to learn more than it hurt his body to struggle, but he told himself it was just another ache in another muscle; a muscle that had never been his strongest. He liked his brain pumped up. Although he didn't use it as a first reflex, he knew it had grown strong.

His 'little guy' was in charge, a younger self that pulled on three levers: his mind, his body and his emotions. The 'little guy' had the last word and always had since the day the dog had attacked his little sister.

They had been walking down a back alley near home when a dog had jumped a fence and gone for them. It was some kind of pit-bull thing, a giant beast to him and the little girl. It had grabbed her face and pushed her to the ground. He had grabbed it by the balls and yanked them as hard as he could. It had turned on him. As it had lunged, its fangs a perfect white, something had gelled inside his soul. The dog had grabbed his arm and pulled him to the ground. He had stuck his thumb into its right eye and pushed until it came out of its socket as the dog shook him. The dog shuddered, but shook him harder.

The pit-bull was going to tear his arm off. He pulled his thumb out of the bloody socket and shifted his grip to press hard on the other eye. The dog let go and sprang back. It yowled, spun backwards and ran a few paces. It stopped, blood running down its muzzle, its right eye hanging gorily.

Danny had jumped up and run to his sister, who sat stunned, her face covered with blood, her cheek torn. He pulled her up and grabbed her around the waist. 'Fire!' he had screamed. 'Fire!' Everyone said people would come to a fire, but not a murder. He knew no one would come to a crazed dog attack. 'Fire!' he cried, and soon they came.

From that moment on, the little boy who had fought the

dog had taken his place on the bench: he was the manager who called the shots.

Danny sat on the British equivalent of a Greyhound bus to London. He looked out at all the little fields. It was rather like Japan, small and neat. There was something kind of cute about the landscape – it was strangely model-like. The people in the country seemed to have reached an agreement to share in a friendly way, too small a space to live comfortably. Through it all, a skinny freeway wove towards the city.

London was meant to be foggy and have soldiers in red there. They always teased the Brits about the London fog and the Brits laughed and teased them back about the dollar being three to the pound. That was good because three dollars to the pound for the gold brick would be great.

It might not be foggy in the UK today but it sure as hell didn't need fog for the weather to be as miserable as sin. No wonder the Brits were everywhere around the world: staying home would be seriously depressing.

Right now the guys would be out to sea again, sailing to the bay to look for more gold. If he wasn't so tired he'd be jigging in his bus seat like a child on his way to the fair. Instead, jetlagged, he was just awake. Tomorrow there was an auction at Christie's of antiquities. He was going to sit in on it and see if anything made sense to him. Then he'd go to the valuation department and get an opinion. An over muscular grin spread across his face. Time was passing way too slowly for his liking.

At the hotel he would stay in until the next day. He was not going out and risking anything. He would wait, eat and sleep until the new day came and his mission really kicked off.

The next morning, getting out of bed was a hard stretch. He could have lain in the nice sheets at the Best Western Marble

Arch for many more hours. The auction was in about an hour and that was enough time to shave, shower and shift to Christie's.

18

Jim sat at the front with his numbered paddle. It said '9'. Nine was a good number, he thought. It was three squared, and three was the basic number of sides for a two dimensional object. Nine was solidity squared and anything solid, squared, had to be his friend. The room was filling and he looked at his watch. He was early as usual.

He took out the catalogue of ancient objects. He had marked each lot with a note. There was a mummy, a Spartan helmet, a spectacular Roman gold necklace, a mysterious glass Anglo-Saxon drinking horn. It was all so insanely cheap. How could a Roman's surgeon's kit be worth less than a thousand pounds? How could a Roman gold signet ring with a fabulously engraved stone be worth little more than that? A Bronze Age axe head for a few hundred quid? Absurd. It seemed like a hoax.

Even the most expensive item, a head of Emperor Hadrian, was only a hundred and twenty thousand – he could flip that out of a dollar-yen trade in a few minutes – yet the statue had been buried in the ground for two thousand years, a unique masterpiece, now apparently little appreciated. The catalogue was like a treasure chest. The prices reminded him of some obvious Internet fraud, yet this was one of the most prestigious auction houses in the world. The objects were real and so were those prices. He thumbed through the catalogue. It all looked so appealing.

His side was throbbing under his arm and, when he pressed it, felt swollen, firm to his touch. He fiddled with his phone as if something on it might interest him. How sad was it that he had no one to call? He SMSed Jane. 'Morning,' he wrote. She would be fast asleep and he wondered whether a beep thousands of miles away would wake her. He felt guilty at the possibility but it would be nice to hear her. Would he tell her he'd had the tracker removed or hold his tongue until they met again and she took off his shirt? Would it make her angry, put her off sex? What would she say?

The thoughts buzzed around his head.

The room was almost full. Would he have to battle with some other rich antiquities addict? Had Stafford clued the auction house in sufficiently for him to buy what he liked without suddenly hitting some kind of credit limit? He fancied the Hercules statue at the beginning of the auction. The hero was bronze and leant against a big knobbly club. It was meant to cost around a hundred thousand pounds and would look good on a shelf in the lounge. In fact, he fancied it all. If he wasn't careful, home would soon look like some dusty museum. He gazed around. The auction was going to start shortly. He was getting rather excited – he could buy the auction house, let alone the contents of the sale. There was something rather wonderful about that feeling of power.

He took a deep breath. Whatever he bought, it wouldn't beat how he felt when he found something on the foreshore. Money couldn't buy that buzz.

Danny watched the young man at the front. He was snapping up the whole freakin' auction. Old guys in nice jackets were frowning and puffing as he bid them out of their league. Was he some kind of joker or some super-rich dude on a roll? A dealer tried to match him on a broken marble foot. The catalogue said it was worth two thousand pounds, but they were soon bidding close to fifty thousand. The dealer looked very serious but the young guy was taking him on. The price hit a hundred thousand, then two hundred thousand. The room had gone very quiet.

Two hundred and ten, went the young guy.

Two hundred and twenty, went the dealer.

Two hundred and thirty.

Two hundred and forty. The dealer was apparently intent on winning.

The young guy didn't bid back.

The dealer smiled.

The young guy nodded and motioned with his hand to admit defeat.

The dealer looked suddenly horrified. The gavel went down. The dealer coughed, got up and walked out of the room.

What was that about? wondered Danny.

The young guy carried on his remorseless pursuit, the crowd now apparently accepting that he was going to buy pretty much every lot.

Danny had no idea what he was watching, but he knew what he had to do.

There was a break in the proceedings and the young guy got up and headed down the aisle in Danny's direction.

Danny got up. 'Hey,' he said, as Jim passed him.

Jim knew immediately that he was looking at a GI. 'Hey, soldier,' he said.

The American double-took, then grinned. 'You got a second?'

Jim had been thinking about getting a coffee and going back for the second session, but he said, 'Sure, mate.'

'Sit down,' said the American. 'Let me show you something.' He moved back two seats and pulled up the duffel bag.

Jim was on a high from all the bidding. 'What have you got?' he said. He saw a flash of gold. He bent down and saw a box inside a green cloth bag, a gold-decorated fabulous jewel flashing up at him like an old coin lying in the mud. 'That's amazing,' he murmured.

'It is,' said the American.

'Brilliant,' said Jim, as if he'd met a lucky bridegroom with his newly-wed wife.

'I'm selling,' said the soldier.

'Are you?'

'Sure.'

'But it's beautiful,' Jim said, as if that meant anything in a saleroom to a seller.

'Isn't it just.'

Jim knew he had to have it. 'How much do you want for it?'

'A million.'

'OK.'

'Or two.'

'OK,' said Jim.

'Can we go somewhere private?' said the American, glancing around.

'OK,' said Jim, standing up. 'I'm Jim.' He held out his hand.

The soldier took it in his giant paw. 'Danny.'

'Good to meet you.'

In the cab, Jim gawped at the article in his lap. It was a heavy lump of gold engraved in the most delicate and refined way he could imagine. 'Where did you get this?' he said.

'Can't say,' said Danny.

'It's not stolen, is it?'

'No,' said Danny.

'I can Google stolen Japanese treasure, you know,' he said, not taking his eyes of the tableau.

'Be my guest.'

'It's amazing,' Jim said again.

Danny just grinned. 'There's at least half a million dollars of raw gold in it.'

Jim didn't reply. What was gold to him? It was just a metal that scared people bought. Gold was only good for Mexican teeth and jewellery. The slab was another matter. It was a masterpiece, carved by a genius. He wasn't a connoisseur of the arts but he had handled enough bits and bobs to know when he was in the presence of majesty.

The cab drew up outside Jim's house and the two men got out. Jim paid off the driver, then went up to his front door. He knocked, and Stafford answered. The butler looked questioningly at Danny. 'Please come in.'

'Danny's got an amazing thing he wants to sell,' said Jim, ushering his guest through to the lounge.

Danny went to the window. The panoramic view of the Thames was impressive and he turned to compliment his host. Before he could speak, he caught a glimpse of a computer on a desk by the far wall. That looked like General Jane... The screen flashed out.

Jim led him to a table in the middle of the room, a rickety old wooden piece. 'Lay it down here,' he said. 'Look at this, Stafford.'

Danny put the GI duffel on the floor, unzipped it and heaved the slab out. He put it on the table.

Stafford bent over it, adjusting his glasses. He looked at Jim silently, in the opaque way he did when he meant something important. Jim could never guess *what* he meant until it was too late for the answer to be useful. 'OK, Danny, what do you want for it?' he asked.

Danny laughed. The little boy with his hand on the levers thought they looked friendly. 'A million.'

'Dollars?' asked Jim.

The little boy pulled the lever that operated his brain. 'Euros…' He hesitated. 'Pounds.'

'Which?' asked Stafford.

'Which is more?' asked Danny, cheekily.

'Dollars,' said Jim.

Danny shifted uncomfortably. He sure as hell knew that wasn't true. 'Are you kidding me?'

'Yes,' said Jim. 'The pound is the heaviest. A million pounds is three million dollars.'

'OK,' said Danny, nervously, 'that will do just fine.'

'Right,' said Jim, 'but I need to make a call.'

'You know, I'm kind of scared of people getting to know about it.'

'Is it stolen?' Jim asked, for the second time.

'No,' interjected Stafford.

Jim and Danny looked at him in mutual surprise.

'I'm sure Danny is an honest man.' Stafford coughed a little. 'Aren't you, Danny?'

'Yes,' he said.

'Just one call, no one sinister,' said Jim.

Max Davas not sinister? He certainly was, as far as many were concerned.

Davas was quietly happy, his Rolex Milgauss ticking quietly away next to the giant superconductive magnets that drove the accelerator. 'Are you sure you aren't going to create a black hole?' he enquired.

'No,' said Professor Eigen. 'To the contrary. I hope we will create many. I'm sure you know they will simply evaporate.'

Davas raised his eyebrows. 'As long as your equation is not upside down.'

Eigen gesticulated. 'We are sure we are right.'

Davas waved at the enclosure beside the magnets of the

toroid at the terminal of the accelerator. 'And this is where the field will be at its strongest?'

'Right here, just before the detector.'

'I want my server as close as possible. I don't want a millimetre wasted,' said Davas, pointing to a space that clearly blocked the alley that ran alongside the giant tube that was the particle accelerator.

'For twenty million dollars a year in funding, we can dig out the wall a little more,' said Eigen, smiling.

'You don't believe in my tachyons, do you?' said Davas, with a grin.

'And you don't believe in my benign black holes.'

'You're right,' said Davas, 'and I seem to be in partnership with both Doomsday scenarios.'

'We are only using the energy of a tiny flying insect. Even though we are expending a teravolt of energy, we aren't at risk of creating an earth-gobbling-sized black hole.'

Davas wagged a finger. 'You forget, Hans, who you are talking to.'

Eigen chuckled as Davas pulled his BlackBerry from his pocket. At the accelerator, everywhere was connected, even deep underground.

Davas would only answer his phone for Jim.

'Tell me if I should pay a million pounds for this,' said Jim. An image popped up on the screen as he downloaded it.

'Yes,' said Davas.

'Anything else?' asked Jim.

'No,' said Davas.

'Can't you say any more?' asked Jim, slightly irritated.

'No,' said Davas. 'Go to five if you need to, and if that's not enough call back.'

'A tachyon field will *not* pull your server into the future,' said Eigen, by way of attracting Davas's attention from the image on his little screen.

'What?' said Davas, looking up. 'Let's forget the experiment, then.'

Professor Eigen merely cocked his head questioningly.

'All right, I was only joking. It's worth an attempt, don't you think?'

'Why not?' agreed Eigen.

Davas smiled. 'I already have a tachyon device. I just need a back-up.'

'Is that so?' said Eigen, looking a little perturbed.

'Really,' said Davas, thinking of Jim reading the future of the markets in the blank space at the front of a stock chart.

Jim hung up and walked back into the room. Stafford was riveted to the gold artefact. 'OK, Danny, a million pounds it is.'

'Three million dollars,' said Danny.

'No problem.'

'In cash.'

'Cash?' said Jim.

'Cash.'

'That won't work.'

Danny looked at him with 'Why?' stamped all over his face.

'In hundred-dollar bills?'

'Twenties.'

Jim's trader maths kicked in. 'That is a hundred and fifty kilos of banknotes,' he said.

'Oh,' said Danny. 'You sure?'

'A dollar bill is a gram whatever denomination. Twenty into three million is one hundred and fifty thousand, that's a hundred and fifty kilos.'

'Right,' said Danny, shifting from his left foot to the right.

'Anyway, even if you could carry it, you can't move more

than ten thousand dollars in cash over borders. Three million is going to be tricky unless you live here, which you don't.'

Danny seemed a little crestfallen, 'What do you think I should do?'

'You don't want a cheque, I suppose.'

Danny shook his head.

'I can do a transfer.'

'You know the bank G D Marland?' interjected Stafford.

'Sure,' said Danny. 'Everyone's heard of them.'

'Show him the account,' said Stafford, mopping his brow with a handkerchief. 'We can do a wire to his account in the States.'

Jim and Danny's eyes met. 'Cool,' said Danny.

They walked to the computer and Jim wiggled his mouse. Jane's picture, his screen wallpaper, flashed onto the screen. She was smiling, crawling under barbed wire through mud. She was a few years younger but she hadn't changed much. Jim always smiled when he saw the shot. He opened the browser and covered the picture. He glanced at Danny. For some reason, the man was clearly mortified. 'You OK?'

'Yes,' said Danny, after a moment's hesitation. 'Who...' he said, before the 'little guy' pulled the lever and his mouth snapped shut.

'Who?'

'Nothing,' said Danny.

Jim opened the account on the summary page. There was a serial number where the balance should have been.

Danny read it. 'How many decimal places is that?' he asked.

'A lot,' said Jim, trying to stifle a smile. 'Let's send you the money.'

'Can we go to the bank and send it from there?' asked Danny. 'That way I can believe it and also ring up my pa and get his bank details. I haven't got mine.'

'Fine,' said Jim. 'Let me call the bank.'

Danny was reading the number but the spacing was too tight for him to reliably make out whether there were nine or ten digits left of the decimal. 'Wow,' he said finally. 'You are some rich guy.'

Jim was already on his mobile. 'Yes,' he said, 'but you know the legend of Croesus.'

'No,' said Danny. 'What is it?'

'Hi,' said Jim. 'Can you put me onto St John?'

'Not a happy story,' said Stafford, shaking his head.

19

Akira sat by his friend's hospital bed and held his mottled, trembling hand. The old man was asleep, his mouth a little open, an oxygen line under his nose. Akira would sit there for another half an hour, then leave. He saw a flicker of eyelids and watched his friend slowly awaken. 'Good afternoon,' said Akira.

'I've seen it,' said the old man very quietly, his voice hollow like the note of a small breathy flute.

'I know,' said Akira. 'Your wife has told me all the details.'

'It exists.'

'I know,' said Akira again. 'Please do not force yourself to speak.'

'It…' the old man squeezed Akira's hand '…is real.'

'I know,' said Akira, a third time, 'and I will find it.'

'It is… so beautiful.'

Akira smiled at his old friend, who perhaps smiled back before falling, exhausted once more, asleep.

Akira made a fist of his short hand, then let his fingers open one by one. Was it a miracle or a curse? he wondered.

Brandon looked out onto the cove. The sky was a perfect blue. The black cliffs looked less sharp than they had on previous occasions and seabirds coasted along them above the surf, crying to their comrades. The water lapped against the fishing boat, a smooth, undulating surface without a ripple to break its salty skin.

He let Casey roll off into the water first, then followed

him. The sea below was empty. The hammerheads had gone and there seemed to be hardly any life in the waters, except the occasional fish that flittered past, almost invisible against the blue light. As he swam down, he heard Casey in his ear: 'Wow.'

The sand below was glittering. Brandon's eyes bugged out. 'Am I seeing things?' he said into the radio.

'I don't think so,' said Casey.

The storm had stripped acres of seabed and where there had been sand there was now rock. The rock was covered with timber beams and flecked with gold.

'Reece,' called Casey. 'How many holdalls have you got up there?'

'How many do you need?' came the reply.

'Plenty.'

Brandon unslung his empty duffel bag, unzipped it and began to pick up coins and drop them in. He picked up a gold blob with a red stone in it. 'This is intense,' he said into the radio.

'Good,' said Reece.

'I mean really fucking intense,' he said. 'This is, like, going to take all day.'

'You're going to have to winch this up, Reece,' said Casey. 'It's thick down here – shame you can't see it for yourself.'

'Love to,' said Reece, 'but after that instant storm last trip I'm staying top side.'

Brandon poured a handful of coins into the bag. 'We can swap places later. I ain't going to be able to get all this up in one dive.'

'What have you guys got down there?'

'You can't get narcosis at forty feet, can you?' laughed Brandon, scooping another handful of coins into the bag.

'You ain't got narcosis,' said Casey. 'If you have, so've I. Would you look at that!' he exclaimed, picking up an ingot the size of a Hershey bar.

'I take it you've got something,' said Reece.

'Lordy,' said Casey. 'It's the mother lode.'

'The mother of all mother lodes,' added Brandon.

'That's good news,' said Reece. 'When you've had enough, I'll come on down.'

20

Reece looked out of the bridge window. Brandon was tying up the boat and there were three Japanese on the quayside, a smallish guy flanked by two policemen. He let out a groan. How the hell could they be there? Maybe they'd broken some local rule. Or maybe they weren't there for them.

He turned the engine off as Brandon stepped back in. His comrade was looking at him worriedly.

Reece's eyes said, 'Leave this to me.' He stepped off the boat nonchalantly and made his way to the bow as if to check something.

The little guy between the two policemen started to walk towards him. Reece undid the rope and tied it again slowly. When he looked up, they were staring at him. 'Hi,' he said. 'Can I help you?'

'Yes,' said the short Japanese man. 'I am Professor Akira Nakabashi of the Imperial Archive.' He smiled and offered his hand.

Reece noticed that he appeared to have only one arm; his training told him that the other was present but stunted.

The short man gazed into his eyes, and Reece knew he knew. He also knew that the Japanese knew *he* knew. 'Thank God,' he said, laughing.

'Thank God?' said Akira. He waved his hand. 'Thank God!'

'You speak English,' said Reece.

Akira smiled. 'So do you,' he said.

'Yes,' agreed Reece.

'Please continue.'

'Thank God you're here. We've made an amazing discovery.'

'I know,' said Akira.

'You do?'

'Yes,' said Akira, 'you just told me.'

'Yes, I did.'

'American heroes like you must be proud.'

'We are,' said Reece. Had they traced the coins he'd sold? 'How did you find us so fast?'

'Intuition,' said Akira.

'Of course.'

'Can I come aboard?'

'Sure,' said Reece. 'See what we've got.'

Akira said something to the policemen, who walked away.

Akira smiled at Reece. 'This is very wonderful.'

'Yes,' said Reece.

'You have done us such a great service.'

Brandon and Casey didn't look very happy.

'This is Professor...' Reece hesitated.

'Nakabashi, but you can call me Akira.'

'This is Akira-san from the Imperial Archive. I've told him what we've found.'

Brandon and Casey shook his hand. They smiled as best they could.

'Can I see?' asked Akira.

Brandon went to one of five heavy-looking bags and, with Casey's help, hauled it onto the table, which appeared to groan under the weight.

'Careful,' said Reece. 'It's kind of full.'

Akira opened the zipper, fished inside and pulled out a long pencil-like piece of gold. He opened it out into a fan of golden fingers. 'Wonderful,' he said. He studied it closely. Then he put his hand back into the bag and pulled out a handful of coins. 'Fourteenth century, only five known till now.' He held out his palm. 'Two of which you may have sold in Tokyo a few weeks ago.' He smiled in a friendly way.

He peered at the three SEALs. 'I watched you these two days on the satellite. I almost sent a warship to greet you, but when I knew who you were, I thought, no, I shall come to greet them personally.' He smiled.

'Thank you,' said Reece.

'You see, this coin can come from only one ship and this one ship could only have sunk within three hundred miles along this coast, and only one set of divers has dived here in all these months.'

'I see,' said Reece.

'That's cool,' said Brandon.

Casey nodded.

'There will be much more like this to be recovered,' said Akira.

'You bet,' said Brandon.

'And I should think,' said Akira, 'that you will be handsomely rewarded.' He smiled.

They smiled back.

'That's great,' said Reece, sighing with relief inside.

'But,' continued Akira, 'I have to ask you a question.'

'Sure,' said Reece, stiffening.

'All this treasure is wonderful and I am overjoyed that it is recovered but more important by far – *by far* – is the whereabouts of a box.'

'Box?' said Reece.

'A gold box, about a metre wide.'

Brandon looked at Casey, who stared at his feet.

'A box? What about a box?' asked Reece.

'It has the picture of the sun rising over the shore and it is a very, very precious thing. Have you found it?'

Reece looked into Akira's eyes. Akira looked back into him.

'Yes,' said Reece, as it dawned on him. The gold slab wasn't a slab at all: it was a box. 'Yes, we found it.'

'Is it here?' asked Akira.

'No.'

'Where is it?'

Reece sagged a little.

Akira grabbed his shoulder with his good hand. 'As long as it is returned to the Emperor, you have nothing whatsoever to fear. Tell me everything and you will simply be thanked. It is almost miracle enough that it is recovered.'

'We've sent it to London.'

'Do not fear,' said Akira, his face blank. 'I will get it back.' He flexed the fingers of his short hand. 'But you must understand that if you do not help me correctly, the terrible things that will befall you will be not as bad as that which will befall me.'

Reece looked into Akira's eyes again. The guy was serious. Whatever they had found was deadly important. He had seen that serious intent before when their missions had held a large slice of suicide attached to them. Absolutely nothing was more important to this Japanese than the slab – the box – not even his own life. 'You can trust me and what I've told you,' said Reece.

Akira bowed in acknowledgement.

21

The doorbell rang. Stafford took a quick look at his iPhone. 'Good Lord,' he muttered.

'What is it?' asked Jim.

'Davas –' He corrected himself: 'Mr Davas, sir. He's at the door.'

'You have the doorbell on your iPhone?'

'Approximately,' said Stafford, exiting.

He was letting Davas in as Jim walked into the hallway. 'Max!'

'Jim!'

Jim hugged him, rather to Davas's surprise. 'It's great to see you.'

'It's good to see you too.'

'You've come to see the box,' said Stafford. It wasn't a question, more a redundant observation.

'Yes,' said Davas. 'And Jim, of course.'

Stafford cleared his throat. 'Of course.'

'Come through,' said Jim. 'It's amazing.'

'He knows that already,' said Stafford.

Davas glared at him, his lips puckered as though he was sucking a lemon.

They went to the weathered old table on which the box lay.

'Did I do well?' asked Jim, as Davas inspected it.

Davas took a deep breath. He looked at Jim as if he was some kind of gifted idiot.

'What?' said Jim.

'Have you got a cloth, Stafford?'

'Sir.'

'Could you bring it?'

'Yes.'

'Will you bring it?'

'In a moment.'

'Thank you.'

'Is it a Kyoto puzzle box?' asked Stafford.

Davas looked at Stafford. 'You know better than I do. Have you tried to open it?'

Stafford didn't reply.

'Have you?' Davas pressed.

Stafford stretched his neck a little. 'It would have been hard to resist.'

'Indeed,' agreed Davas.

Jim was staring at the two old men with irritation. 'What the fuck are you talking about?'

'A cloth, please, Stafford.'

'Certainly.' The butler left the room.

'This isn't a solid slab, Jim, it's a Kyoto puzzle box.'

'A box?'

'Yes.'

'A box of what?'

Davas gave a small smile that spread across his face. 'We will see.'

'Did I make a good buy?'

'Yes,' said Davas. 'There are no known Kyoto puzzle boxes in private hands. There is one in the British Museum, of course, then two in the Japanese Imperial Collection. This is the only one of four known. However, whatever the value of the box, any contents will be worth ten times more – perhaps a thousand times.'

'What's a puzzle box worth without anything in it?'

'Five million, perhaps ten million dollars.'

Jim felt a wave of satisfaction flush through him. He had known the slab – the box – was a treasure just as he knew when stocks would move. Instinct had told the truth again. 'Ten million empty. I wonder what's inside.'

'We'll see,' said Stafford, returning with a hand towel and a tea towel over his arm.

Davas took the tea towel and laid it over the lid. He placed a finger over the whale in the bay and pushed down hard with his thumb. 'I don't want to damage the box,' he said.

'I tried that,' said Stafford.

Davas put his palm on the rising sun and pushed down again, then twisted. Nothing happened.

'I tried that too.'

Davas picked up the box and examined the edges.

'I couldn't see anything,' said Stafford. He handed Davas a device. 'I couldn't see any joints with my eye, a magnifying glass or this.'

Davas took the little pen-shaped device and pressed the button on its barrel. He ran it around the edges of the box. His face remained empty of discovery. He laid the slab flat and swept the red beam across the face. He looked at Stafford. 'I take it you tried that too.'

'Indeed.'

'Let me have a go,' said Jim.

Davas held up his wrinkled hands. 'Of course.'

Jim put his left hand on the golden sun. He pressed on it.

'I tried that,' said Davas.

'I know,' said Jim, pressing firmly.

Stafford looked on impassively. If he hadn't found the catch to the Kyoto box, it simply wasn't a puzzle box.

Jim applied a little twist to his pressure. There was a hiss. The sun sank into the box and turned. Two lugs at the front flicked out.

'Wait!' cried Davas.

Jim lifted his hand off the sun and spun the circle as if to unscrew it. It clicked and lifted out. He tried to lift the lid by the lugs.

'No!' cried Davas. 'Don't! Stop!'

Jim pushed the lugs in and two lugs at the back popped out. The lid lifted a little and Jim began to slide it off.

Davas barged him violently and Jim skidded away from the table.

'What did you do that for?' he panted.

'These things can be sabotaged, booby-trapped.'

'Right,' said Jim, going back to the box. 'But not this one.'

'At least stand to one side of it,' said Davas, still hanging back.

'OK,' said Jim, and moved to the left of the box. He lifted the lid. Inside, there was a dark red burgundy mass. Nothing shot out; nothing exploded.

They peered in.

'What is it?' wondered Jim.

'Beeswax,' said Stafford. 'It's used to pack something precious so it won't rattle around.'

Around what appeared to be the locking mechanism there was a circle, to the right of it a square, and a long thin rectangle at the bottom of the box. Stafford touched the ancient wax surface of the square. It was fixed solidly to the inside of the box. He took out a pocket knife, put the blade into the corner of the square-shaped mass and tried to push the blade into it. The wax was hard, like the grout between two bricks.

'Let me have a go,' said Jim. He pushed his two thumbs into the corner. There was a cracking sound. The cube of wax sank in at one end and popped out at the other. Jim prised it free.

Davas was still standing back, his arms folded.

Jim twisted the wax block as if it was a loaf of bread. It

shattered. Within, there was a tearing of paper. Then he saw a flash of emerald and gold. He pulled out a green necklace. 'Wow.' He held it up. It was a string of deep green stone fingers, like a Native American necklace of bear claws. It was held together with a gold chain woven with highly detailed floral patterns. He opened the necklace and went to put it on.

'Don't do that,' said Davas.

Jim put it on. 'What do you think?'

'Very regal,' said Stafford.

Davas shrugged.

Jim turned back to the box. He pressed down on the circle of wax and heard another dry crack. He pushed and prodded the area until the circular wax cake popped out.

Davas and Stafford craned their necks and stood almost on tiptoe to watch him. Jim broke open the wax and unwrapped a mirror, with a knob in the form of a flower bud on the reverse. He looked at himself in the polished silver face: he saw a blurred distorted image of himself, but he looked kind of handsome and heroic in a cartoony smudgy way. Behind him, Stafford and Davas looked like two awed schoolkids with some visiting dignitary. He laughed. 'Nice mirror,' he said, and laid it on the towel. Davas picked it up.

Jim put a thumb at each end of the oblong and pressed hard; the block flipped up and out and almost fell out of the box. Jim caught it. He twisted the wax block, which broke, paper tearing beneath.

Davas put the mirror back on the towel. 'Dear God,' he said, as Jim pulled a Japanese sword from its crumbling wrapping.

'Kusanagi,' said Stafford.

'What?' said Jim, removing the sword from its plain but beautiful scabbard. He held the blade up to the failing light from the window. The sky was leaden and a wind was blowing down the Thames. A funny bleached light highlighted the object, giving it a strange thick outline. He grinned, experiencing a flash of aggression. 'Cool,' he said. 'What a cool thing.' He turned to Davas and Stafford, held up the scabbard and slid the flashing blade back into it. 'What do you think they're worth altogether?' He put the sword down.

Davas and Stafford sagged. 'Can we sit down?' said Davas, motioning to the two sofas by the window.

'Let me get some drinks,' said Stafford.

'Brandy,' muttered Davas, weakly.

'The Napoleon,' said Stafford, stumbling away.

'What's up?' Jim had finally registered their confusion.

'Let's sit down, Jim,' said Davas.

22

Outside, giant grey clouds had opened and rain was pelting down. Jim held the mirror and studied it intently. The mottled surface certainly improved his looks: it seemed to elongate his face and warp out his jaw to make it look chiselled. 'This is very cool,' he said, rolling it around in his hand. As well as the flower-bud handle, there were engravings of foliage across the back. 'Amazing,' he said. 'The design here is incredibly complicated.'

He caught sight of Davas in the mirror. He looked younger in the distorted surface and happier than usual.

Davas leant over and lifted the necklace over Jim's head. 'Priceless,' he said.

'Is it jade?' asked Jim.

'The most perfect jade I've ever seen,' said Davas. 'Yasakani no Magatama.'

'Is that a kind of Japanese jade?' said Jim.

'No,' said Davas. 'Yasakani no Magatama is the Jewel of the Japanese Imperial Regalia.'

'Is this like that?'

'No,' said Davas. 'This *is* Yasakani no Magatama.' Set against the greyness of the view from the window, the green shone with a glowing depth as if it had an internal light.

Jim looked at Davas as if he was talking nonsense. 'What?'

'This is the Yasakani no Magatama. And that mirror you are holding is the Yata no Kagami.'

'And this?' said Jim.

Stafford entered, carrying a tray with three glasses and an ancient bottle of cognac. 'The sword Kusanagi,' he said.

'I think so,' said Davas.

Jim laughed. 'Come on, guys, what the hell are you on about?' He caught a glimpse of Stafford in the mirror. In the eccentric field of the polished silver, he looked younger, slimmer and very military.

'These items,' said Stafford, 'if I'm not incorrect, are the Imperial Regalia of Japan.'

Jim wanted to say, 'Don't be stupid.' Whatever the Imperial Regalia of Japan were, he couldn't be in possession of them. 'What do you mean?'

'You do not mean, "What do you mean?", Jim,' said Davas. 'You mean, "How can this be?"'

'OK,' said Jim. 'How can this be the Imperial Regalia of Japan? Have they been stolen?'

'No,' said Davas, 'they have not.'

'Right,' said Jim, putting the mirror down and picking up the sword. 'Let's start at the beginning. What's regalia?'

'The British Crown Jewels are regalia,' Stafford told him, before Davas could reply. He picked up the mirror and began to examine it. He glanced at Jim, then returned to the object.

'Yes,' said Davas. 'They are approximately the same. When your queen was crowned, she was given the orb, which here is the mirror; the sceptre, which in this case is the sword Kusanagi, and–'

'The crown, which here is Yasakani no Magatama, the green necklace,' interrupted Stafford.

Davas helped himself to a shot of cognac.

The rain tapped on the window like a handful of gravel. Jim pulled the sword a little from its scabbard. The steel shone iridescently, the surface whirled with blue, black and red, which shone and flickered in the light. 'How can these be the Japanese Crown Jewels?' he said, grinning at the two old men as if they had gone mad. 'Wouldn't they have noticed they were missing?'

'Yes and no,' said Davas.

Stafford was shaking his head at the mirror. He picked up the necklace with his other hand. 'These were responsible for coaxing the sun back into the sky,' he said. He coughed. 'According to Japanese legend.'

'Well, Jim,' began Davas, giving Stafford a look of frustration, 'these objects predate recorded Japanese history. They are both real and legendary. The sword was retrieved from one of the tails of a many-headed dragon and, as Stafford pointed out, the mirror and the jewel were hung on a tree to coax the sun goddess out of a cave where she was sulking. She of course, ascended back into the heavens. More important than the stories is the probability that the regalia were lost in a shipwreck in the fourteenth century.'

'Oh,' said Jim.

'The trouble is,' said Stafford, handing the mirror to Davas, 'the Japanese preferred not to mention it. You see, the objects are symbolic of Imperial legitimacy. Lose them, lose legitimacy, lose power.'

'Right,' said Jim.

'And,' continued Stafford, 'it's even harder to admit they're gone when the next coronation comes around. Then the next one and the next. So the ugly truth simply doesn't come out.'

'The regalia appears at coronations wrapped in paper,' said Davas. 'I've always thought it ironic.'

'How do you two know all this?' said Jim.

'You appear to be surrounded by connoisseurs,' said Davas.

Jim offered him the samurai sword, which he took. The scabbard was of a dense dark wood, with a matt finish that felt secure in his grip. 'Ama no Murakumo no Tsurugi,' said Davas, pulling the blade out. 'Amazing.' He held it up. 'The Sword of the Gathering Clouds of Heaven.' He sheathed it. 'The Japanese

Excalibur.' He offered it back to Jim.

'Excalibur?' queried Jim.

Stafford nodded. 'The fabled "grass cutter" of Japanese legend.'

'So is it a Flymo or an Excalibur?' he said, pulling the blade right out and holding it up, as Davas had done. The wind was whipping down the Thames and a flash of lightning sent a white afterglow around the wall. 'All this and special effects,' he said, putting the sword back into its scabbard. 'If you're right, this lot's worth an absolute bomb! How much?'

'I dread to think,' said Davas. 'Do you want to sell them?'

'Not really,' said Jim. 'They're amazing. I think I want to own them for a bit. Then I could give them to a museum. I mean, the Japanese would be really happy to get them back, right?'

'I'm not sure they could admit to receiving them,' said Stafford. 'What would that do to the legitimacy of the royal line? You'd have to give them back secretly.'

Davas was thinking hard.

'That would be no good,' said Jim, scowling. 'It wouldn't be fair.'

'They'd pay a king's ransom,' said Davas, just before a rumble of thunder passed overhead, 'but you don't need money.'

'Well, there's no hurry,' said Jim. 'If it's all been missing for six hundred years, a few more won't matter. I can leave it to Japan in my will.' He took the sword out again and postured with it. He felt the base of the blade with his thumb. 'Razor sharp.'

Davas was gazing out of the window at the storm. He seemed to be pondering something unpleasant. 'If you want to hang on to these objects, you'll need to keep it very quiet. I cannot imagine what the Japanese would do to get them back. It will be like living with the *Mona Lisa* and the Turin Shroud, having had them stolen on demand.'

'At the very least,' interjected Stafford.

Davas hauled himself to his feet and walked to the window with his brandy. He watched the churning river sweep towards the sea.

Jim stood up and held the blade to the light. 'I'll keep them for a bit, then maybe see if we can do a deal. They should be pretty happy.'

'Very wise,' said Davas, 'and probably very lucrative also. Tell me when you want to go ahead and I will act as go-between.'

'It could prove hard to get off on the right foot,' said Stafford.

'It probably will,' said Davas, absently.

'How hard can it be?' Jim brandished the sword. 'Excuse me, mister, how would you like your Crown Jewels back?' He sheathed it. 'That's sorted then.'

Davas was holding the necklace to the light. He was smiling to himself. 'Remarkable,' he breathed.

Jim took it from him and put it on again. He picked up the mirror and the sword. 'Am I the Emperor of Japan now?'

'I doubt it,' said Davas.

The necklace felt rather good. It lay softly on his shoulders and sent a rather comforting sensation through him. The last person to wear it had been a Japanese emperor, five hundred years ago. Jim decided to wear it for a bit.

23

Akira had only ever seen the Emperor in person twice before and then only as he had passed through the Archive on a tour of the objects.

The Emperor smiled, his entourage flanking him on both sides. He was a god. No matter what the Americans had said, no matter what papers were signed, he and his forebears were gods and his offspring would be gods too. Not that Akira believed in gods, but he did believe in logic. Before the Second World War the Emperor had been a god and nothing could logically remove godly status. Rabbits were classed as birds in Japan, but whatever their classification, a rabbit could not fly and was a mammal. They could count rabbits as they wished and eat them on fasts with birds, but still rabbits were mammals. So a god was a god, whatever humankind cared to call it for their own convenience.

Akira withdrew the fingers of gold. 'This is the fan of the concubine Yosihida.' He opened the golden supports, bereft now of their exquisitely painted silk. 'It has been recovered. I beg a private audience with the Emperor.'

The Imperial party stood rooted to the spot.

A fat old man appeared from the far right and approached the Emperor. He whispered into his ear. A conversation followed.

The Emperor smiled. 'Please leave me and the professor alone.'

The room cleared, rather hesitantly.

Akira bowed deeply. 'I believe Kusanagi, Yata no Kagami and Yasakani no Magatama have been recovered.'

The Emperor's brow furrowed. 'So,' he said, the word elongated, part agreement, part question.

'They are in London and I believe I can bring them home.'

'Enough,' said the Emperor. 'To continue our talk we must be truly alone.'

Akira's mouth fell open in shock and disappointment. He bowed.

Kim's private restaurant was famous. The billionaire was perhaps the only man in the world to own his own personal five-star restaurant and keep it for his sole purposes.

Hananaka was often entertained in luxury restaurants. As a junior member of the Cabinet Secretariat he was frequently fêted. One of his functions was to indicate intentions to powerful people outside the government, and he did this in any number of ways, most of which were invisible to the Western eye. This was the first time he had called on Kim and for once it was to his own benefit.

In his quiet way Hananaka had become a desperate man. He was supporting his family's four ancient and decrepit parents and was slowly but surely sinking into terrible debt. For him, it was not hard to borrow money at a minuscule interest rate, but he could no longer repay it. Meanwhile the debt was ballooning as he borrowed more to pay for the parental care and the interest he could not cover. Soon he would have to resort to moneylenders, the ruthless underbelly of Japanese financial life. Then his only escape would be an arranged accident to pay out insurance on his death.

Now life had dealt him a terrible temptation. A simple way to pay off all his debts.

The head waiter ushered him through the restaurant, which had a dozen tables. All were empty. Two shuffling geisha in red and white silk kimonos joined them in procession. He was ushered into a small dark dining room. There was a fish tank across the far left wall with coral, and tropical fish that drifted back and forth. To the right of the tank hung a painting he recognised as by Toulouse Lautrec. A dresser in heavy lacquer stood against the back wall, a Tang camel prancing across it in desiccated biscuit terracotta. The fish tank seemed very deep, as if it was the size of a room all by itself.

Kim looked up from his phone. He smiled like someone who had just heard that something awful had happened to an enemy. He stood up and they bowed. Hananaka felt Kim bowed too low, and he tried not to overcompensate. They exchanged pleasantries, then drink and food started to appear. As Hananaka had expected, it was all exquisite.

Hananaka began to appear more drunk than he was. The only way he could make his proposal was to be drunk and then it could be rejected, laughed away or denied at will. He was laboriously pouring his heart out about the state of his family. How his own sainted parents and his perfect wife's beloved mother and father were so fragile.

Kim was nodding, smiling happily in the knowledge there was advantage to be had and, apparently, at the small cost of four old people's care. 'So, so, so,' he punctuated Hananaka-san's sad story.

Hananaka steeled himself. He had made it plain what he required in return for what he was about to give. Kim was duty bound to supply it. What he was about to give was worth infinitely more than he could ask, so there would be no quibbling. Kim would not disappoint him, even though, under his perfect Japanese exterior, he was from Korea, of a despised people.

The door opened. The two geisha scooted in and cleared the middle of the table. They manipulated various invisible latches and the centre collapsed. The cloth parted and there was now a large hole between Hananaka and Kim.

Kim turned as a trolley was rolled in and slotted between them. Under a cloth there was a large mound.

Hananaka smiled and nodded. 'What is it? A giant fish?'

'*Nyotaimori*,' said Kim, with a hungry smile. He smacked his lips.

'Oh,' said Hananaka. He wondered how Kim's restaurant would serve such a dish.

The geisha lifted back the sheet to reveal a naked girl. A selection of thinly sliced sashimi lay across her body, covering her like a silken dress. Between her legs there was a gigantic pile of Beluga caviar.

'Oh!' gasped Hananaka.

'Come,' said Kim, 'tell me your news.'

Hananaka looked at the perfectly still girl, whose only sign of life was her breathing. He hesitated. What if she heard?

'Please go ahead,' said Kim, spooning some caviar from the girl's groin with a carved bone utensil.

Hananaka sat up a little. It would be rude to remain silent and, after all, the sashimi plate was only some stupid girl.

'The Imperial Regalia have been recovered and are in England. I am sure if you came by them, all my debts and yours would be extinguished.'

Kim seemed to freeze, a spoonful of caviar poised just before his mouth. He looked down at the girl. She knew her life depended on her discretion. 'This is almost too hard to imagine,' he said.

'Yes,' said Hananaka. 'I knew you would understand.'

Kim put the spoon into his mouth and savoured its load as he thought. He swallowed. 'And you will help me acquire them.'

'Acquire them before anyone else does.'

'So, so, so...'

24

Stafford sat up in bed. His iPhone was vibrating on the table – an intruder alert. He looked at the outlined figure poised at the first-floor window, trying to open the latch. He allowed himself a little smile as he saw the blade slide between the sash frames and flick the latch. The agile balaclava-clad man who balanced on the slim sill would get nowhere trying to raise the window. It was dead-bolted with screw-in keys. Stafford had been fortifying the house, taking every opportunity, whether Jim was around or not, to make the riverside warehouse into a fortress.

Jim was a serious target, be it for the money he was worth or for the skill he had in calling the markets. A rich man needed good security, whether he cared for it or not. It was now being tested.

He wondered about calling the police, but as he did so he saw the intruder swing off the sill and climb down the drainpipe. From a different camera he watched the expert motions of the cat burglar. This was no junkie after money for drugs. He watched the figure walk up the street and disappear into a side road about a hundred yards ahead.

25

The moonlight was almost perfect. He could see as well as if he was working in daylight. He liked to run across the rooftops: it was a skill that made him different. He was no common criminal. He didn't kick down doors when people were out to steal their jewellery and cash. He was a craftsman. He had never been caught.

In one sense it was a simple job: get in, get the object, get out, leaving as little trace as possible. His trusted network of dealers would call on him when they needed something purloined. It was an expensive collector's game, robbing between the rich. It paid very well indeed.

He was no leery villain, off down the nightclubs to big it up. He was a professional with perhaps another ten years of lucrative work ahead of him.

He was learning to drive a London taxi, not because he would ever need the money but because the wait between jobs would get to him and make him anxious. He was addicted to the challenge and without it he needed a distraction.

One day he might fall off or through a roof but for now he scampered over the building tops with acrobatic grace, a happy man.

The job was immense. Fetch three items for one million pounds. It was almost too good to be true. These days, Oriental collectors must be rich beyond belief. They must be going crazy with their new-found wealth. Everyone knew the Far East was taking over the world. He tried not to think as he walked across the eaves: balance was skill and pure concentration.

Stafford sat up in bed again. 'Good grief,' he muttered. Someone was on the roof. He looked at the image on the phone. It was another intruder, the second night in a row. The same balaclava-clad figure was taking tiles up on the roof. He would be coming in through the attic. Someone so skilled and resourceful would be inside the house in moments. He got out of bed and threw on his dressing-gown over his silk pyjamas. He put his slippers on and went to his bedside drawer.

He took out the PPK and quickly screwed in the silencer. He left his room and made his way upstairs. He had to protect Jim's bedroom and he had only seconds to get into place. If he called the police now, he would lose the video feed and tracking of the intruder.

He castigated himself as he went as fast as he could up the stairs. They had no panic room or alarm buttons. The house was practically unprotected. It seemed he had spent too much time on securing the perimeter and on surveillance. He had let the side down badly.

The black-clad figure lowered himself through the hatch in the roof space to the floor below. He held himself and judged the drop. It was little enough that getting back up would be no problem. He lowered himself and dropped the last feet to the floor. Normally he would have gone in through a ground-floor window, but this house was well secured. However, no one protected their roof. He would most probably leave through the front door. Getting out was always much easier than getting in.

The tricky bit would be finding the items. He had a copy of the plans bought from the firm that had put in the alarm of the previous owner. He would start in the waterside lounge and go from there.

Stafford stood by the doorway to Jim's room and watched the figure on the screen make his way quickly down the stairs. If the intruder turned into the hall where he was waiting, he would shoot. His palm was hot and slippery and he remembered the feeling of excitement and dread from all those many years ago when he had waited, gun in hand, for the shadow of a returning target.

The figure was coming down the stairs and would either keep going to the floors below or turn right towards him. Right would mark the figure as an assassin, straight on, as a robber.

The shadow flickered by and was gone downstairs.

Stafford walked carefully away from Jim's door and after the robber.

He stopped by the open door and listened. He always took stock before crossing a threshold. He went in. He was looking for a rectangular gold box with the rising sun on it. There it was, right in front of the window, on a table.

Brilliant, he thought. He trotted gracefully over to it. He took out a penlight, the end of which was covered in cloth. It threw a faint light. He picked up the box, which was extremely heavy, and turned it to catch the moonlight from the window. Bingo, he thought. He pulled out a fine nylon holdall that filled his left trouser pocket. It would take the box.

The light went on.

Shit! He twisted around, blinded by the light.

'Put it down,' said the voice of an old man.

He laid the box down, buying time for his eyes to adjust.

He turned. An old man was holding a gun on him, aiming straight between his eyes. It was a bluff – the gun was a replica. He reached for his belt and pulled out a long knife.

Stafford fired instinctively, as he had many times before.

The body fell.

Stafford sighed. 'Oh dear,' he said. He laid down his gun and slipped off his dressing-gown. He folded it and put it under the bleeding head of the robber. It would catch most of the blood. He tried to take the man's pulse. He was dead.

It had been a long time since he had taken a life and he would have shed a tear if it wasn't for the fact that there was work to be done.

He called the main number; a female voice answered. She wasn't well spoken like the women of the old days: she sounded like a checkout girl in a supermarket. 'Removals, please,' he said.

'Identification.'

'Bertie fourteen.'

'Do you have a five digit number?'

'Just fourteen.'

'Triple zero one four?'

'Perhaps.'

'I have it,' she said. 'Biometrics failed.'

'Good Lord,' he said. 'Can't you just put me through?'

'Let me try again with that voice print.' There was a click. 'Putting you through.'

'Night supervisor.'

'Is that Removals?'

'No – I don't know why you've come through to me.'

'Can you transfer me?'

'I'm not sure.'

'Good grief,' muttered Stafford. 'Look, can you be relied upon to get a message to Removals?'

'Well, I don't know.'

'Listen, my man, the message is, "Bertie fourteen has a removal at his address."'

'I'll try.'

'You know what a removal is?'

'I think so.'

'Well, then, please try hard.'

There was the clattering of a keyboard. 'Yes, sir.'

Stafford hung up with a sigh.

26

There was a knock at Professor Nakabashi's office door.

'Come in.'

A tall, thin man in a black suit entered. His shirt was very white against the harsh black of his jacket. His cuffs almost shone as they poked out from under his sleeves. His hair was heavily oiled.

Akira stood up and bowed politely.

They exchanged cards.

'Sensei, I have brought you your travel itinerary. The delay has been unfortunate.'

'I am nonetheless eager to go.'

'I have been asked to warn you that news has travelled far and wide.'

'Then I am honoured that I have been selected to go.'

'You will have two companions from the DID for your protection.'

'I am grateful.'

'You fly tonight.'

Jim noticed the Persian rug in front of the table with the golden box. If he had been curious enough he would have lifted it and found that an area of carpet beneath it had been cut away. He went to his computer and checked his email. Nothing from Jane. He opened his currency charts. Interest rates were going to explode in the coming month: he could jump on them and short bonds into the ground.

Davas wouldn't like that because Davas was the guardian of

the US Treasury bond. He was the fund manager famous for his currency calls and his powerful hedge fund, when in reality he was the US Treasury's market manipulator who propped up the giant superpower by being one step ahead of the market. Jim had no desire to play Samson and pull the temple down on everyone. He felt no need to dispel the illusion of money. The Turkish lira looked like it wanted to be tweaked; he could knock it back for a few million. He curled his fingers and stood up. 'Argh,' he grumbled. He had to get used to leaving the markets alone.

Stafford came in with his morning cup of tea. He noted Jim was wearing the necklace.

Jim noticed that Stafford was not his normal rosy-cheeked self. 'You OK?' he asked.

'Yes, thank you, sir,' he said. 'The storm has damaged the roof tiles and I've been clambering around in the loft.'

'Don't go straining yourself,' said Jim.

'I'll try not to,' said Stafford.

Jim pressed his ribs. They were feeling much better.

'I think perhaps, sir, that we might put the items in storage at a bank. Selfridges has a very good facility, or the bank on the Strand.'

'Why bother?' said Jim. 'You've turned this place into Fort Knox.'

'Very good, sir,' said Stafford, smiling weakly.

There was a fanfare from Jim's computer and he shot out of his seat, clattering the cup down on the low coffee table. The fanfare meant only one thing: an email from Jane.

Hey Jim, got leave. You free?

He called but her phone went straight through to voicemail.

Of course. I'll clear all the decks. How long have you got?

He sent the email on its way. It was three a.m. on the east coast, he thought. Maybe she was east of him instead.

He paged through stock charts as he waited, occasionally buying stock in companies that looked like they were on the up. He was spreading some good news. He stumbled on an Italian retailer that looked like it was going to go bust unexpectedly. He looked up news on the company and it was all good. Interesting, he thought. He was naturally inclined to short its stock there and then. He groaned. Why bother?

The fanfare sounded and he sat up straighter, a smile on his face.

Don't know. Meet in Naples?

Jim liked Italy – or, rather, he liked Venice where he had stayed with Davas. He pulled up Naples on Wikipedia. There was a picture of a bay. 'Oh, shit,' he muttered.

It's got a flipping volcano. Can we meet somewhere else?

If he never saw another volcano he'd be a happy man. A brush with death in the one at Las Palmas had been the start of it. Then, in short order, a lethal escapade in Congo under the erupting Mount Nyiragongo had nearly done for him. The thought of meeting Jane near Vesuvius just seemed like a bad idea.

The idea of Naples pulled him back to the Italian store with the imminent collapse in its chart pattern. He looked at it closely: it would fold in a year or so. Negoziomundo seemed to the entire world a hugely successful company. It sponsored the World Cup and Formula One. He fancied that its office must be set on the slopes of Vesuvius, just like Pompeii, ready to be swept away by an unpredictable and instantaneous disaster. But it wasn't sited under a volcano: whatever the disaster was going to be, it wasn't a geological one.

The fanfare blasted.

Ha, ha. OK, I'll come to London. Going dark.

When?

There was no reply.

Jim looked at Negoziomundo's stock price. It took all his willpower to stop himself firing up his trading robots to sell the company into the ground. He looked out at the river. The tide was going down nicely. He had forgotten: there was going to be a very low tide this morning.

Stafford hadn't. He entered the room with Jim's boots and his green padded coat. Jim jumped up. 'Thanks, Stafford,' he said. 'You've saved my life.' He went to the window and pulled on the boots. 'Jane's coming,' he said.

'Very good, sir.'

Jim slung on the coat.

'Perhaps Sir might like to leave the priceless crown of the Japanese behind?'

'Oh, yes,' said Jim, sliding it over his head. 'Wouldn't want to lose that in the mud.' He noticed his butler had perked up. 'See you later.'

Jim laid out the contents of his pocket on the coffee table. He pushed aside the modern coins.

'The Romans threw away their small change,' noted Stafford, picking up a bent piece of metal. 'Part of a silver watch case.' He sniffed. 'Various buttons, Victorian or later. Harrington farthing from the reign of Charles the First. Rather charming. Rivet heads.'

'I thought they might be corroded coins.'

'Sadly not.' Stafford picked up two twin brass disks held together by a wire.

'Georgian cufflinks.

That's it,' said Jim, rummaging in his pockets. 'Hold on, there's this.'

There was a buzz from the front door.

'Musket ball,' said Stafford, and tugged out his iPhone. 'There appears to be a Japanese gentleman at the door.'

'Holy crap,' said Jim, a phrase he had picked up from Jane. They went to the door.

'Hello,' said Stafford, intent on the video of the view outside that had appeared on a console by the door. The Japanese man was looking at the door, awaiting a response. He was alone.

'Yes,' said the caller. 'I have come to see Jim Evans-san.'

'Do you have an appointment?'

'No. I am sorry.'

'What do you think?' said Jim to Stafford.

Stafford didn't reply. 'Who may I say is calling?'

'Professor Nakabashi from the Japanese Imperial Archive.' The letterbox opened and a card fell into the cage.

Jim fished it out. 'It's all in Japanese.'

Stafford took it from him. 'So it is.'

'Let him in.' Jim smirked, 'I mean, it stands to reason, doesn't it?'

Stafford frowned. He looked at the image of the man, then at a broader view around the door. There was still no one in sight.

'Please come in,' he said.

Jim turned the lock and opened the door.

The professor looked up at him. 'Nice to meet you,' he said, offering his hand. They shook and he followed Jim along the hallway; Stafford brought up the rear. They went through into the lounge and the guest stumbled. Jim turned, grabbed his guest's left hand and steadied him. He discovered that the hand came straight from the man's armpit. 'You OK?' he said, letting go.

'Yes.'

'Let's sit down.'

Akira Nakabashi was trying not to look at the box, Jim thought, though his eyes were drawn to it. He took out a handkerchief and mopped his top lip.

They sat. 'How can I help you?' said Jim.

Akira coughed and tried to clear his throat.

'Could we have some tea, Stafford?' said Jim.

'Certainly.' Stafford didn't budge an inch.

'That would be very kind,' said Akira.

'It's OK,' said Jim to Stafford. 'You go ahead.'

Stafford looked doubtful. He pulled out his iPhone and dialled. He was going to keep a remote eye on proceedings.

'So, how can I help you?' said Jim again.

'I had heard that you were in possession of a very rare plaque.' Akira turned in his chair. 'I see it there. I am very keen to examine it with a view to purchasing it for the Japanese Imperial Collection.'

'Oh,' said Jim. 'I've only just bought it.'

'Yes,' said Akira, 'but I'm sure I can make you a good offer. May I look at it?'

'Go ahead,' said Jim. They stood and walked over to it. 'You said plaque,' remarked Jim, 'why do you call it a plaque?'

'It is a figure of speech,' said Akira. 'My English is very

weak.'

'It's very good.'

'Thank you,' said Akira. 'May I pick it up?'

Jim nodded.

Akira awkwardly lifted it. 'If I may sit down with it?'

'Go ahead.'

Akira went back to the sofa and laid the heavy gold box on his legs. 'It is very beautiful,' he said. 'May I ask what you paid for it?'

'Three million dollars.'

'You bought well,' said Akira. He took his handkerchief out again and mopped his brow.

'I bought it because it's so beautiful, and with gold heading for two thousand dollars an ounce, well, there's a big intrinsic value there too. I love old things.' He smiled at Akira, who, he knew, was well aware of what he was holding. 'Did you see the table?'

'No,' said Akira, looking up from the box.

'That's second-century Roman. It's the only Roman wooden table in private hands. I bought it off the Pope.' Jim laughed.

'And you use it?'

'Of course,' said Jim. 'Some abbot had been having his lunch off it for a thousand years in some monastery somewhere. I didn't see any reason not to carry on.'

Akira's eyes returned to the box.

'I've never heard of plaques,' said Jim.

'No?' said Akira. 'Very popular in medieval Italy. Also quite a fashion in the Edo period in Japan.'

'Oh,' said Jim.

Stafford reappeared with Japanese tea in rough-hewn clay mugs.

'*Domo arogato*,' said Akira, with a little nod. 'Will you

consider an offer?' He took the teacup in his short hand. He put it down again and picked it up with the other.

'Yeah,' said Jim. 'Of course.'

'Thank you.' Akira's mind raced. He knew Jim had paid $3 million and he was planning to offer $6 million on the basis that a hundred per cent profit might prove irresistible. He noticed Stafford was floating in the background. Should he offer $10 million and clinch a deal, or $4 million and not appear too keen? 'Six million dollars.'

'Ten million,' said Jim, 'and you're done. Get me the money and you can take the…' he almost said 'box' '…plaque.'

'One request,' said Akira, almost dizzy with tension. 'May I have some time alone with the object to examine it further?'

'No, that won't be possible.' Jim smiled but Akira saw he was angry suddenly.

'I need to examine it very closely if I'm to pay such a price.'

'You can examine it right here, right now. Take it or leave it. You see, I was thinking of donating it to the British Museum. They'd name the plaque after me – you know the sort of thing. The Portland Vase, the Evans Plaque.'

Akira winced. 'I see.'

'The Elgin Marbles,' offered the butler, from across the room.

'The Elgin Marbles,' echoed Akira. Those magnificent treasures had been stolen by the British two hundred years ago and they refused to return them to Greece. His heart sank. 'Ten million dollars. I agree.'

Jim stood up. 'I'll get you my bank details. As soon as the money hits my account, you can come back and pick her up.' He went to his computer and, with a few clicks, was printing out a page. He handed the A4 sheet to Akira and heaved the box from his lap. He placed it back on the table.

Akira stood up. 'Thank you,' he said, with a bow. He touched the old table. It was also a treasure. He felt sad.

'Please follow me,' said the butler, pointing to the door.

'Until our next meeting,' said Akira.

A few minutes passed, then Stafford came back into the room. 'Was that wise?'

Jim had the necklace on again and was holding the sword in a fencing pose. 'Fucking bastard was trying to rip me off.' He waved the sword and watched its blade flash. 'I'm not going to lie down for that.' He held the sword above his head in a cod-samurai stance. 'He can have the box for what Davas says it's worth. He's going to have to pay a fuck of a lot more to get the rest.'

'Perhaps you might consider tempering your annoyance.'

Jim lowered the sword. 'Yeah well – probably.' He put the sword back into its scabbard. 'But you can see my point. In just five minutes he managed to piss me right off.'

Stafford sighed. 'Very good, sir.'

27

Jim's mobile burst into a loud rap tune. He grunted and struggled to find it. 'Yeah,' he said, trying to sound more than ten per cent conscious.

'Evans-san,' said a Japanese voice.

He sat up. 'Yes?'

'This is Professor Nakabashi.'

'Hi,' he said, sitting a bit straighter.

'Did you receive the ten mirrion?'

'Mirrion?'

'Dorrars. The ten mirrion dorrars.'

The pronunciation clicked. 'Don't know,' said Jim. It was one minute past nine. 'Can you call me back in ten minutes?'

'Yes, certainly.'

'OK.' He dropped the line. Damn, he thought, he had to stop hanging up on people like that. He wasn't a trader anymore. He put on his dressing-gown, the gold embroidered D of the Davas crest sparkling in the gloom. It was another gloomy London day.

He stumbled down the stairs, slumped in front of his computer and fired up the banking software. He checked his email. Nothing from Jane as usual. He opened his statement. There was his ten million dollars.

He smiled to himself. He knew well enough why the professor was so eager. Inside the ten million dollar box was a hundred million dollar treasure. The polite, unassuming Japanese professor *was* trying to swindle him.

He checked his mobile in case there was a missed SMS from

Jane. As he was shrugging in disappointment the phone rang again.

'Evans-san, did you receive your payment?'

'Yep,' said Jim. 'It's there.'

'When can I come and pick up the plaque?'

'When do you want to come?'

'Right away.' There was a short pause. 'Ten.'

'Ten thirty?' suggested Jim.

'Yes, thank you,' said Akira.

Stafford was holding a tray in his left hand. On it was a folded newspaper. 'Professor Nakabashi,' he announced. He looked distinctly unhappy and peered down his nose at Akira.

Jim got up and smiled. He held the smile with a certain difficulty that made his cheeks bulge.

The Japanese seemed to regard him as a card sharp would a stupid player. Blank but somehow sneering.

Akira bowed and shook his hand. 'So glad you received the funds so quickly.' He took the bag from his shoulder with his short hand and passed it into the other. 'I won't take up your valuable time.'

Jim pointed to the Roman table and the box. 'Help yourself.'

Akira went to the golden box and, for a second, studied the ancient wooden table. He touched it with the palm of his hand. 'This is very special,' he said, looking back at Jim. His eyes twinkled and Jim caught the glint of appreciation.

'Thanks,' he said, softening towards the guy.

Akira unzipped the bag and Jim slipped the box into it. 'I am very grateful,' Akira said, zipping it closed. He swung it onto his shoulder. 'This object has a deep meaning and I thank you.'

Jim felt Akira's sincerity and his heart sank a little. He nodded but didn't say anything.

'I will leave you now. I have a flight to prepare for.'

Stafford was standing in the doorway.

'Goodbye,' said Akira.

'See you,' said Jim. He turned away and went to his desk, watching with one eye the professor making his way quickly to the door. He might be buying an empty box on purpose but his eagerness to leave was a little too obvious. He slumped in his chair. The situation felt very, as Stafford might say, unsatisfactory. Why couldn't people just be straight?

Akira studied the box with his magnifying glass. He pored over every carved surface, every corner, indentation, scratch and mark. He could see no evidence of a latch, hinge or joint. He knew the release was the rising sun, which shone in the top right of the tableau. He knew it was the key, but he had tried it gently and nothing had given him the slightest impression that it was anything but a carved surface.

He had studied the box for three hours. He was now left with two choices: take it home for X-ray and microscopic analysis or exert more force on what he believed to be the lock mechanism. He pressed the fingertips of his right hand to his forehead. It would be madness to risk damaging such a treasure to satisfy his personal curiosity. It would be the height of arrogance to try to open the box for his personal satisfaction and glory. He took his right hand from his forehead and stared at the golden sun. He leant down and pressed on it with the palm of his short hand. He grunted with the effort and there was a click.

'Ho!' he gasped. With his left hand, he touched the sunken sun, tweaked it, and found it turned anticlockwise. His mouth was open as he rotated it. Suddenly it rose up and he pulled on it. There was another click. Two lugs protruded from the side of the box. Two golden catches. He knew the Imperial box had no traps in it. He pushed the catches in and two rear ones opened. The front of the box lifted slightly.

He took a deep breath, took the lid and raised it.

He shrieked and jumped to his feet. The chair flew, with a crash, to the floor.

He could see the wax the regalia had been embedded in. It was freshly broken. Evans had found his way into the box, had taken the regalia and sold him the empty shell. He fell to his knees and held his head, his left hand across his face, his right on his cheek. He was overwhelmed by utter despair.

28

The door buzzer sounded. 'Yes?' said Stafford, into the intercom.

'It is Professor Nakabashi.'

'Yes,' said Stafford, who had known this the moment his iPhone had flashed on with the CCTV feed.

'May I come in?'

'I will ask.'

Jim nodded from further down the hallway. He felt a little nervous. This was going to be interesting, he thought. As he went into the lounge, he heard Stafford say, 'Please wait a minute.' He took the sword from the coffee-table and put it under the sofa. He dropped his jacket over the mirror and necklace and sat down on the sofa. 'Ready,' he called. He took out his mobile and looked at it. There was a message he hadn't heard come in. It was Jane.

He opened it.

On my way tough guy. Jim's face lit up. He hit reply and was about to start typing when Professor Akira Nakabashi entered the room. Stafford stood behind him.

Jim sighed and put the phone down. 'Hi,' he said.

The professor looked very tense. A leather briefcase in his hand, he stood to attention and bowed. 'I'm so sorry,' he said, 'but there has been some misunderstanding.'

'Really?' said Jim.

'The box.'

'The box?' said Jim.

'The box.' ·

134

'What box?' Jim stared at him challengingly.

'The box I bought from you.'

'The plaque, you mean. Plaque, as in solid-lump-of-metal thing.'

'Yes.'

'What about it?'

'There has been a misunderstanding.'

'I don't think so,' said Jim. 'You wanted to buy it and you have.'

'But I need all of it.'

'All of it?'

'Well, you should have said. Why didn't you?'

Akira stood frozen to the spot. He understood Jim's anger and felt ashamed. 'Do you have the contents?'

'What might they be?' said Jim.

Akira was sweating. He was almost lost for words. 'I'm sorry,' he said. 'Very sorry.'

Jim pulled back his coat. 'Is that what you're looking for?'

'Oh...' Akira groaned at the sight of the mirror and the jewel. He sat down on the sofa across from Jim. 'You know,' he said.

'Yata–'

'No Kagami and Yasakani no Magatama' said Akira. 'May I?' he said.

'Sure,' said Jim.

Akira picked up the mirror and looked into the distorting polished silver surface. His short arm appeared almost the normal length; his face seemed fresh and handsome; and he seemed blissfully happy. He was holding a legend, the sacred mirror that even the goddess of the sun could not resist looking into. The craftsmanship was almost divinely fine. He put it down gently and held out his hand towards the necklace. He looked at Jim for permission.

'Go ahead,' said Jim.

Akira picked it up. It was made of the finest jade he had ever seen. The claw-shaped stones had a purity and depth of colour that even the most perfect stones normally only held in their very heart. He imagined that stones of this quality must have been found when the world was empty. Then gems and gold had lain in streams awaiting humankind to stumble upon them and scoop them up. Now we scuttle over the denuded globe, he thought, scratching for the leftover crumbs of a world once fecund with natural treasures.

He had always argued that the jewel was a crown in the form of a necklace. Myth had the Yasakani no Magatama as a single gem and he had disputed it in private with other scholars. The priests who were meant to have the object could have settled the argument and all the experts knew why they didn't. Anyone who cared even to consider making a study of the Japanese Imperial Regalia quickly came to the conclusion that it no longer existed.

The very objects that supported the legitimacy of emperors back over half a millennium were a mirage. They had been lost for more than six hundred years, and generation after generation had held faith with their symbolism and the legitimacy with which they imbued the state, while in fact they had been lost at sea. Who would have guessed they would return? Was it a miracle or a curse?

He looked up from the deep green gems. The Englishman was holding something. His eyes bugged out. It was the sword Kusanagi. Akira froze. Evans-san held Kusanagi, the grass cutter! He put down the necklace as if in a trance.

'May I, please?' asked Akira.

'Sure,' said Jim, holding it out.

'Excuse me, sir,' said the butler. rather urgently, but it was too late.

Akira held the sword, the hilt in his short hand. He felt a surge of excitement and the world was suddenly bright and crystalline. The sword was destiny. In its metal, forged by legend, was a power so great that he who wielded it was invincible. Even the elements would obey him. The hero who held Kusanagi could not be defeated in battle or wounded. It vanquished all enemies. To carry it was to vanquish armies. Kingdoms fell before its blade. It had held the courage, valour and might of Japan for a thousand years.

He sprang up and pulled the sword from its scabbard.

Jim jumped out of his chair.

'I must take these,' said Akira, loudly, raising the blade to threaten Jim. 'Put the jewel and the mirror in my case.'

There was a crash.

Akira looked round.

The butler had dropped his tray and was aiming a pistol straight between his eyes. Even though he was fifteen feet away it was as if he could look up the barrel of the pistol.

'Put the sword down,' said the butler, clearly.

'There are no guns in Britain,' cried Akira.

'Please don't make me shoot you.'

Akira wasn't backing down. 'I must take what is rightfully Japan's.'

'This is your final warning. Put the sword down.' Stafford sighed. 'Let me demonstrate.' He turned his aim slightly. The pistol reported and the picture window behind Akira shattered. The weapon was instantly aimed again between Akira's eyes. 'You will not hear the next shot. Please spare me your execution.'

Akira stared pleadingly into the man's eyes; his life was over anyway.

'Put the fucking sword down,' shouted Jim.

Akira sheathed it and Jim snatched it from him. 'Fucking hell,' he spat. Now it was in his hand, he wanted to pull the sword out and chop the professor in half. He clenched the hilt in his hands, then let out an angry grunt and sat on the sofa again.

'I think you'd better leave,' said Stafford.

Akira hung his head. He picked up his case and walked to the door. 'I'm sorry,' he said. 'I'm so very sorry.'

Jim picked up the necklace and put it on. He felt a little better. He picked up the mirror, the sword on his knee.

Akira looked back as he left the room. The light moan he let out was the muffled echo of a deep inner cry.

Stafford watched the professor wander like a tipsy man down the road away from the house. He straightened his waistcoat and returned to the lounge. He walked in and went to Jim, who sat sullenly looking at his phone. 'May I sit down?'

'Sure. Thanks for saving my neck.'

'My pleasure,' said Stafford, lowering himself awkwardly onto the oversoft sofa. 'I'm afraid I need to bring you up to date on the events of a previous night. I didn't want to bother you with them.'

'What events?'

'Unfortunately I had to shoot a man trying to burgle us two nights ago.'

'Where?'

'Just by the table behind me.'

'Is he OK?'

'No.'

'You killed him?'

'Yes.'

'Oh, bloody hell. Where's his body?'

'Gone.'

'I shouldn't ask. Should I?'

'No.'

Jim got up, went to the Persian rug and lifted it, grimacing in preparation for what he might see. A neat square had been cut from the carpet. He dropped the rug.

'We need to put the items somewhere safe.' Stafford stood up again. 'Unless you say otherwise I'll see to it today.'

'Why couldn't he have just done a deal?' Jim scratched his head.

'Maybe they can't afford to.'

'Really?' said Jim, sceptically. 'That doesn't seem likely.'

'Maybe the professor can't afford to.'

29

How Akira came to be standing in the park by London's Houses of Parliament, he didn't actually know. He had just walked away from Evans's house and kept going. He was in a daze, shocked by himself and by his reaction to holding the regalia. He was numbed by defeat and loss. He found himself musing about things in an almost disembodied fashion.

Compared with Tokyo, London was a scruffy, worn city of noise, dirt and smells. The pavements were broken and crazed, the roads pot-holed, chaotic and dug up. Apart from a few modern buildings the streets were a muddle of construction from different eras, haphazardly laid out, in a way like much of Tokyo. While the grubbiness had seemed quaint to him on arrival, it now seemed desolate and apocalyptic. It seemed to reflect the fact that he had failed and that his worthless life was over. His disgrace was total.

When people looked at him, they saw a monster. They had been right all those years. He actually was the deformed, diseased and twisted soul everyone knew he must be by the signature of his body. He had not only failed himself and his family, he had failed his country and his race.

His spirit and heart were broken.

He looked over the park wall at the river. He had been here before. His life had returned to the wall and the water that lay beyond. Now there was no challenge to achieve, no test to validate him. There was only the awkwardness and effort of climbing the low parapet to tumble into the waters below.

Only a few hours before he had touched the sacred, yet now

he plumbed the depths of an inner hell.

He looked at his short hand, the fist tightly curled. He would open his fingers and place them on the wall, then vault up and over. He flexed his fingers a little but they were not ready to open. Instead his palm went into spasm. The cramp squeezed his fingers tightly shut. With his other hand he began to prise the fingers open. The pain was exquisite. The agony forced the fist closed as he pulled with all his might. Opening his palm was the only way to end the pain in his hand, then the pain in his heart and soul.

The sun was falling.

'*Big Issue*?' said a voice.

He spun around.

'You all right, mate?' said the high, fluttering voice of the homeless man, trembling as he held his magazines.

'No,' he said, the cramp suddenly gone.

'You don't look all right neither,' said the tramp, smiling sadly, his yellow stubs of teeth painful to see. 'Thinking of ending it?'

'Yes,' said Akira. He looked at the tramp, his wild mane of grey hair and white-streaked beard. 'My life is over.'

'I know what it's like, mate, that's for sure.' He smiled, a tremor flickering up and down his face as his body quivered. 'But, you know, if your life's over and you're still standing, then everything else is a gift. If you're all washed up and you're still alive, then every spin of the wheel is a free shot.'

Akira was dumbfounded. 'Free shot?'

There was a bang, splutter and roar on the road behind. Akira started. He knew that sound.

He turned and gasped. It was a black Harley Davidson, its rider, in leathers, wearing a black helmet. Akira screwed up his eyes to get a clear view of the biker as he passed behind the trees and onto the bridge beyond. The Harley banged and belched as he ran to the wall and leant forwards desperately to see the impossible. The black crash helmet flashed in the dying sunlight above the pediment of Lambeth Bridge, then was lost from view.

He turned back to the tramp – and froze at the sight of a young fox. It stretched its neck out to him, its right forepaw lifted. Its brush swept from side to side and its tongue flicked pink from its open mouth. It seemed to bow.

Akira stepped forwards and the fox skittered back. 'Wait,' he called, holding out his long arm to it.

The fox trotted a few paces away.

Akira stood still and watched it retreat. It stopped, glanced back at him, then disappeared into the gathering gloom. Akira looked around him. It was getting dark. He wanted to cry. 'Everything I do now is free of constraint,' he told himself, as he staggered towards the road and the possibility of a taxi.

30

Stafford opened the door. He looked down at Akira. 'What can I do for you today, Professor?'

'May I come in?'

'Mr Evans is not here and neither is the regalia.'

'May I come in anyway? Perhaps you will allow me to explain myself and then relay a message.'

31

Jane's kiss was a bit like a punch in the mouth, and her first embrace like a mildly modified judo throw. Her body was even more snaky and athletic than when she had left him three months before. Her skin was tanned mahogany, her black hair burnt to ash brown. She was lifting him off the ground with one arm. She was hard beneath her slim-cut clothes, not filling them as she had when she had left.

There was a bedroom in his jet and he was going to tell the pilot to fly the long road back.

'Let's get out of here,' he said.

'OK,' she said.

'But first you've got to put me down.'

Jim had never really wondered about the relationship between danger and the need to procreate but it was certainly going through his mind as the Gulfstream sped down the runway. Jane was unbuttoning his shirt when the real acceleration kicked in and suddenly the physics of weight, acceleration and their relationship became very clear in his mind as they flattened him on the bed.

Jane was laughing as the lift-off sent them down the mattress and into a heap on the bedroom wall. They arranged themselves in a sitting-up position as the plane rose into the air. She unpicked his buttons. 'We'd better wait till we level out,' she remarked.

'OK,' he said, 'but I've already got my seat in the upright position.'

'You sure have.' She pulled his shirt open and ran her finger over the fresh scar across his ribs. 'This is new,' she said, giving him a sarcastic look.

He gave her one back. 'I've been meaning to talk to you about that.'

He started to unbutton her blouse. Below where her dark tan faded at the neck, the skin was perfectly white. He eased the buttons open and began to kiss her chest. Her body seemed to be melting under his touch, hard, bunched muscles suddenly fluid, white skin becoming pink.

She giggled. 'Gee, it's been way too long this time.' She grabbed a handful of his hair.

He couldn't wait until they got to thirty thousand feet. He pulled her belt end and unhooked the buckle.

She pushed him off and rolled him onto his back, pulling his hand away from her pants. She pinned his shoulders down and licked his fresh scar. He shuddered, the disrupted nerves firing in a cascade of strange signals.

'Tasty,' she said.

He unclipped her bra and pulled it off. Her nipples stood out from her flat muscular chest. As he rolled her back she had somehow managed to get his jeans undone.

'Stop,' she commanded.

He propped himself up on one hand. 'What?'

'Take your socks off, you goddamn Brit. At once!'

He laughed. 'OK, OK!'

It proved difficult with his legs pointing up in the air as the jet soared into the blue.

The front door swung open. Stafford was on the other side.

'Oh – hello,' said Jim.

'Afternoon, sir.' He nodded. 'Afternoon, General.'

Jane smiled. 'Colonel,' she said.

'Colonel?' enquired Jim, turning back.

'I've been busted down. How else do you think I can get out and about?'

Jim's concern showed on his face.

'Don't worry,' she said, smiling. 'I asked for the demotion. It was either that or a permanent desk job.'

'I'm sorry,' said Stafford, 'but you have a visitor.'

'Visitor?' said Jim, his happy bubble popping.

'From Japan.'

'The professor?' he exploded. 'You are joking?'

'Going back to school?' asked Jane, innocently.

Jim groaned. 'It's a long story I was saving for later.'

'Sounds interesting,' she said, following him.

'Well, actually, now you come to mention it, it is.' He laughed.

Akira got up as they entered.

Jim noticed Stafford had had the window replaced. That was quick, he thought. 'Professor,' he greeted him, smiling as best he could. Akira bowed. Jim shook his short hand. He could feel the man's tension. 'This is my girlfriend, Jane.' She bowed and Akira reciprocated. 'How can I help you?' He threw himself onto the sofa.

'I want you to sell me the objects.'

'OK, sit down,' said Jim. 'No funny games this time, eh?'

'No,' said Akira, perching uncomfortably on the edge of his seat.

Jane sat on the sofa arm.

'First I must apologise for my previous actions. I do not know what devil entered me.'

'What did he do?' asked Jane.

Akira squirmed a little.

'Nothing really,' said Jim. 'Just tried to chop my head off.'

Jane looked at Akira, who wasn't making any attempt to

contradict what Jim had said. She seemed perplexed. 'OK,' she said. 'That's fine, then.'

'It's all right, Professor,' said Jim. 'I don't hold grudges.' He flexed his shoulders as if that might not be totally the case. 'Anyway, I accept your apology.'

'Thank you,' said Akira. 'I would like to make you an offer for the objects.'

'Go ahead.'

Jane threw a glance at Stafford, who stood by the door with a tray in his hand and a white cloth on it. There was a pistol under the cloth – she could tell even at that oblique angle. She stiffened and stood up.

'It's hard for me to know what to pay,' said Akira. 'What would you suggest?'

'Make me an offer and we'll go from there.'

'As you know, they are very precious.' He put the fingers of his long arm to his lips. 'A hundred mirrion dorrars.'

'A hundred billion dollars,' replied Jim pretending to mishear. 'OK, I'll accept a hundred billion.'

'No, no, no,' said Akira, his eyes bulging. 'Mirrion not birrion.'

'A hundred million,' said Jim, laughing. 'That's like a nice Van Gogh, right? A hundred million is peanuts.'

Jane was giving him a questioning look.

Akira closed his eyes. 'I'm sorry,' he said, opening them, 'but I cannot negotiate these kinds of vast sums. I simply do not have the authority.' He suddenly looked desperately sad.

Jim felt a bit sorry for him. 'What do you think they're actually worth?'

'The regalia are beyond price,' sighed Akira.

'Are you talking about the Japanese regalia?' asked Jane.

Jim nodded.

She seemed confused.

Jim jumped up. 'Let's ask Mr Google,' he said, striding to his desk. He opened a browser. 'What is the value of the British Crown Jewels?' he typed. 'The British Crown Jewels are worth thirteen billion pounds, apparently.'

'What's the *Mona Lisa* worth?' asked Jane.

Jim typed. 'Wow – only a billion. Anybody got any other comparisons?' he asked. 'It says here that the Emperor's palace was worth seven trillion dollars in 1989, more than all the real estate in California. So if his house is worth that, how much for his Crown Jewels?'

'The Japanese Crown Jewels,' said Jane. 'What's this all about?'

Akira stood up. 'Please,' he said, 'I'm sorry, I understand you are angry with me and I do not wish to make things worse. Can I suggest a plan?'

'Why not?' Jim said, grinning.

'I will bring a small group of experts to examine the objects.'

'Wait a minute,' said Jim.

'No, no, no, please,' protested Akira. 'They will examine the objects on your terms. They will then advise others on any offer. Then it will be for you to make arrangements with the correct authority as to what price is fair and reasonable. Does this seem possible to you?'

Jim shrugged. 'Yeah, sounds fine.'

Akira bowed. 'Then it is agreed.'

Jim nodded. 'Yes.' He waved a finger at the professor. 'But no more tricks.'

Akira bowed again. 'No more tricks.'

Jim glanced at the window. 'Oh, shit! It's low tide and what a beauty! It must be full moon.' The stony foreshore now fell nearly twenty feet to the neap tide line. 'Come on,' he said to Jane and Akira. 'Let's take a look before the tide turns.' He went to the window, opened it and raised his foot over the sill. 'Come on, Professor, let's see if we can find some more treasure.'

Jane came down the twelve steps after him in three easy movements.

Jim breathed in the muddy scent of the Thames. He loved the dank clay odour. He trudged to the waterline across the shingle that clattered under his feet. He gazed back at the row of Victorian and eighteenth-century warehouses that fronted the river. It seemed to him that he was looking into another era, as if time had moved at a different pace on the steeply sloping foreshore, leaving it as a gateway to another age.

He could almost hear the sounds of the past, the barked messages and greetings along the once frenetic riverbank. The Thames had been a heaving thoroughfare. For most of the city's life, the river had been the key artery by which people had preferred to travel, rather than braving the smelly, polluted and crime-ridden streets. Now it was placid and empty, with only the occasional boat travelling on it. Like a deserted Roman road buried in a field, an empire had fallen and its broadways had been forgotten.

Akira struggled down onto the beach and walked towards them.

'Look here,' said Jim, as he arrived. 'See where the stones stop and the mud starts? This is where the metal is dropped by the tide. You look here for things – along this line.'

Akira bent down to pluck out a fragment that flashed silver. He pulled and a glistening black and silver chain snaked out of the mud. 'Like this?' he said.

Jim looked into his blank but nonetheless questioning eyes. 'Let me see.' He was amazed at Akira's instant success. He took and examined the watch-chain. It was made of links meshed together in a tightly interwoven cord. 'I've never found anything this good in the hundred times I've been down here,' he marvelled.

'Then keep it,' said Akira, 'as a token of goodwill.'

'No,' said Jim. 'I couldn't. It's special. You found it so it's yours.'

Akira bowed.

Jim smiled. 'Let's see if you can find anything else.'

Akira turned and bent down. Jim caught a glimpse of something else silver on the ground.

Akira picked it up and offered it. It was a bottle cap. 'I'm afraid my luck has ended.'

'Oh!' squealed Jane, from ten yards away. 'Now that's more like it.' She held up a gold-red tube. It was a wartime .303 round. She spotted a scatter of red laser light at the professor's feet and looked up at Jim's apartment: a top-floor window was open. She shook her head. 'We've really got to have a talk with Stafford.'

32

Kim looked out over Tokyo from the fifty-fourth floor. On a clear day the view to Mount Fuji was breathtaking but it had been a long time since anything had lifted his jaded mood. He had thrown up many such great blocks by the power of his will. He built what he liked because no one dared stop him. He built with the huge debt he was allowed.

He owed his banks so much money that only by constructing newer buildings, bigger and higher, could he justify his empire having the assets necessary to cover its giant liabilities. Like a staggering man about to fall, he had to run headlong to stay upright. Without forward momentum he would come crashing to the ground.

Money was a fiction, an illusion built on confidence. They saw his towers and could not value them, so everyone was happy when he told them he was easily able to continue to pay what was due. Yet they all knew that it was only the negligible interest rates in Japan that let the fiction roll on.

If they had to be sold, Kim's assets could not cover his mountains of debt. His ten billion dollars of loans were secured by no more than five billion dollars of property, if he was forced to sell them in the depressed market that had dragged on in Japan for more than two decades. Once he had been a mighty billionaire, but the grinding deflation of the last generation had ground once stratospheric property values back to earth. Yet the debt stayed, and all that kept it serviced was yet more borrowing. He was now a minus billionaire, living like a king off the vast loans that piled ever higher.

If he could lay his hands on the regalia, he could pay everything off in one transaction.

The lights of the buildings lit the heavy clouds, and the rain shone as it fell. He stared out over the vast city.

Tokyo was built inside the crater of a giant active volcano. Mount Fuji was merely a pimple on the rim of a huge, festering boil. One day it would explode and everyone would die. The skies would fill with ash and the world would fall into a decade of never ending winter. Civilization would wilt and humanity shrink back to a level not seen for a thousand years. Sometimes he wished it would happen in front of him and end his predicament in a disaster so great his calumny would be drowned in its overwhelming monstrosity. Now he had a different hope.

He turned to his desk and poured sake into a tall glass. He took a net on a short stick and fished in a bowl, catching an almost transparent prawn. He flicked the prawn into the glass of sake. He lifted the glass and watched the creature twist and turn. He wondered what it felt. He wondered if it thought and, if so, what it was thinking. Was it in agony? He could see its black eyes twisting, the blood that pulsated through its delicate veins into its brain. Man could not even dream of creating such a complicated and refined thing. He tilted his head back and poured the contents of the glass into his mouth. The prawn struggled as he bit on it with a crunch.

The sharpness of the sake contrasted nicely with the slight oiliness of the flesh. The living always tasted so much finer than the dead.

33

The cab drew up and the driver lowered his window to look out at the shop's sign. 'Here we are, gents, Karate Arigato.'

The cab was made for five people but the five Japanese men barely fitted.

'Please wait,' said the big guy on the kerbside jump seat.

'Sure, guv'nor,' said the cabbie. There was forty pounds on the cab's clock, and the prospect of another forty or fifty for the drive back was music to his ears. 'I'll happily wait here for you rather than go back to central London empty.'

The Japanese grunted, taking it for granted that the cabbie had agreed in the affirmative.

Karate Arigato survived mainly on its mail-order business to martial artists, fans and fantasists. It was at the end of a row of scrappy shops set on a main road heading out of town towards Walthamstow in the far north-east of London. In the window there was a picture of Fred, the owner, advertising karate lessons. Fred taught kids karate at night and ran the shop in the daytime. He had been a pretty good fighter when he was young but now his hips and knees were blown. Perhaps thirty years ago, before huge shopping malls and parking restrictions were invented, the row of shops would have been bustling, but now they were barely visited, clinging precariously to commercial existence.

Fred didn't notice five large Japanese get out of a black cab in front of the shop. He was busy listening to the radio and reading the newspaper at the same time. This meant that neither the news nor the discussion on the radio made much sense to him.

However, the activity passed the time. It was a pleasant surprise when the buzzer on the door went as it opened. He stood up to see five burly Japanese men walk in. They seemed rather too big for both their suits and his shop.

They were soon admiring his samurai swords. Swords had been illegal for a few years now but no one had bothered him. It wasn't clear which were or weren't banned. His swords weren't sharp and they were handmade. Fred reckoned that made them legal, but he was glad he hadn't been challenged by the authorities. The swords were just for decoration, he reckoned, to be hung on the walls of those, like him, who admired martial arts.

The only people who normally cared about his throwing stars, cod warlock broadswords and num-chucks were his fun-loving clientele. Through the door to the back of the shop there was a pile of packing material to send this paraphernalia on its way to the bedroom samurai and closet Wiccans who collectively kept the financial wolf from his door. Some of his gear might look a bit wicked but no one ever did any harm with it.

The Japanese smiled a lot and bought themselves a sword each. It was nice to have a till full of fresh fifty pound notes. They bought sharpening stones too.

'*Sayonara*,' said Fred, as they left.

34

Jim had one hand in his jacket pocket. He was gazing into Jane's eyes across the table. She looked completely wonderful in her little black dress. She was absolutely perfect. 'How was your pudding?' he asked.

'Just great! I loved the way they blew it up in the saucepan.'

'Yeah,' he said, 'it was magic.' He smiled broadly. 'I've got a question for you,' he said, gripping the object in his pocket.

'What's that?' She glanced away as someone at the next table stood up. She looked back at him and smiled distantly.

He took the box from his pocket and opened it. 'I wondered if you'd marry me.' He held out the box. The diamond in the solitaire was about the size of an American quarter.

She hesitated. She picked the box up and examined the canary yellow stone. 'No,' she said. 'I'm not ready.'

Jim closed his eyes and sat back. He dropped his head.

'Sorry,' she said, 'it's very sweet of you.'

'Put the ring on and think about it.'

She took it out of the box and put it on. It was loose on her finger. The giant stone flashed and twinkled.

The head waiter was trying to catch Jim's eye. Jim shook his head: now was not the time to bring in the string quartet.

'It looks ridiculous,' said Jane, eyeing the huge sparkling rock. 'It's great but it doesn't look right on me.' She slipped it off, pushed it back into the box and closed the lid with a snap. She peered at Jim as if she was a naughty little girl. 'Jim, do I look like someone ready to get married?'

'What are you waiting for? Someone better to come along?'

'No,' she said. 'Just a better time. I'm just not finished yet.'

'Finished? What's not finished? You mean maybe you've not finished yourself off yet?'

'Come on – let's not spoil the evening.'

'Hold on,' he said, 'you told me you're not ready yet.' He held his hand up. 'OK, so this is not a negotiation. I said, "Will you?" and you said, "No." That's right, isn't it?'

'Yes, that's right. Not now.' She took his hand across the table. 'You mean a lot to me, you really do…'

'But?'

'But however much I think of you, I love what I do more.' She squeezed his fingers. 'I just haven't had enough of what I do. I don't want to give it up, not for anything, not even for you.'

Jim looked grim. 'How long will it be before you want something more?'

'I don't know. I can't make any promises. It doesn't have to come between us.'

'No, I suppose not.' Jim looked over his shoulder. The musicians who had briefly filled the doorway were making their way out again with their instruments, ushered by the head waiter.

Jane was watching them. 'OK,' she said. 'Let me ask you something.'

'What?'

'Will you stick around for me?'

'Yes,' he said.

She was pushing the box back to him. 'Good,' she said. 'I'd like that very much.'

He put it back in his pocket.

'Can I ask you something else?' she said.

'Go ahead.'

'How much was that ring?'
'You don't want to know.'
'No, you're probably right.'

35

The chief priest of the Shinto shrine sat cross-legged on the floor. Behind him four priests stood by drums they were beating in a set of interlocking rhythms.

He read the scroll again. The calligraphy was the work of the high priest of the Ise Shrine.

A lost mirror
Reflections from the deep sea
Now are seen again

He laid the parchment in the urn of glowing charcoal, the heat bathing his hand. He watched the cylinder of paper first crease, then smoke. A flame licked up around it, rose up the sides and began to dance. He fanned his face. He closed his eyes and fell into meditation. He knew that the Yata no Kagami was a myth, as was the sword Kusanagi, which his temple guarded. It had been his first act when he had been elevated to check the package for the sacred item. He had retraced the same path as his predecessors, their careful study a tortured path he had followed years after them. Every fold had its many fathers and they, too, had found nothing inside the package but a thin gold bar to weigh down the box and a sheet of paper with a letter written in archaic script. He had held the letter and tried to read it but the writing was faint and indecipherable. He had closed the package and refolded the paper, as had his predecessors, and sealed it with his own seal as they had done in their time. Like the generations of chief priests before him, he had been left to ponder its meaning. It was a profound journey that only a few had been privileged to experience over those many centuries.

Now the mystery had evolved once more, as the smoke from the parchment thickened on its passage to the heavens.

He opened his eyes and lifted his head, the tassels on his black hat flicking from side to side. He straightened his arms and his golden sleeves fell down like curtains. He pulled out his mobile and SMSed the high priest of Ise Shrine. **I know of this, what are we to do?** He prayed that the answer would not come by scroll.

The phone was ringing. It was Davas's ring tone. Jim looked at the clock: it was the middle of the night. He grabbed the phone off the bedside table.

'What have you done?' the old man practically shouted.

'What's up?' said Jim wearily.

'Have you seen the yen?'

'No,' said Jim, slipping out of the sheets naked. 'You know I don't do that any more. I try not to even look.'

'Well, the yen is all over the map.'

'Really?' said Jim, pulling on his dressing-gown.

'My models tell me something big is going on. Who knows about the regalia?'

Jane was awake now.

'Don't know,' said Jim, opening his bedroom door. 'The professor. The guy that sold it me.' He went down the hallway in the pitch black. 'Whoever they've told.'

'They've told many. The whole causal nexus is lit up like the aurora borealis.'

'Hold on, let me get to my screens.' He plonked himself down and opened up his trading battle screens. 'Shit,' he muttered. The yen was down nine per cent in a straight line. 'I did ask for a hundred billion dollars at one point,' he said. 'I didn't mean it, though.'

'That's rather excessive,' remarked Davas.

Jim groaned. 'This fucker's going to roll all over the place,' he said, watching the currency shudder from one price level to another. 'You sure a bit of Japan hasn't fallen into the sea or something?'

'Certain.'

'They're coming tomorrow to take a look,' said Jim.

'Who is?'

'Well, the Japanese government, I think.'

'You need to be very careful, Jim,' said Davas. 'You're up to your ears in trouble here. This is a game you shouldn't play. Just give the regalia up and be done with it.'

'Max, they're coming tomorrow. They can take a look, make me an offer and it's all done and dusted. No need to panic.'

'Panic!' shrieked Davas. 'There is every reason to panic. The markets are never wrong.'

'Max, it's going to be OK. It's under control.'

'Jim, you're dabbling with forces you don't understand. Please be very careful.'

'I will, Max,' he said, watching the yen spike up a whole per cent in a gigantic move that might have taken half a day in a normal market. 'Now I'm going back to bed.' He hung up.

Jane was standing in the doorway. 'Care to fill me in?'

'Always,' he said, 'but later. First I've got a scar that needs some kissing.'

Jane wouldn't let him fall asleep after his exertions. 'No, you're going to tell me now.'

'Later.'

'No, sir, now. You've had your fun, and now you have to tell me everything, as promised.'

He moaned. The blood was definitely draining from his brain.

'Sit up and talk.' She pulled a hair from his chest.

'Ouch.'

She plucked him again.

'Get off,' he said, and sat up. 'All right.'

'Waiting to receive.'

'Well, what I didn't tell you was that the night before the professor showed up we had a night visitor, who, unfortunately, Stafford shot dead.'

'Oh,' said Jane. 'That's not good.'

'And now the yen is going mental. As we both know, information spreads like honey and all of a sudden the yen is going nuts. So, we can assume a lot of people are getting to know about this.'

'Nuts and honey,' observed Jane. 'That sounds tasty. Are we talking muesli here?'

'Maybe we are – things are definitely getting flaky.' He grinned. 'But the reason the yen is going nutty might be because they think I want a hundred billion dollars in yen for their Crown Jewels. That's quite a lot of money to print in a hurry. Or it might be something else altogether.'

'Like what?'

Jim looked out of the bedroom windows. The moonlight flooded in through the open curtains. He grimaced. 'Well, I've read up on their Crown Jewels. They're basically the things the Emperor needs to be crowned with to be the Emperor. Clearly he wasn't, was he? So is he actually the Emperor or not? For that matter, have any of the Emperors been properly crowned since the jewels disappeared? You could imagine that the whole royal line way back into the past has never been legitimate. It's been rumoured that the regalia were lost in the middle ages but, you know, it's not really an issue unless they suddenly show up somewhere else. Then the whole family tree and royal line would be technically up the creek.

'It's like a bomb under the structure of Japanese society. It's like us waking up one day and finding the Bible was written centuries after Jesus.'

'The Bible *was* written centuries after Jesus,' said Jane.

'Oh,' said Jim. 'Was it?'

Jane nodded.

Jim shrugged. 'Well, you get what I mean. Anyway, something's throwing a spanner in the works with the yen and Max seems to think it's me – he's probably right.'

'Would a hundred billion dollars do that?'

'Who knows? And who knows what rumours are going around? Maybe they think it's a trillion dollars.' He snorted with amusement. 'That would be daft, wouldn't it?'

'And pretty dangerous too,' added Jane.

'Well, we'll see tomorrow when these people show up. The professor said he was bringing experts who are national treasures, but I think he meant experts to see the national treasures.'

36

To any child of the seventies, the cult temple looked like a tank out of the Atari arcade game Battlezone. This seemed to be missed by the followers who worshipped there. The shrine looked incongruous among the low-rise buildings of Azubudai, but it took a little effort to see it at all in its bizarre entirety among its higgledy-piggledy surroundings. The entrance had a distinctly fifties sci-fi feel to it. Above the jutting alien spacecraft lines, a long steep staircase loomed into a bay, like a portal, at the front of the building. For anyone with more imagination than it took to join a Japanese cult, Gort the robot from the *The Day the Earth Stood Still* seemed quite likely to step out onto the top step and welcome visitors.

Perhaps the massive tax breaks afforded to cults partly explained why a giant UFO-shaped building had been raised in central Tokyo. But it wasn't for financial reasons that a follower was sprinting up the loading ramp into the heart of the mighty earthbound spacecraft. He burst through the temple portal and ran down into the belly of the craft. He had to get to the master at any cost. He was panting and exhausted. Finally he reached the inner chamber. He could hear the chanting. He threw the doors open.

Around the giant pool stood the students, dressed in their white jumpsuits, their backs to the water. They were humming, their arms outstretched. The master watched the desperate man, red-faced and sweating, who was racing towards him. He clapped his hands and the students fell backwards into the pool. Then, with a shower of laughter, they surfaced and began hugging each other.

The man fell to his knees in front of the master. 'Forgive me,' he puffed, 'but I have momentous news you must know immediately.'

It was the same news that across town, an hour before, had brought together the grim brothers of the far right. They and others believed in the old way, the way of the samurai, an era when a nobleman could summarily execute a peasant for nothing more than a funny look. In their cause to rebuild the old Japan, they sent lorries with giant speakers around Tokyo to shout their slogans and preach their creed of ultra-nationalism. When they got too close to sensitive embassies, the Tokyo police would pull barriers across the road and make them move on.

There was a gentleman's agreement between the extremists and the authorities that the protests could continue so long as the protestors played by the rules. You could be rude as long as you were polite about it and the ultra-nationalists were proper in their outrage and protest. Their extremism was moderate, in as much as the state's moderation was extreme.

Japanese life was a tight web of unwritten and unspoken rules. But now all the rules were dead: the very spine from which these silent understandings hung had been broken. The Imperial Regalia, long lost but in spirit still present, had been discovered. The myth of its reality was a lie and the reality of the myth was true. The sacred objects of Japan were tangible. Now history had been reset six hundred years back and could be started again from there. If only they could get their hands on the regalia, they could crown their own Emperor and wipe the slate clean.

Nobody said anything. They simply sat and smoked and drank their whisky.

Hori-san was young, but resolute. Barely thirty, he would have been junior but for his ability to raise funds and provide muscle. His connections were not particularly honourable or his methods obvious. He won respect through his activity and zeal. With maturity he would be an important man. He stood up. 'I will act,' he said raising his glass.

The others looked around to gauge the reaction of the group.

Hori-san held out his glass.

Mimura-san hoisted himself up, coughed and picked up his glass from the table. Another stood, then another.

Hori-san raised his glass higher. '*Campai.*'

37

Jim looked into the glass front of the bank and safe-deposit centre where Stafford had stashed the regalia. It had on display a large orange fibreglass cow covered with diamonds. There appeared to be a jungle and a waterfall inside. It wasn't like the antiseptic bank he had worked in. It looked more like a greenhouse gone wrong than a powerhouse of wealth management.

The crazy movement of the yen was playing on his mind. For starters the situation just screamed out to be traded. Sitting on his hands was like asking a little kid with a plate of chocolate biscuits shoved under his nose not to eat them.

If that wasn't off-putting enough, the thought that it was connected directly to him and the regalia was weighing on his mind. Davas was right: he was dabbling with things he didn't understand. It was like being in possession of Excalibur or the Holy Grail. Something was bound to go horribly wrong.

He tried to put that thought out of his mind as he headed for the revolving door with his un-fiancée and his un-butler.

They were shown down to the vault.

There were three ancient men with Akira Nakabashi as they entered the meeting room of the safe deposit section. The professor stood, and two tiny old men struggled to their feet. The third, in a wheelchair, simply nodded.

Jim suddenly felt a little too informally dressed, in his tennis shirt, slacks and jumper. It was wet and cold outside and he held his raincoat over his arm. 'Please sit down,' he said, dropping the coat over the back of a chair. The two old men must have been at least ninety and looked as though a draught from the

166

door might blow them over.

'Thank you,' said Akira. Nobody sat. 'I am most honoured to introduce to you three living national treasures. Saito-san,' he said, pointing to the ancient man in the wheelchair, 'is our living national treasure in touretics.'

'Nice to meet you,' said Jim.

Stafford and Jane were bowing. The old man nodded, his small knobbly hands gripping the arms of the wheelchair.

'What's touretics?' asked Jim.

Akira paused. He seemed to be searching hard for a good word.

'Metal carving,' said Stafford, quietly.

'Exactly,' agreed Akira.

'This is Stafford and Jane,' said Jim, rather put off by the prospect of complicated introductions.

'This is Fujita-san, living treasure of sword making,' said Akira.

Fujita-san bowed stiffly. The stiffness expressed a degree of anger rather than advanced age.

They bowed back.

'This is Suzuki-san, living treasure of *bachiru* and also most respected expert of *magatama*.'

'Ivory carving and jade gems, like the necklace,' whispered Stafford.

Suzuki-san smiled and bowed, bobbing up sharply with a wide grin of broad yellow twisted teeth.

They all bowed again.

They sat down.

'They're bringing the things in a second,' said Jim, to the frail assembly of Japanese men. 'Did you all just fly in?' he asked. A long flight might have been enough to kill people that decrepit.

'Yes,' said Akira.

Suzuki-san spoke.

Akira translated. 'Suzuki-san says it will be a fine end to his life if he sees the Three Sacred Treasures.'

'That's nice,' said Jim. He glanced around the room. It was like a bunker. There were no windows. The tired panelling was punctuated with bland abstracts that might have been fashionable in the seventies but were now the height of kitsch and rather grimy to boot.

To his relief the meeting room door opened. The three old men sat up in their seats and watched intently as the safe deposit manager brought in a long, thin, silver-coloured box. Stafford took a key from his pocket and the manager produced another. They unlocked the box together.

The manager left the room.

Stafford opened the box and removed what looked like a felt bag that might have held an expensive pair of shoes. He took out the mirror and placed it on the table on top of the flattened bag.

Akira passed it to Saito-san, who held it as if it was as fragile as a butterfly. He blinked at it as if dust had blown into his eyes. He turned the mirror in his hands, barely touching it, as though even the slightest contact was some kind of violation.

Stafford took the necklace from another bag and laid it on the table.

Suzuki-san let out a cry of what might have been pleasure or the result of an excruciating blow to the funny bone, such as Jim had experienced as a child. He plucked up the necklace with the middle finger of his right hand and held it to the light. He uttered a long series of oohs.

Jim took out the sword and suddenly the room was still. He offered it to Fujita-san.

Fujita-san stood up, as if sitting down would be disrespectful. He took the sword in both hands and looked down at it without moving. He breathed in, scowling, then exhaled and pulled the blade half out of its scabbard. He looked at it, then at Akira.

He spoke and Akira nodded.

'What did he say?' said Jim.

'I said,' replied Fujita-san, 'this must surely be Kusanagi.' He laid the sword, back in its scabbard, on the table and sat down.

Suzuki-san and Saito-san had swapped items and were engrossed in their reveries.

'Don't you want to look at the sword some more?' Jim asked Fujita-san.

'No,' he said curtly.

'Why?' wondered Jim.

'It is not for me to handle the sword Kusanagi.'

'It is difficult,' interjected Akira. 'These are sacred items.'

Jim wanted to point out that the other two living treasures weren't having similar difficulties but instead he picked up the sword himself and took it from its scabbard. It seemed to bathe in a kind of cold white light. He turned it. They were staring at him and at the flashing blade. 'I'll be sorry to part with this,' he said finally, sheathing it with a satisfactory flourish.

Akira turned to his living treasures and spoke to them in turn. They each replied, '*Hi.*'

'I think they agree,' said Jane, softly.

'I think you are right,' said Stafford.

'Thank you, Evans-san, Stafford-san,' Akira seemed to ignore Jane. 'Thank you so much for letting us see the regalia. I look forward to quickly resolving this matter with you.'

Suzuki-san stood up and touched the hilt of the sword, drawing his hand back slowly. He smiled and bowed.

Fujita-san led the living treasures out of the room, Akira pushing Saito-san in his wheelchair. Suzuki-san was the last to leave, and as he went to close the door behind him he paused and gave Jim a long, mysterious smile.

The door closed.

Jim sat down and slipped the necklace on. 'I like this,' he said, sliding it under his tennis shirt. 'I might keep it.' He picked up the sword and mirror and posed regally. 'Maybe I can be Emperor of East London.'

'You'd look good,' said Jane.

'Allow me,' said Stafford, taking the mirror. 'In a few minutes our car will pull up outside and we will go on to the new vault.'

'Who's the driver?' asked Jane, suddenly.

'An old friend of yours. Superintendent Smith.'

'That's good,' said Jim. Trust Stafford to rustle up the best.

The door opened and the vault manager brought in a briefcase with a handcuff attached to the handle.

Stafford put the mirror into its soft bag and passed it to Jim, who pushed it into the pocket of the raincoat he held over his arm. Stafford cuffed the briefcase to his hand. 'It's a long time since I've been a decoy,' he said. 'Let's hope this instance turns out happier than the last.' A flicker of reminiscence flashed across his face. He blanched and snapped back to the present. 'Would you like to wear the Magatama or do you think it might be better in your other pocket?' he asked Jim.

Jim touched the necklace under his shirt. He always felt a little sad taking it off. The stones felt warm against his skin, even though they weren't. 'I'll leave it on,' he said. He picked up his raincoat and put it on. He straightened it on his shoulders, feeling the mirror wedged deep in its left pocket. He opened the coat and slotted the sword into the inside pocket. Kusanagi slid down into the lining snugly. Stafford had made it with a needle and thread, sewing as expertly as Jim's nan had when she'd darned his socks all those years ago.

'As soon as Smith calls, we will go,' said Stafford, sitting down with the briefcase. He adjusted the handcuff on his wrist and set his face to a determined frown.

Jim felt Jane kiss his cheek. 'Never a dull moment around you,' she said, smiling.

'Likewise,' he responded.

38

Jim suddenly appreciated the broad plate-glass windows of the bank. They gave him a clear view of the street ahead. No one alarming was standing on the pavement outside. Stafford got into the revolving door and pushed ahead as Jim entered the next compartment. No sooner was he halfway round than he realised Stafford was pushing hard on the door to get out and saw, from the corner of his eye, figures rushing from the left towards them.

A door of their car, a Mercedes people carrier, was opening, and Stafford was now squeezing out of the revolving door in an attempt to sprint for it. He was a couple of strides across the pavement when the figures were on him. One tried to rip the case from his grasp but managed only to have the briefcase suspended between him and Stafford's outstretched arm. Another held Stafford fast.

Jim was out of the revolving door, shouting at the top of his voice: 'Hey!' There were four men as far as he could see. There was a flash of metal as one of the men pulled a sword, and another as Jim drew Kusanagi. The bulky Japanese standing side on to him was raising the blade to cut Stafford's arm off.

Jim didn't hesitate: he slashed Stafford's attacker. As the blow struck Jim felt resistance in his sword. The bulky figure fell, cut in two.

There was a flash to Jim's right, which he instinctively blocked with Kusanagi. The attacker's sword shattered, fragments striking Jim's head. His eyes focused on his opponent, whose arm was outstretched, his hand still clutching the broken blade.

Jim thrust forwards and skewered him.

He turned. Jane was landing a punch to the throat of the man still pulling on Stafford's briefcase. He focused on the man holding Stafford's other arm. He could see the shot, a diagonal blow through the base of the neck to the hip. He could just sweep his arm around and down and swat the man like a fly. It was the right blow, the perfect cut. He would touch him with the finger of death. There was terror in the man's eyes. Jim could see his fingers loosening on Stafford, could sense his enemy's realisation that he was about to die. He could see everything clearly in the cold bright light.

He blinked. The Japanese let go of Stafford and Jim waved the sword at him. The guy turned and fled across the road.

Jane was bundling Stafford into the people carrier, and Jim realised he was splattered with blood. Horrified faces lined the windows of the bank and the pavement was covered with gore. He slipped the sword into its scabbard and jumped into the vehicle. He slammed the sliding door and Smith drove away.

'What the hell was that?' shouted Smith, before calling in the incident over his radio.

Stafford's wrist was bleeding and he cursed quietly to himself as he tried to take the handcuff off.

'First aid?' called Jane.

'In the boot.'

'Going to need it fast.'

'Need to get clear of the scene first,' called back Smith.

'Got a gun?'

'Yes.'

'Pass it back and stop the car.'

Jane took the pistol from Smith and as the people carrier stopped, she jumped out and opened the boot, retrieved the kit and sprinted back into the vehicle. 'Go.'

Jim was looking at Stafford's bleeding wrist. It didn't seem as bad as Jane reckoned it was.

'Hold still,' said Jane. She pressed a wad of bandage onto Jim's head. 'Hold that there.'

'What?'

'Just press firmly and hold still.' She wrapped another bandage around his head and under his chin and fastened it with a large plaster.

Stafford had freed himself of the handcuff and was staring fixedly at Jim's head.

'What?' said Jim, angrily.

'You have a large gash in your scalp, which is rather hanging off,' said Stafford.

Jim looked at Jane, then back at Stafford. 'Doesn't seem to be bleeding,' he said, 'and it doesn't hurt.'

'Give it time,' said Jane. 'Smith, we've got to get these guys to a hospital.'

'Not me,' said Stafford. 'I've got to get these somewhere safe.' He started to bandage his wrist.

Smith had put a magnetic blue light out of the window and it was now flashing.

Jim lifted the necklace over his head and put it into the other pocket. He slid out of the raincoat. 'You'd better take this,' he said, as he handed it to Stafford. Now there was a shooting pain in his head.

Jane slipped off her jacket and unbuttoned her shirt. She folded the blouse quickly into a square. She added it to the bandages, which were sodden with blood. 'Press on this, Jim – you'll be OK.'

'Let me out here,' said Stafford. He looked at Jim, blood trickling down from beneath the bandages. 'I'll see you all later.'

Jane buckled Jim in. All he could hear was thunder in his ears.

Akira was sitting next to the little table by his hotel bedroom window. He glanced out through the grubby net curtains onto the grimy wall of the building's inner well, put his mobile down and sighed.

'Samurai Carnage,' said the newspaper's website.

He had seen the black suited men on the pavement as the people carrier containing himself and the living treasures had pulled away.

Why hadn't the butler, Stafford, answered his call? Why did people never seem to have their mobile phones switched on anymore?

His eyes closed and he saw the fox in front of him again, its pink tongue pulsating with each breath. The image was the only thing that gave him strength. He had begged the head of Imperial Security for help but the response had been stony. He was piling disgrace on himself and his family.

He dwelt on the tramp and the fox.

39

Smith was reading a copy of *New Scientist* as he sat in the waiting room at the private clinic. Jane was motionless, her face blank. He put down the magazine. 'So, what's this all about?' he asked finally.

'Hell knows.'

'May I be frank?'

'You can be whoever you like,' she replied, with a trace of a glare.

'You don't have to tell me, but I do have to say that Jim and you have managed to put me in a rather tricky situation.'

'I can see that. What are you going to do?'

'Nothing – at least, not immediately.'

'That's good of you,' she said.

'Remind me. Do you have diplomatic immunity?'

'Most certainly.'

'Very good,' he said. 'Funnily enough, this is right up my alley. SO13, et cetera.'

'So you're working there now?'

'Yes,' he said. 'Now, you did tell me you were moving some valuables and I did agree to help, and I was looking forward to dinner with you both, but I do have to ask, what exactly were you moving?'

'Antiques.'

'You told me that.'

'I know.'

'What sort of antiques?'

'Japanese antiques.'

'And were you expecting to be bushwhacked by a posse of ninjas?'

'There was a very small possibility, hence our request.'

'How small a possibility?'

'Infinitesimal.'

'What kind of antiques are they?'

'Old ones.' She sounded irritated.

'How old?'

'I'm no expert in antiques.' Jane glared at him.

'Do you know who attacked you?'

'No.'

'If you did know, who would it be?'

'Look, John, don't try to interrogate me. We worked together long enough for you to know better than to try that.'

'OK,' said Smith. 'One more question, though.'

'Go ahead.'

'You saw Jim use that sword.'

'I was a bit occupied but, roughly speaking, yes.'

'You saw what he did?'

'I saw the aftermath.'

'Since when did he learn how to use a sword like that?'

A flicker of doubt flashed over her face. It reddened. 'I don't know.'

Smith had been through a lot of shit with Jane, and she had practically been his best friend for three whole years. He missed working with her. 'I'll try to smooth the way,' he said, sitting back, 'but I can't promise I won't have to arrest Jim. I've had all the CCTV seized.'

She knew as much. Her phone had intercepted the texts between him and his unit and she had read the traffic as it went back and forth. Smith had taken charge of the incident and branded it a matter of national security on the basis Jane was involved. He was a clever operator but not as smooth as she was. She didn't allow herself a smile. 'So I guess dinner's off,' she said.

'That's a pity,' said Smith. 'I was really looking forward to it.'

Stafford unwrapped the replica samurai sword. He honed it in the knife sharpener until the machine started to overheat. Eventually it cut out. He washed the sword several times, then put it in the cupboard with the Hoover and the mops. He imagined the police would certainly pay a visit and want to take away the sword involved in the incident. He prepared Kusanagi's stand-in accordingly. He was once again perverting the course of injustice and it pleased him deeply.

His phone was vibrating again. It was the professor for the umpteenth time. He huffed and answered. 'Yes,' he said, extending the word to three syllables.

'Stafford-san,' asked Akira, 'is everybody OK?'

'No,' replied Stafford, stretching the negative for three seconds.

'Is someone hurt?'

'Yes.'

'I'm so sorry,' said Akira. 'I don't know what happened. I saw men on the street and tried to call you.'

Stafford had noted that he had received a call around the time of the attack. 'That was good of you.'

'I must see Evans-san. I must explain to him personally I had nothing to do with it. Is he all right?'

'I will pass on the message,' said Stafford, somewhat tersely.

'And you and the lady, are you all right?'

'Thank you for calling.' Stafford hung up, feeling he had perhaps given out too much information. He nursed his shoulder. It was starting to stiffen even with all the painkillers coursing through his veins.

A people carrier pulled up outside the front door and, at a

glance, he recognised it as Smith's vehicle. He made his way up the stairs to the door. Jim was fumbling with his keys when it swung open. 'Thanks, Stafford,' he said, walking quickly but unsteadily inside. Jane followed him.

'How's your hand?' she asked Stafford, as he closed the door.

'Intact,' he replied.

She touched his shoulder and gave him a smile. 'I'll take a look at your injuries in five.'

'I'm quite all right.'

'I'll be the judge of that.'

Jim was slumped on the sofa in the lounge. Jane sat next to him, 'You want to talk?'

'Not really.'

'You did well.'

'What a disaster.'

'How do you feel?'

'Fucked.'

'You're going to have the mother of all headaches tomorrow.'

'That's good,' said Jim.

She took his hand. 'It's going to be OK.'

'Yeah, of course,' he said, squeezing her hand.

They sat in silence until Stafford came in, holding a tray rather awkwardly. Jane sprang up. 'I thought tea was called for,' he said, as Jane relieved him of his load.

'Thanks,' said Jim, blearily.

'Professor Nakabashi called,' said Stafford.

'I hope you told him to go fuck himself,' said Jim, his head rolling back.

'Not in those exact words,' replied Stafford.

'You get the first aid pack out and I'll be down in two minutes,' said Jane, putting the tray in front of Jim.

Jim looked down at the tea. 'You go ahead. I'm all set up here.' He smiled a little.

'OK,' said Jane, taking her mug. 'You just take it easy.'

Jim lay down on the sofa and tried to arrange his head on the arm so there was no pressure on his scalp wound. It was tricky, but as soon as he found a comfortable position he was asleep.

It was a crushing feeling in his head that brought him around. His skull seemed to be in the tight grasp of a huge hand. He opened his eyes. They didn't focus to begin with but from the pale light it looked like early morning. He felt stiff all over and his body was reluctant to move. His head was throbbing to his pulse. He levered himself up with difficulty, the duvet that covered him falling to one side.

Jane was asleep on the facing sofa.

There was a glass of water on the table and a pot of painkillers, with two laid out by it waiting for him. He reached for the pills and swallowed them, then drank the water. He got up groggily and went to his computer. Yesterday was all over the news.

He squinted at it. 'North Korean terrorists attack tourists.' He wondered if he was dreaming. Mystery have-a-go hero fights back. He noticed Jane standing behind him. 'Smith must have done a cover up,' he said.

'Well, it wasn't me,' said Jane, 'Maybe they were North Koreans.'

'Why?'

'There's plenty of bad blood between North Korea and Japan. Imagine what stunts they could pull if they got hold of the regalia.'

Jim's head was pounding. 'I think I'll go upstairs and get some more kip.'

'Good plan.'

It was eleven o'clock. Jim was watching the FTSE 100 trade. His head was still hurting badly and the painkillers didn't seem to be working. It was a grey, overcast morning, the cloud hanging low over the river, which was rising to high tide.

Jane was reading a book on Burma. He got up and sat beside her. 'I feel awful,' he said.

She put the book down. 'You're in shock.'

'I'm not,' he said.

'Denial is normal,' she said gently.

'I'm not in denial.'

'It's OK,' she said.

'I'm not in denial,' he insisted grumpily.

'Don't be angry. It's absolutely fine.'

'I'm not angry,' he said, standing up. His head rewarded him for the sudden jolt with a shooting pain. He held it in both hands. 'Argh.'

She raised an eyebrow and pursed her lips.

'OK. I might be angry, but not with you.'

The front door buzzed. 'Who the fuck is that?' he snapped, and stormed off towards the hall.

'I'll deal with this,' said Stafford, as they met by the door.

'Who is it?'

'The professor.'

'What?' Jim exploded.

'I'll send him away. Please – leave it to me.'

'No,' said Jim. 'I want to tell him personally to take a long fucking walk off a short fucking pier.'

Stafford turned to let him pass, looking down at the CCTV feed from the front door. Their unexpected caller was alone.

Jim swung the door open. Akira reeled back, clearly horrified to see Jim's head swathed in bandages.

'What do you want?' snapped Jim, slightly disarmed by the professor's expression.

'Evans-san, I'm so very sorry to trouble you. Can I come in?'

'No.'

Akira's head dropped. 'I understand. This was not my doing.'

'Really? Do you expect me to believe you didn't send those Koreans?'

'They were not Koreans.'

Jim's mind went temporarily blank. 'How do you know?'

'I saw them as I left. They were Japanese. I tried to call.'

'How do you know they were Japanese?'

'They did not look like North Koreans, they looked like Japanese. Forgive me to know the difference.'

'Who were they, then?'

'I don't know.'

Jim struggled to think over the pulsating pain in his head. 'I'll tell you what. Until things get back to normal I'm doing nothing. This fucking nonsense has got to stop. If I get one more problem, I'll throw the fucking regalia into the sea and that will be an end to it.'

'Or donate them to the British Museum,' came Stafford's voice from inside.

'No,' said Jim. 'I'll fucking chuck them in the North Sea.'

'Please believe me,' said Akira, stooping as if he was carrying a hefty weight, 'I only want to recover the regalia. I mean you no harm. I'm so sorry for what has happened. I understand you can't forgive but please believe me.'

'Just make sure nothing else happens. When I'm ready I'll get in touch,' said Jim.

'But I can't ensure that. What is happening is out of my hands. Too many people must know now. I cannot calm the tempest. It is out of control.'

'That's your problem.'

'No,' said Akira. 'It is our problem.'

'I'll be in touch.' Jim closed the door with what was almost a slam.

Stafford watched the professor turn away. He looked bereft. Stafford stroked his chin.

Jane cut off the patch into Jim's CCTV and put her mobile down. Jim walked in. 'What was that?' she asked innocently.

'That bloody professor. "I know I tried to chop your head off a couple of days ago, but this time it wasn't me."'

The door buzzer went, and simultaneously Jane's BlackBerry, face down, skipped across the table.

'Who the fuck's that?' exclaimed Jim, spinning around as Jane snatched up her phone. 'He's not back again, is he?'

'It's Superintendent Smith,' called Stafford.

'What ho!' Smith greeted him – with an edge of sarcasm, it seemed to Jim.

'Do come in, *Inspector*.' Stafford gave as good as he got.

Jim's mood lifted. 'John,' he said, going into the hall. He shook his friend's hand.

'How's the head?'

'OK,' said Jim. 'Hurts like crazy but it's OK.'

Jane got up from Jim's computer. 'Hey, John, what's the story on the NKs?'

'Koreans!' He shrugged. 'A likely story.'

'We thought you might have made it up,' said Jim, sitting down on the sofa.

'Not me.' He turned to Jim. 'Who was that at your door just now?'

'John,' intercepted Jane, 'can we do without the interrogation?'

'Not for much longer,' he replied.

'Where did the story about the Koreans come from?' asked Jim.

Smith closed his eyes. 'You know,' he said, 'this is all wrong. I'm meant to be making the enquiries here.'

'Come on, John, you know I'm going to find out as soon as the west coast wakes up.'

'Is this some kind of DIA operation?' said Smith, propping himself on the edge of the ancient table.

'Just help me here,' said Jane. 'I'll fill you in as soon as I can.'

Smith looked down at her thoughtfully. 'All right, but you're getting nothing further from me until then. Japanese intelligence told us it was North Koreans.'

'And?' prompted Jane.

'Well, let's just say we aren't exactly in regular communications with the Japanese on this kind of matter, so we took what they said at face value. It's a convenient story for everyone.'

'But you don't believe it.'

'I associate heavily tattooed Orientals with the Yakuza,' said Smith. 'There you are. Now I've broken my own agreement to say no more.'

'The Japanese Mafia,' put in Jim.

'Yes,' said Smith, 'and all very fishy if you ask me – or should I say all very sashimi? Who was your visitor?'

'Can't say,' said Jane.

'Look,' said Smith, getting off his perch, 'this is not on. I could just throw you all into a cell and then you'd have to spill the beans.'

'That won't work,' said Jane. 'My leave ends on Friday and I have to be back in Virginia.'

Smith looked sourly at her. 'Isn't abuse of friendship a felony in your country?'

'No,' she said. 'It's a misdemeanour.'

Smith turned to Jim. 'I hope you know what you're doing, mate,' he said. 'I can't help you if you won't let me in. I mean, don't get tangled up with the DIA – they'll eat you up and spit you out.' He gave Jane a penetrating look.

She responded with a pointed glare. 'We're not so bad,'

she said.

As Smith talked, Jim was thinking about the asking price for the regalia. The Japanese had tacitly agreed to pay a hundred billion dollars for them. Something burst in his head, with a crack like exploding bubble wrap. He realised he was being a complete idiot. His, Jane and Smith's lives were simply not worth a fraction of a hundred billion dollars. A hundred billion was more than the GDP of Libya. Thousands of lives could be blotted out with a hundred billion dollars – and there he was, taunting the world with it. He had got himself into a high stakes game he didn't know how to play and all their lives were in the pot. They would all be sacrificed without hesitation to the winning of that prize.

'Thanks, John' said Jim, holding down the emotions that were rising inside him. 'It'll all turn out OK. Once it's done and dusted I'll tell you about it over a beer.'

'I'll let myself out,' said Smith, gruffly.

Jim was staring out onto the river, watching the water run downstream towards the sea.

'What are you thinking?' asked Jane.

'I'm going to give them back,' he said. 'Screw the money.'

'Wait,' said Jane. 'Let's not do anything too quickly. We've got to go over all the options. We can't afford to do anything dumb.'

'I'll just ring up the professor and hand them over to him.'

'That's a good idea,' said Jane, 'but don't do it right this second. Let's think it over properly first. We have to get this right.'

'These attacks aren't about the professor,' said Jim. 'I believe him. What would a history professor have to do with killers?'

Jane nodded. 'Nakabashi is Japanese government, right? They wouldn't use Yakuza muscle. That's coming from somewhere else.'

'This is just an almighty fuck up,' said Jim.

Jane nodded. 'Yep, and it's getting messy – fast. The configuration is looking bad.'

'This gear is like plutonium,' said Jim, almost to himself. 'It's toxic. We're in some kind of death spiral, I can feel it. It's like when the market crashes – suddenly things take on a life of their own and you can't fight it.'

'Sometimes you've got to just drop the ball and high tail it out of trouble, but you never do it without thinking it through,' said Jane. 'Let's make sure we don't land ourselves in deeper shit by handing the stuff over too fast. We'll do some planning.'

40

Stafford looked askance. 'Are you sure?'

'Yes,' said Jim. 'It's the simplest solution.'

Stafford glanced at Jane, then back at him. 'Very well.'

'Where did you put them?'

'I pawned them,' said Stafford. 'It seemed the only solution in the circumstances.'

Jim gasped. '*Pawned* them?'

'Yes.'

'Cool,' said Jane. 'What did you get for them?'

'Do you really wish to know?'

'You can get them back, can't you?' asked Jim.

'Of course.'

'Thank goodness for that!'

'Are you certain you want to do this?' said Stafford, disappointment in his face.

'Yes. It's just too dangerous. I think we're all hanging by a thread,' said Jim. 'I'm going to call the professor and tell him to pick them up tomorrow. Then we'll be shot of the whole mess. After that Jane and I are going to fly to Washington Dulles, so I can see her off.'

Stafford nodded, with an element of reluctant agreement. 'I'll collect the items first thing tomorrow morning.'

Jim felt a welling sense of relief. He could tell he was making the right decision by his sudden mood change. Cutting a trading loss early felt like that: the relief was based on the understanding of the bad things the future would hold if you held on. Deep down, he knew he had to give the regalia back unconditionally.

41

'*Muschi, muschi*,' said Akira, answering his phone. 'Ah, Evans-san. Good to hear from you.' Why was the man calling him so soon after they had last spoken? Had something else happened? Something terrible?

'Professor, I've got some good news.'

'Good news?' repeated Akira, a wave of confusion sweeping over him. Had Evans-san given the regalia to the British Museum? Or, indeed, thrown it into the sea?

'You can come and get the jewels tomorrow morning. Just come round the house and pick them up.'

'Say again, please.'

'You can come and get your treasures tomorrow. I'm giving them to you.'

Akira leaped up from his chair. 'You are giving them up?'

'Yes.'

Akira wanted to ask why, but he didn't. He tried to imagine what Jim was thinking that he could hand them over for nothing. Anxieties raced through his mind. What was he going to do with them once he had them? He had planned to take them to the embassy but now, with killers on the loose, that wasn't a simple matter.

'Hello,' said Jim. 'Are you still there?'

Akira snapped out of his shock. 'Yes, yes.' He felt a little weak and sat down again. 'Evans-san, what time shall I call on you?'

'Eleven o'clock should be fine.'

'Thank you so very much.'

'No problem,' said Jim, and hung up.

'What a crazy trade,' he said, grimacing. 'All this excitement and bugger all to show for it.'

'Look on the bright side,' said Jane, giving him a hug from behind. 'You've got a groovy duelling scar out of it.'

'You're right. I've always wanted one on my head to add to the collection.'

42

'*Hi*,' said Akira, meaning yes. 'Tomorrow morning I plan to pick up the regalia.' He nodded to the caller far away in Tokyo. '*Hi*, there is no further payment involved. *Hi*, Evans-san will give me all three objects.' He was standing to attention in his small, tired hotel bedroom. 'I will need a guard to transfer them to the embassy.' He was nodding. 'Twenty people seems more than adequate. Will they be armed?' He was listening intently. 'May I suggest that only legitimately armed guards be used? We should avoid embarrassment.' He groaned. 'Only three armed attachés available?… I see. Would enlisting British help be too difficult?… I see. I appreciate you will do all you can to help me.'

His face was locked in a mask of pain. Tokyo could not act fast enough. They could not ask for help: they did not have the right people in London and he had to act in the morning.

He stiffened himself. All he had to do was pick up the regalia in the presence of three armed guards and get it five miles to the embassy. It was a stressful prospect but it would surely end well.

'Thank you,' he said, to the compliments from Tokyo. 'Goodbye.'

43

'Excuse me, sir,' said Stafford, back in his official cover role as butler.

'Yes?' said Jim, turning away from his computer. Jane looked up from her book on Burma.

'Professor Nakabashi just walked past our front door.' Stafford looked down at his iPhone. 'There he is again.'

Jim got up and stared at the screen. Akira's form was disappearing up the road. 'I'll go and see what he's up to.'

The fence was made of plywood and painted blue. Akira could see through the cracks onto the construction site beyond. From the evidence of rigs poking out above the barrier, excavation was going on and he could see snatches of it. He paid attention to the details: the street and the alleyways that led off it.

He turned the corner and jumped. Evans-san was looking at him quizzically. 'Oh,' he said, bowing. 'You surprised me.'

'What the hell are you doing?' said Jim, as genially as he could.

'Yes, yes,' said Akira, 'very good question.' He squinted hard at Jim. 'I am learning the lie of the land. Tomorrow I can't leave anything to chance. I am walking the route between your house and the embassy.' He held up his phone. 'I am taking notes and photographs. I want to leave nothing to fortune.'

'Oh,' said Jim. 'Good thinking.'

'Thank you,' said Akira. 'I am a little frightened, I must admit. What happened to you could happen to me.' He smiled nervously. 'I'm not big and strong like you.' He clenched the fist of his short hand. 'I only have this arm to fight back with,' he said, swinging the blow five inches by pushing out his shoulder. He immediately regretted his joke.

Jim was smiling. 'Sorry to bug you,' he said. 'I'm a bit wound up right now.'

'I understand,' said Akira. 'I am likewise wound up.'

Jane was walking towards them, 'Hi there, guys, what's up?'

'The professor's casing the area for tomorrow's pick-up,' Jim told her.

Akira bowed to her.

'Good job,' said Jane. 'Why don't we all do dinner tonight?'

They looked at her as if she had said something either really clever or really dumb.

'I'm getting bummed out being cooped up day and night,' she said.

'OK,' said Jim. 'I'm up for it.'

What would they do if he refused? wondered Akira. Would it be a big insult? Would they change their minds about giving up the regalia? What would happen if it all went terribly wrong? Would they be safe? Would he be safe? Were the regalia safe?

'How about you, Akira-san?' said Jane.

The woman Jane was excessively forceful, even for an American, but she sent an exciting shiver down his spine. 'Yes,' he said. 'Please allow me to entertain you tonight.'

The trees of Green Park and the traffic of Piccadilly are all that separates the Japanese Embassy from Buckingham Palace. Half Moon Street is around the corner, and partway down there is a Japanese restaurant called Kiku. Quality and proximity to the embassy means it is very popular – and Akira decided it would accomplish two purposes: it was a place to eat, and going there would offer him a chance to check out the area directly around the embassy before dinner.

He had arranged to meet Jim and Jane there at seven and had then carried on his research, finally walking the whole way back to the embassy along his chosen route of the next day's vital mission.

London would be so much nicer, he was sure, if only it was cared for a little better. Nothing was quite finished. The pavements were never properly flat. The trees were badly pruned and often vandalised, the grilles around their trunks not perfectly set. Chewing gum was left stuck to the paving. There was graffiti and, like any backward country, litter. London was scruffy.

It amazed him that no one saw the benefit of just a little more diligence and attention. London could shine like a jewel, such as Kyoto. Instead it was dog-eared and splattered with besmirching corrosion. He didn't understand why.

44

Jane was poking the razor clam with her chopsticks. It seemed to be curling up in response. 'This is real fresh,' she noted.

Akira nodded. 'Do you like it?'

Jane was chewing. 'Very good,' she said, a few moments later.

A waitress put down three lidded porcelain mugs set in wicker baskets. A glazed cartoon creature adorned the lids, a smiling ball shaped fish. It looked a little like a very fat whale.

The waitress took out a matchbox and struck a match. She took the top off Akira's mug and ignited the liquid, which quickly sputtered out. Some black and grey flakes were floating in the clear liquid below.

'*Fugu sake*,' said Akira, happily.

Now she lit Jim's drink – there was a puff of blue flame.

Jane smiled. Europeans served women first, but with Asians men took priority. Americans had lost the gender plot almost entirely. 'Tincture of neurotoxin,' she said, saluting. 'Exciting.'

'*Campai*,' said Akira.

'What is this?' said Jim, clinking his cup with Jane and Akira.

'*Fugu*,' said Akira. 'Puffer fish fins in hot sake.'

'Lethal puffer fish fins in hot alcohol,' said Jane, and sipped.

'Right,' said Jim, adjusting his bandage. The liquid was bitter and heady, the fascinating solvent like fumes of the sake mixing with the bitter but intangible kick of the fins with their magic neurotoxin.

'A bit of liver from this fish and you drop dead on the spot.'

said Jane. 'That flavour is a tiny trace of one of the world's most powerful poisons shooting up the nerve ends in your tongue to your brain.'

'Not so much poison, I'm sure,' said Akira, 'though accidents do happen, but not with the fins.'

'Tastes great, doesn't it?' said Jane.

Jim was trying to notice the effects of the potentially lethal toxins in his mouth. It just tasted pleasantly harsh to him, rather like a big sniff of spray glue. 'What's that?' he asked, gesturing at a pile of orange stuff wrapped in a black papery substance.

'Sea urchin egg,' said Akira. 'Very good.'

Jim picked it up with his chopsticks and got it into his mouth rather inelegantly. He nodded in appreciation. He wanted to say, 'It tastes very eggy,' but if he had he would have likely sprayed the professor with it.

He washed it down with his toxic fish fin toddy. 'How would I know if I'd been poisoned?'

'You get paralysed,' said Jane.

'So, so, so,' said Akira.

'You suffocate,' she said. 'You're wide awake but you can't breathe. 'It's like about ten people a year die from *fugu* in Japan - right Professor?'

Akira nodded. 'Very little chance of dying from eating *fugu*.'

'More people die from bowing accidents in Japan than from eating blowfish.'

'You know a lot about Japan, Jane-san.'

'Thank you,' said Jane. 'I wish.'

'Die from bowing?' said Jim, wondering whether the puffer fish poison had got into his ears.

'Bashing your head when you do it,' said Jane, 'or getting it trapped in a train door – you know the kind of thing. Enough people doing anything is going to result in fatalities. Tens of thousands of people die every year just getting in and out of the bath.'

'That's good to know,' said Jim. 'I'm sticking to the shower from now on.'

'What do you think?' said Jim, as soon as the cab pulled away.

'He's legit,' said Jane. 'He's quirky but no gangster.'

'Did you notice that every time we put him on the spot, his funny hand would start flexing or making a fist or something?'

'No,' said Jane. 'Really?'

'His face is, like, pretty much blank all the time, and his funny hand does all the talking.'

Jane scowled. 'I totally missed that.'

'I could be wrong,' said Jim.

'What did it tell you?'

'He's totally terrified. His hand was, like, screaming in panic every time we mentioned anything to do with the regalia.'

'You can't blame him.'

'I can't say I'm feeling brave myself,' said Jim.

45

The full moon beamed down like a searchlight on the river, illuminating the scene with a clear colourless light. The Thames glittered in chiaroscuro, the water shimmering like the scales of a fish.

There was a sharp banging noise. Stafford awoke. His phone was ringing. He took a second to realise where he was, in his new position at the top of the house in the granny flat. He picked the phone up and tried to turn the lights on. The power was out. The general alarm should have gone off.

'Good grief,' he said, pulling open the bedside table drawer and hauling out his pistol. Men were piling out of a black RIB outside and racing up the ladder towards the lounge.

'Get into the bathroom and lock the door!' Jane was shouting at Jim, a gun in her hand.

'No,' said Jim.

From the noise, a lot of people were coming their way.

'Just do it!'

'No,' said Jim.

'All right,' she said.

Stafford looked out of his doorway. He couldn't see anything in the dim glow of the emergency lighting.

There was a burst of cracks and whistles and he dodged inside his room as the wall and doorframe erupted under a hail of bullets. 'Gosh,' he heard himself cry out. He braced himself, put his arm outside and fired two shots.

Jim resisted the urge to look towards where the gunshots were coming from. He could hear feet thudding down the hall.

The door burst open and Jane opened fire, the first figure tumbling forwards. She shot the second. There was a report from the doorway and something struck her. She collapsed to the floor. Jim ran to her.

There was another shot and something sharp slapped Jim's arm. A flash of white light lit his world and he felt a twist of agony. He was stricken and powerless with pain.

A black figure, crowned with night sights, bent down and jabbed a hypodermic into Jane's thigh, then another into Jim. The figure pulled the Taser round out of Jane and threw her over his shoulder. The other Taser shooter dropped his weapon and helped up the second figure Jane had shot. He had been saved by a bulletproof vest. The first man into the room had a bullet between his eyes and was going nowhere.

Stafford had barely put his arm out of the door before the next salvo whined past it. He snatched his hand back in.

He heard running downstairs. They were leaving. He listened hard. There it was – movement from the man at the foot of the stairs. He swung out and let off three rounds. There was a muffled cry. He ducked back.

A boat engine was roaring outside. Stafford slammed the door and hurriedly closed the latch. He ran to the window and threw it up. A figure was jumping into the RIB with Jane on his shoulder. He couldn't see Jim. There were seven figures and Jane. He took aim at one of the RIB's twin engines and fired. Torchlights swung and he ducked back. The window erupted into a shower of broken glass. He shielded his face. He ran to cover and peered out. The RIB was tearing away through the shadows along the Thames.

Stafford picked his way through the broken glass and put his slippers on. He unlatched the bedroom door. He swung his pistol out and aimed down the stairs before following his extended arm out onto the landing.

He went slowly down the stairs. There was a body in the hall. The man had managed to crawl a little way before expiring. He walked past the corpse and looked into the main hallway that ran the length of the building. It was empty. He waddled gamely to Jim's bedroom. A body lay in what looked, in the moonlight, like a puddle of water. He knew it was blood. Then he saw Jim. 'Oh dear,' he muttered, as he went to him. A hypodermic was sticking out of his leg, which Stafford removed.

He took Jim's pulse, which was strong, then called Smith.

'We're already on the way,' said Smith. 'Two of my men have been seriously assaulted outside your house.'

'A fast boat is heading down the Thames with seven heavily-armed men in it. Colonel Brown is onboard and being held captive. I'm in control here.'

'Got that.' Smith hung up.

Jim was only partially aware that he was walking. Stafford was struggling to steer him down the hall. They careered into a guest bedroom and towards the double bed. Stafford let him drop onto it, then picked up his feet and pushed him further into the middle. 'You rest there. I'll deal with Smith when he comes.'

Jim didn't hear him.

Jane was in some kind of crate. She was handcuffed in a foetal position and there was a mask over her face. She felt as if she was dreaming but knew from the pain in her wrists that she was at least partially awake.

The machine that monitored her vital signs noticed the increase in activity and pumped more of the drug into her. She lost consciousness.

46

Smith was pacing around the shattered lounge. 'You mean to tell me you know nothing about this?'

'Not exactly,' said Stafford, 'but it's clear to me that this is not about Jim. It's about Jane. They took her and left him. That fact is patently obvious.'

'Are you suggesting the group of Yakuza who attacked you on the Strand were a different group from the Japanese who stormed you tonight and who are unconnected again with the one-armed Japanese guy, who happens to be the Japanese Emperor's curator?'

'Is he now?' said Stafford. 'How interesting.'

'Look, Bertie…'

Stafford gave him look of displeasure.

'There are bodies strewn all over the place. Two of my men sat outside have been attacked and disabled. You have to tell me what's going on.'

'You know I can't.'

'I don't care if you *are* MI10, and I don't care if it's a national secret. *I need to know.* I don't care about the DIA either. You simply have to tell me.'

'I can't,' said Stafford.

'You will.'

'John, there is something you need to know.'

'Go on.'

'If I tell you what's happening, your own life will be at great risk.'

Smith stared at him down his once broken nose. 'Tell me

how that could be?'

'I'm afraid we're involved in something so big that nobody can be considered safe or indispensable.'

'Go on.'

'I have nothing more to say.'

'Stafford, do you think I care for one moment about being in danger? You know the score between Jim, Jane and me. Frankly, I'm pissed off that I'm frozen out here.'

'You have my word that, in the circumstances, you are best left in the dark.'

Smith looked around the room in thought. Indeed, he had seen nothing like it. He couldn't imagine what could be so dangerous that he wasn't safe knowing about it – but, then, he couldn't imagine what could have unleashed this tidal wave of violence either. It didn't make any sense. Whatever it was it certainly couldn't be about some antiques.

47

The top floor of Kim's headquarters was famous. It was taken up with his private zoo. The building was renowned across Japan as the most opulently extravagant of any in the nation. He was the biggest property magnate in Tokyo, and it was a symbol of his power and wealth. It was part of the bluff that his wealth was so great that all his creditors were secure in their investment with him.

He would seldom allow visitors, and then only if they were the most influential of people, and then again, only if they had something he wanted.

The keepers were Koreans, with families in the North.

Those who knew realised he had business tendrils that stretched over the 42nd Parallel into that brooding, malevolent country. The source of his initial capital and the lack of substantiation of his personal history was always a topic of conversation among his detractors, but it hadn't held him back.

What held him back was debt. A two trillion yen financial black hole.

With the regalia, he told himself yet again, he would escape from his increasingly unbearable burden. With it, he would pay off all his debts.

He chopped the fish liver, his hands in surgical gloves, then added it to a small mound of minced Kobe beef, which he rolled into meatballs. He went to the lift from his office suite to the floor above. Whenever he entered the zoo, the CCTV that monitored all the animals went off. The screens on the tenth

202

floor would go blank the moment he stepped out of the lift. His enjoyment of the animals was not for others to watch.

The cages were bare, like prison cells without beds. Each animal sat in an antiseptic space, bars on all sides, with perhaps a ledge to jump up on or a bar to swing from.

Kim walked past the hyena; its paws made a scampering sound as it turned so that its eyes could follow him up the aisle. The cheetah in the next cage was pacing in circles and figures of eight. It didn't pay any attention to him. The lion watched him pass.

Kim stopped by the Tasmanian devil's cage and watched for a moment. It, too, was circling its cage, marching in its piggy way in a never ending circuit.

The tiger's cage, the biggest, was at the far corner of the floor. She rose as Kim approached. She looked at him, the pupils in her brown eyes tight elliptic slits. Kim opened the food door and put the bowl in. He closed the door. The bowl popped into the cage and slid a little across the floor. The tiger looked at the bowl and then at Kim. She stepped over to it and sniffed. She ate.

Kim watched and waited. The tiger swayed and began to pant. She sat back on her haunches and batted her eyes as if surprised at something. Her mouth dropped open and there was a thud as she fell forwards onto her side.

Kim swiped his cufflinks across the cage lock. There was a clunk and he opened the door. He knelt by the paralysed tiger. 'You are so very beautiful,' he said, stroking her warm fur.

After he had finished with her, he would serve her at his restaurant and another occupant would take her place in the cage. The traces of *fugu* toxin in her muscles would add flavour.

48

Jim was sitting by the shattered window when Stafford returned with his bag. 'Give it to me,' he said. He took out the necklace and put it on. He arranged his tennis shirt so it fell under it. He held the mirror in one hand and the sword in the other. 'They've grabbed Jane to swap her for these. She's probably halfway to Japan by now.' He put the mirror down and pulled the sword out of the scabbard. 'I'm going to have to go there and get her back – and I'm going to kill whoever's behind this and stick their head on a spike.'

'Very good, sir,' said Stafford, raising an eyebrow.

Jim put the sword away. 'The professor is the key.'

'How so?' queried Stafford.

'I don't know, but he is.'

Jim's phone rang. 'Hello.'

'Good morning, Jim Evans,' said a Japanese man's voice, in clear English. 'We understand you have lost your lady friend. We would like to help.'

'Is she OK?'

'For a small fee, I'm sure we can locate her and she can be returned to you well and happy.'

'Small fee?'

'Some objects with which you are familiar.'

'Well, that's going to be difficult, isn't it, seeing as you've got her in Japan and the objects are in London?'

There was a silence. 'I'm sure these problems can be overcome.'

He picked up the sword again. 'First you need to prove to me

Jane's alive. Then we can talk.'

'She is alive.'

He was clenching the sword very tightly. 'Have you thought about how many of your people I have already killed?' he hissed. A white light was filling his vision. 'Your life expectancy is directly connected to hers.'

The line went dead.

Kim looked at his keyboard. Indeed, he had not considered how many of his men had been killed in trying to secure the regalia. He felt a sensation of unease in his chest. He took the battery out of the phone and dropped the sim card into the maw of his shredder. It shattered.

Jim studied his distorted face in the undulating surface of the mirror. He looked very determined and there was a hard, mean glint in his eye. He appeared much older in the shimmering silver lens, his face careworn and craggy.

Jane had saved his arse in the Congo, and now it was his turn to even the score. She had moved heaven and earth to get to him in the jungle, risking her career and her neck. Without her, he would have never made it out alive. Now it was down to him to save her.

He stared at the face in the mirror. He could hardly recognise himself.

The driver pulled over and parked. Akira looked around the street nervously. There were two uniformed policemen at Jim's door. He instructed his guards to stay in the car. The police were armed with machine guns.

They didn't look very happy as he approached. 'I'm here to see Evans-san,' he said.

'Is he expecting you?'

'Yes.'

The older and fatter of the policemen buzzed through to the house and explained.

Stafford came to the door. 'You'd better come in,' he said to Akira.

Even though Stafford had cleared up the mess, Akira immediately noticed something was awry in the house. A breeze was blowing up the corridor and the lounge, as he passed the door, was in a shambolic state. Stafford showed him into a study, where Jim sat brooding.

'What has happened, Evans-san?' said Akira, his horror written on his face.

'We got attacked last night. They took Jane.'

'Oh, no,' said Akira. 'Do you still retain the regalia?'

'Yes,' said Jim.

'And you will trade it for her?'

'Yes,' said Jim.

'I must beg you not to.'

'I know,' said Jim. 'I will if I have to.'

There was a silence.

'But,' said Jim, 'I have a deal for you.'

'Anything in my power.'

'If you take me to Japan and find Jane, I will give you one object. If I can rescue her, I will give you another. If we get back here alive, I will give you the sword Kusanagi.'

Akira stood, his head bowed. His eyes were closed and he was thinking. 'I agree. There may be a way.' He opened his eyes.

Jim was holding Kusanagi, the back of his hand pressed to his lips. 'Good,' he said. 'Prepare to leave immediately.'

'And the regalia?'

Stafford had entered the room without Akira noticing. 'I will make sure it's safe.'

Why Stafford had decided he needed the Maybach limousine, Jim didn't understand. They didn't use it because cabs were so much more convenient than negotiating the whale of a car around London. Getting it out of the underground parking bay was bad enough. The huge vehicle seemed to have a giant momentum and Jim suspected that Stafford had had it bullet proofed.

They were heading for Heathrow and a Virgin Atlantic flight to Tokyo. The Gulfstream couldn't make it in one hop to Japan, so a commercial flight was best. The professor was shouting into his phone. Whoever was at the other end was getting both barrels. Gone was the respectful, polite little curator: he had been replaced by a rabid wolf. He was growling and shouting at the top of his voice.

'We have been betrayed,' he said, after hanging up. 'Everything I have relayed is relayed on and people are knowing what should be secret. I have demanded *carte blanche*. That way we will not have to revert for permission.'

'What does that mean?'

'It means I can do as I please and get what I demand.'

'Great,' said Jim.

Akira's short hand was twisted into a claw. 'It is the only way.'

49

Kim ran his hand over the naked woman. She had an impressive figure, muscled and honed, the body of an athlete. It was covered with many interesting scars.

How had this woman come by these divots and little white lines? She might be dangerous. That was unexpected but delightful. He felt her stir and pulled his hand away. She began to move and he stepped back. She was waking up. How was that possible?

He walked out of the cage and closed it, growling with frustration. She must be very strong to recuperate so quickly. He looked at her through the bars. She was even more beautiful than the tiger.

Jane always thanked God when she woke up after seeing action. One day she would go to sleep and not wake up, and she sometimes wondered whether she would have to forgo admission to the nice place.

She sat up on a low, tiled platform and planted her feet on a ceramic floor. She was naked but not cold. A gorilla was gazing at her through the bars of the next cage. Where the hell was she? She looked out of the window and glimpsed Mount Fuji in the far distance. Tokyo, she thought. She climbed off the platform and sat on the floor by the gorilla, her head slowly clearing. Looking mournful, she made eye contact with it.

It didn't seem necessary to force herself to think about why she was there. She was in some zoo, and that was weird enough to contemplate with her barely functioning mind. The gorilla was female, she thought. They regarded each other. Who would have a zoo up a skyscraper? Maybe she had died and gone to hell after all.

The gorilla took a bar in its right hand and she gripped the one next to it. Looking into the gorilla's sad brown eyes, she sensed its gentle soul. For a fragmentary moment she remembered herself as a little child. A lot had changed since then. She got to her feet and went to the window behind the bars. She stared out to the snow capped peak.

What was it about Jim and her and volcanoes? Was it a cosmic irony, or evidence of 'dead pixels in the sky'? She pressed her head against the bars. They were too close together for it to fit through. No point forcing your body through a gap if your head can't follow.

She sat down again beside the gorilla and held the bar once more. The gorilla grasped the one next to her hand. She wondered how tame it was.

Jim hadn't flown much in the traditional way and wasn't used to the delays and security of an airport. When he wanted to fly somewhere, he rolled up to his jet, got on and took off. At the other end they looked at his passport and waved him through. His projectile progress from urchin to mega-rich had spat him out of the East End into a netherworld where common realities only occasionally intersected with his life. The normal world felt somehow refreshing, like a breeze blowing through an open door into a stuffy room.

He wandered into an electronics store, the professor in tow, and looked at the cameras. It was all so normal. It felt good. Heathrow was heaving with travellers milling about. They headed for the Virgin lounge.

When they went in, Jim found it a bit strange, like the sort of place he might create a spec for if he was drunk. You could get a free haircut there or sit in a chair hung from the ceiling. It had a kind of upmarket café in it and at the door a man offering to polish his shoes. There was a pool table at the far end and big flat screen TVs everywhere.

'What are we going to do when we get to Tokyo?' he said, as a waiter left with an order for a sausage roll and a beer for him, a plate of sushi and a cup of green tea for the professor.

Akira flexed the fingers on his short arm. 'We will visit an old friend and then we will see.'

'What will we see?'

Akira closed his eyes. 'Evans-san, I must find your lady and to do that I have only one plan and that is to see my friend.'

'And if it doesn't work?'

'If that does not work, then the Kitsune will have to show us the way.' He gazed blankly, but sadly, at Jim.

'Kitsune?'

'The celestial spirit that guides me.'

Jim wanted to put a finger in his ears and try to fish out whatever had made him hear what the professor had just said. 'Right,' he replied, 'I get it.' What was he going to do if the professor's friend came up blank?

Akira wanted to explain to Jim that he wasn't a religious man, but Shinto beliefs permeated his life, just as Christianity saturated Jim's environment. He had seen a Kitsune and it had spoken to him, just as Jesus would speak to a typist in Birmingham. He threw coins into the box at the Meji shrine, clapped to the gods and never expected an empty heaven to reply.

Now he had been sent to bring back the sacred items of the gods and they were manifest. Akira looked down at his feet. 'It is difficult,' he said.

Jim nodded. 'It really is,' he said. 'Who is your friend?'

'His name is James Dean Yamamoto.'

Jim's eyes widened. 'For fuck's sake,' he said, slumping back in his seat.

'Yamamoto-san is a powerful man,' said Akira, pursing his lips defiantly. 'His connections run through all Tokyo, from Kagoshima to Hokkaido.'

Jim couldn't help but smile. 'OK,' he said, 'but you know I'm totally depending on you.'

'In the circumstances I believe I am depending on you.'

The guard put a plate of sushi into the trap and pushed it into the cage. He followed it with a flask.

Jane was standing by the bars, her hands demurely over her crotch. The guard was young, stupid looking and sweaty. His eyes darted all over her naked body. She smiled a little. His eyes glinted. He was flirting with her from a position of absolute power.

She, on the other hand, was flirting with him from a position of utter powerlessness. He moved closer to the bars, a lascivious grin spreading across his face. So this was the boss's new game. Perhaps he could play it for a while. The gold wires holding his teeth in place twinkled through the saliva.

She lifted her hands up to cover her breasts.

He looked down.

She grabbed his head through the bars and smashed his face into the steel. He didn't sag enough so she smashed his face again into the blood splattered steel cage. He fell. 'No pass, no keys, no phone.' She cursed.

She stripped off his shirt and was removing his trousers when she heard running feet and the sudden howling of the animals. She got the trousers on just in time.

The two new guards looked down in horror at their comrade. His nose was spread right across his face and blood was pouring out of it, his mouth and ears. He was out cold.

She was doing up the grey shirt as she watched them. If the second guard moved a couple of inches further she was going to give him a nasty surprise. Then he did. She grabbed him by the shirt collar and smashed his face into the bars. Her grip broke and the guard fell groaning. The other man jumped back and looked at her aghast as she did up the last of the buttons. The shirt was a bit small for her. The trousers were a bit big and short in the leg, but it was better than being butt naked. She wondered about reaching through the bars and killing the first man, but thought better of it. She picked the plate up and gave the sushi a sniff.

The guards struggled off in a kind of shamed silence.

She sat down by the bars of the gorilla enclosure. The gorilla was watching her. She gave it a pout and watched the gorilla scratching its black furry shoulder. Then it picked up some straw and threw it gently into the air.

She ate the sushi and examined the plate. It was metal: she would sharpen its edges and make it into a lethal weapon. She put down the wooden chopsticks: yet more raw materials.

It was dark outside and the lights of Tokyo gleamed in the heavy rain.

Kim watched the monitor, fascinated but horrified. The waiter brought him his plate, a live fish, its side stripped, sliced and laid out. He watched the fish panting and shivering as he ate its flesh. Its eye twitched back and forth as it suffered its slow agonising death. Could it see Kim looking down on it?

Jane lifted her head. The floor had gone silent but for heavy footsteps coming towards her. The gorilla ambled over to her and strained to see what was on its way. Jane felt its big hand touch her shoulder. It was huffing.

A short fat guy walked past the gorilla cage to her enclosure.

Jane put her hand on the gorilla's. She glanced laconically to the figure by the cage. He was standing well back. She pouted at the gorilla, an expression it seemed to relate to. Jane kind of related to it as well.

'You,' said the man finally, in a sharp voice.

Jane left it for a few seconds. 'You talking to me?' she said.

'Yes, you.'

She rolled forwards from the gorilla's touch. It huffed anxiously. 'Me,' she said.

'Who are you?'

'That's a goddamn funny question,' she said, moving to the bars. If only he would step a few inches closer.

He didn't.

'You will not attack my guards again,' he snapped.

'Sure,' she said, 'no problem.' She was wondering if the plate would fly like a lethal Frisbee once she'd hacked it. Unlikely. She probably wouldn't get time to do anything fancy. Hostages got dead pretty quick in her experience. Her chances of survival were dropping exponentially with time.

'You know,' she said, 'you should probably let me go. If you do, I won't kill you. If not, I can't promise.'

'I ask you again, who are you?'

'I shouldn't worry about me, I'm just a gal. You should worry about my boyfriend.'

'If I am given the regalia I will let you leave.'

'OK,' said Jane. 'Give me your mobile and I'll organise it.'

He looked at her sullenly. 'Don't frustrate me.'

'Frustrate you? I'm sorry, why don't you come in here? I can fix that frustration for you.'

'I can make this very unpleasant for you.'

'Really?' she said. 'That's interesting – but can I ask you something?' She looked at him from the left eye, then the right, then both, scanning up and down his body. He recoiled.

'How do you want to die?' She let the question hang in the air. 'Because right now I think I'll be able to grant you that wish.' She nodded. 'Yup. You should let me go.' She sat down by the gorilla cage and took hold of the bar. The gorilla clutched the one just above her hand.

Kim was bright red with rage. He could shoot her, he could drug her, he could have her bound and gagged. He would have to think of something much worse that would yet leave him with a bargaining chip.

50

Jim was cursing himself. The professor had told him categorically that the bus was the best way into Tokyo. It hadn't occurred to him that he was being cost conscious rather than picking the quickest route. It was early morning. The robot voice in the coach was telling him not to use his mobile because it would annoy the neighbours, but his phone didn't connect with the Japanese system anyway. Without his phone, he felt as if a limb had been severed. It was like losing his voice. His satellite phone was in his bag in the belly of the coach. It had helped save his life in Congo and might have to do so again in Tokyo.

The door buzzer sounded and Stafford looked at his iPhone. Smith was outside. He prepared himself for a grilling. 'Good evening, John. To what do I owe this pleasure?'

Smith was carrying a heavy bag. He sniffed. 'Can I come in?'

'Of course.'

Smith walked past him and into the lounge. 'Repair men have been quick.' The view was a little blurred and the ladder to the window was gone.

'The best bulletproof glazing money can buy,' said Stafford.

'Good,' said Smith. He swung the holdall onto the ancient Roman table. 'You don't mind if I stay the night, do you?'

Stafford was a little startled but quickly recovered himself. 'Of course not.'

Smith unzipped the bag, 'I've brought some party things.' He lifted out a short machine gun and held it towards Stafford.

'My word,' he said, 'this is a beast. I take it we're expecting

215

visitors.'

Smith sniffed again. 'I think so.' He took a handkerchief from his pocket and blew his nose. 'I apologise if I give you my cold.'

'That's perfectly all right.'

'Where's Jim?'

'I'm sure you know.'

'I hope he knows what he's doing.'

'I doubt it.'

'I've pieced it all together.'

'Good.'

Smith took out his own machine gun, ejected the magazine and replaced it. 'I hope you realise that London's swarming with criminals from every corner of the Far East. We've been stopping them at Immigration all day but we can't have got every last one.'

'So it'll be just the two of us here holed up against an overwhelming foe?'

'What do you expect when I've got no back story to tell my lords and masters?'

'I see your point.' Stafford cocked the machine gun. 'Did I do that right?'

'Yes,' said Smith, taking the mini back and uncocking it. He handed Stafford two odd looking snub pistols. 'These new Berettas pack a good punch. Fragmentation rounds.'

Stafford took the handguns. 'A bit modern for me.'

'You'll catch on.'

'Do you think we'll be attacked tonight?'

'Let's just say I don't fancy a bottle of Jim's fine wine this minute. We'll need to be wide awake till further notice.'

Stafford seemed put out. 'I wish Jim would stop playing with these people's currencies. He's clearly annoyed them this time.'

Smith looked hard at him. 'That's a pretty good blag, but it doesn't wash with me. Whatever you lot are up to, it must be a total mare. I really do dread to think.' He took out ammunition and stacked it on the table. 'If it does kick off, my boys should come running, but you never know. How about yours?'

Stafford shook his head. 'I rather doubt it.'

Smith raised his eyebrows. 'You will tell me what this is about after it's all over, won't you?'

'Of course.'

Jim's trading battle screens flashed into life. A virtual bell began to ring and a chart of the yen appeared. The forex market was going crazy and the yen was knifing down.

51

The pretty young secretary trotted quickly into Yamamoto-san's office. She held a plastic tray in both hands. Yamamoto smiled at her, his eyes friendly and paternal. The tray contained a book barely held together by decayed old rubber bands. It was his accounts from his shady days. The boy Akira flashed into his mind.

'Oh,' he said, long and low, and picked up the relic of his past. 'Who brought you this?'

'A Professor Nakabashi and his friend present their compliments and ask if they may see you.'

Yamamoto nodded slowly and got up. 'Please bring them in to me.' His round, lined face was suddenly shiny with perspiration.

Akira was here: Akira, the honoured Imperial Curator, the esteemed professor, his determined little friend from his previous, half forgotten shadowy world. Akira was part of his past life as an outlaw, a life that was, in practice, only just submerged below the surface of a successful businessman. He supported himself on his desk. He had always wanted to see Akira again, but his new life precluded it.

As he had risen in wealth, standing and legitimacy, so had Akira's prestige. It had never seemed fitting that Yamamoto should re-establish contact. It seemed not in the best interest of his lost friend, the renowned Professor Nakabashi. He could not risk embarrassing or compromising Akira. Yet now Akira was here, the plucky one armed kid who had carried his nefarious packages to his no-good clients. Those were the days.

He stood upright as his office door opened. He recognised Akira immediately, not from his pictures in the media, but from the remnants of the child in his face and by the signature of his stunted arm. A tall American was with him.

'Yamamoto-san,' said Akira, 'it is so good to see you.'

Yamamoto felt a tear roll down his face, 'Akira,' he said, embracing him. 'It's been so long.'

Akira was surprised and clearly moved. 'James Dean-san it has been too long. It has been forever.'

Yamamoto looked up at the American and blinked.

'I'm Jim.'

He was Australian.

'This is Evans-san,' said Akira, 'from England.'

'Yamamoto.' He pulled himself together and bowed.

'Jim Evans,' said Jim, bowing awkwardly.

'We need your help, James Dean-san,' said Akira. 'We are in desperate straits.'

'Anything, Akira, anything in my power. What is it?'

'My friend Jim's girlfriend has been kidnapped and is here somewhere in Japan.'

'Kidnapped?'

'By someone very powerful. Very, very, powerful.'

'Oooh,' muttered Yamamoto.

'I am hoping that you can help us find her. She is American.' He took a photo from his inside jacket pocket.

The picture showed a woman soldier crawling under barbed wire. She was very pretty. 'Kidnapped here in Tokyo?' He was confused.

'No, in London but brought here.'

Yamamoto looked incredulously at Akira. 'Kidnapped in London and brought to Tokyo?'

'Yes.'

'Are you sure?'

'Yes.'

'Interesting.'

'Can you help?'

Yamamoto was staring out of the window. 'Yes.'

'How can we repay you?'

Yamamoto laughed. 'You can't, Akira, not unless you have a spare ten billion yen. Maybe in a couple of years you can buy some ramen noodles for a broke old man.'

'Perhaps Evans-san can help you while you look for his girlfriend.'

Mrs Yamamoto had about thirty thousand pounds in her forex trading account. It looked like she had started with a hundred and fifty thousand but had traded it away. For everyone but Jim, forex trading was a random game where you won and lost on a fifty-fifty basis but chewed through your capital with broker expenses.

The trading software was configurable in every conceivable language. Helping people trade away their savings with forex was a huge worldwide business and, with gambling restricted in most countries, it was a proxy for the slot machine or the roulette wheel.

He clicked the link and the software was in English. 'Fuck me,' said Jim, inspecting the yen chart. 'That's going up.' The account had a hundred times leverage, which meant that fifty grand could represent five million. 'All in,' he said, 'buying five million in yen.' Ten minutes later the yen was up 1.5 per cent. Mrs Yamamoto's account registered a profit equivalent to 15 million yen, about $150,000. Yamamoto's eyes bugged out. Akira stood impassively behind him.

'Let's do that again,' said Jim, this time shorting. The yen seemed to collapse just after the trade went on. 'Fuck me,' said Jim. 'This is like shooting fish in a barrel.'

'What is he doing?' whispered Yamamoto, as another ten million yen profit popped onto the screen.

'Trading well,' said Akira, quietly.

'I can see that – it's as if he's telling the yen what to do next.'

'He is a professional.'

'Professional? If professional traders could do this they would own the world.'

'They do,' murmured Akira.

Yamamoto didn't know how to respond. Traders might own the world but even they could not trade like this. The Englishman had tripled the account in twenty minutes. 'I will follow up with my people,' he said, his eyes still riveted to the trading screen.

'Any chance of a cup of tea?' called Jim. 'And have you got any antacid tablets? My stomach's killing me.' He laughed. 'Look at that! Blimey! Bombs away. Something really is fucking up the yen.' Then he realised it was probably him and his stupid demand for untold billions of dollars in return for the regalia. The news and associated mutating rumours were flying around the market creating financial carnage. Was the bill a hundred trillion now? Were they talking about nuclear weapons hidden in Japan instead of a few mythical artefacts? Whatever the news had become it was causing consternation and panic.

A motorcade of silent police bikes was making its way around the Imperial Palace. It was heading for Yamamoto Tower. In a pouch there was a letter, no text, with the 'chops' of the Emperor and the prime minister at the bottom.

52

Eating dog in Japan wasn't against the law, but it was rare. The way he had it prepared, though, was illegal. Tradition held that dog meat was healthy, and Kim enjoyed it, particularly if it was from the right place and was prepared correctly. The dogs were flown in from Korea in small versions of what he used for human cargo.

To the outside world Kim was a highly successful property tycoon, but the engine of his empire, the business that generated the cash he leveraged into bricks and mortar, was smuggling. His illicit gains from trafficking had funded his property empire. Clandestine money gave him the edge, letting him outbid all comers in the legitimate world and kept him from going broke.

Japanese business relied on borrowing huge sums of money at negligible interest rates, which made it easy to hide financial realities. Money borrowed at one per cent could be squandered without anyone realising it was gone and would never be repaid. You could repay one per cent of the capital for decades without anyone suspecting the bulk was long gone. Borrowing money at one per cent was a never ending financial merry-go-round. One per cent interest rate loans need never be repaid or shown to be in default.

In the financial environment when all businesses were addicted to massive levels of debt at low interest, it was hard to see that Kim's deals didn't make commercial sense and that other sources of money had to be keeping his sprawling property empire afloat. But, even with his vast illegal earnings, the property still didn't make financial sense. He was slowly being crushed by the economic Godzilla of Japan: deflation.

Japan had suffered deflation for two decades. Simply put, prices fell in Japan: every year things got cheaper. Which meant in its turn that every year debt got bigger because the money owed became more valuable. The Japanese economy had been on the rack of deflation, unable to escape its vicious circle, since the asset bubble crash of the late eighties that had seen the land of the Emperor's palace become, at one stage, worth more than all the real estate in California. It had been followed by a crash from which the economy had never bounced back.

Kim's property empire had been crumpled by cycles of deflation and he was indebted to such an extent that even the proceeds of his global crimes couldn't bail him out of an impending commercial implosion. He smuggled people, money and now, as his financial pressures worsened, drugs and animals. The drug trade was profitable but the lynch pin of his operation was still smuggling people to and from North Korea. He ferried in people and shipped out the fake dollar bills and euros that the North Koreans printed.

Smuggling rare animals had started as a sideline, a symptom of his desperation for cash. But it had also become a hobby – then an obsession. Exotic animals and their body parts were highly prized and Kim shipped them wherever they needed to go. Meanwhile it allowed him to indulge himself with his zoo. The animals were his only passion. People meant nothing to Kim: they were like puppets to be bent and twisted to his plans. His masters, North Korea, always needed a fresh supply of people to teach languages. They especially needed Japanese but they also needed Europeans and Americans. North Korea needed kidnap victims to teach its spies their languages. It was of utmost importance to know exactly what the enemy was saying and be able to transplant agents with fluent local language skills into the countries it wanted to monitor.

Foreigners never lasted long in the North: before they could acclimatise enough to have a hope of escape they were done away with. Because of this, Kim was tasked with providing a constant supply of new tutors. This meant he had to capture and smuggle more than a hundred people every year to North Korea. It was a huge task, paid for in gold, fake money and in kind.

He had run the operation ever since he was a young man sent to Japan to spy on Tokyo and now, thirty five years on, he could not stop. For sure, he didn't want to: he had to make his empire financially solid again. He had delivered living flesh into North Korea for most of his life. He wasn't scared of that business. It was the drug running he feared. There were many clever enemies to confound him in that business and at some point they would make a breakthrough.

His edge was that his operations were manned by North Koreans. Back in North Korea, his workers' families lived or died on his command. So while his smuggling ring spanned the globe, his security was absolute. Now if he could capture the Imperial regalia he could buy his way out of his predicament and perhaps, at last, disengage from his more dangerous activities. One day, bad luck would catch up with him and destroy the façade. With the risks he was now taking, that moment could not be far away. This might be his last opportunity to escape the noose of his karma.

The dog tasted good.

Before it had died, it had hung by its broken legs, trussed up in his restaurant's kitchen, for two days. It would be tender and have the special taste that only animals that die in torment develop. The thought of its suffering gave him comfort and peace.

53

Yamamoto stood in the door of his office as the police guard marched towards Akira. Sweat pricked his brow. After all these years of being almost straight, he had police in his office. Something terrible was happening.

Jim looked up from his screen. There was no reason to get excited, he thought. The policemen were extremely respectful. One handed the professor a package with military precision and bowed low. They saluted and marched out. 'What was that about?' he asked.

'My *carte blanche.*'

'Maybe you could get the government to pay Yamamoto-san his hundred million instead,' said Jim. 'This is getting boring.' He grinned at the professor. 'Only joking.'

'How is it?'

'Er... two million dollars.' Jim waved his palm back and forth. 'Ish.'

Yamamoto was on the phone, jabbering away. He hung up, 'Now I'm in trouble. That was my wife. The trading company has been on to her. They want to know if she is OK. She wants to know what I'm doing.' He was sweating heavily. 'I told her not to worry. She will be hard on me.'

'Do we have any news from your sources?' asked Akira.

'No,' said Yamamoto, 'but I fear when we do, it will not be good.'

'What do you mean?' said Akira.

'Let us wait till there is news. I do not want to invent ghosts.'

'Fuck,' swore Jim. 'This thing won't let me put on more than fifty million in a trade. Never mind, I can batter the Swissy as well – that looks choice.'

'What's wrong?' Yamamoto hadn't understood what he'd said.

'Nothing,' said Akira. 'Just a little local difficulty.'

Kim watched the cage through the closed-circuit TV. The gorilla was grooming the woman's hair through the bars. Kim was biting his lip, chewing on it almost hard enough to break the skin. A thought sent a shiver through him. He took a pistol from his bottom drawer and went towards the lift that rose straight up to the zoo.

The animals quietened. Jane heard footsteps on the tiles.

'You,' a voice said.

'Me?'

'Who are you?'

'Who are you?' she replied, getting up. The gorilla pushed its arm through the barrier to try to hold her, but she was out of reach.

The man reached into his pocket and pulled out a pistol. It was a dart gun. He aimed it at Jane but he was not taking a proper bead.

She cocked her head at him. 'You should let me go.'

He lowered the pistol, walked over to the gorilla cage, aimed and then fired. The gorilla grunted, jumped up and ran at him, grabbing the bars. It screamed, then fell silent, staggering back dazed. It sat down, head tilted forwards, breathed heavily for a time, then rolled onto its side.

Jane saw the man run his wrist across the door and heard a clunk. The cage door opened. He knelt down by the gorilla and began to stroke it gently. He was looking at Jane and starting to strip off.

You're kidding me, thought Jane, looking away in disgust. She sat on the tiled ledge and gazed out of the window at Tokyo. She considered how surgeons violated a patient's body with their scalpels when they worked feverishly to save a life. The patient would awake from the ordeal none the wiser as to the awful details. The anaesthetic would leave their mind unsullied. She wasn't worried for herself but for the ape.

Then she thought about him opening the door with his wrist. Was there a tag in his watch, or a simple band on his arm? Maybe he had an implant, a small RFID under the skin. She would continue to sharpen the plate, and if she could get hold of his hand she would slice it off and open the cage. She wondered what Jim was doing. Had he called the cavalry? Would they come? Would he come for her? She didn't think so. She was probably alone. That was nothing new.

Things were going to get even uglier.

The nose of the Antonov opened and a ramp lowered onto the tarmac. The containers were unloaded and hitched up to trucks, which filed out of the airport gates. High value electronics were constantly being flown into the UK as consumer crazes came and went. One day it would be phones, the next games consoles, then flat screen TVs. Whatever the next big thing was, it would be flown in from the Far East as quickly as possible. By weight, the newest fad gadgets were worth almost the same as a precious metal, but, unlike gold or silver, they went off like strawberries and were soon valueless.

The containers were heading for an anonymous warehouse in Dagenham. It was run by Koreans who minded their own business and never paid late or broke any rules. It wasn't a busy warehouse: it shipped three or four consignments a year. Just another mean, grubby building in a zone of such.

Yet the business of the warehouse was remarkable. The consignments it marshalled were of people, plucked off the streets almost at random. These unlucky souls would be added to the ranks of the missing and were sent to spend the rest of their short lives teaching English in North Korea. This time they were taking delivery of a dozen grey plastic containers, each containing a man.

53

'Do you mean to tell me there's not a single television in this mansion?' said Smith, to Stafford.

'It isn't a mansion,' Stafford informed him. 'It's a large townhouse.'

'I stand corrected,' said Smith. 'Now, about the TV?'

'I'm afraid we do not have one.'

'You must get bored out of your mind,' said Smith, disgusted.

'Indeed not,' said Stafford. 'I have my books and my journal to occupy me.'

'What about Jim?'

'He has his Internet.'

'It's unnatural,' said Smith, 'and very suspect if you ask me.'

'I think not,' said Stafford.

Smith sat up and took out his mobile. 'A RIB,' he said, 'coming up the river. Surely they aren't going to try to repeat the attack. That would be crazy.' He looked at Stafford. 'It might be kicking off again.'

Stafford picked up the machine pistol from the floor by his chair. 'What is the plan?'

'As soon as an attack starts, hopefully my lot'll be swarming all over this place. We'll have to keep them at bay for a bit. Do you have a panic room?'

'Unfortunately not. It is planned.' Stafford was considering another attack from the river. 'They won't be able to get in from the river this time.'

'Why are they coming back?' Smith answered his phone

and listened to the caller. 'OK,' he said. 'Good.' He looked at Stafford. 'False alarm, Bertie,' he said, relief in his eyes.

'I wish you wouldn't call me Bertie,' said Stafford. 'I might get used to it again.'

James Dean Yamamoto was dumbfounded by what he saw on the screen. Jim had wheeled the chair back with every appearance of contentment.

'How can this be real?' Yamamoto asked Akira. 'How will I explain it?'

'I hope it won't be too inconvenient.'

Yamamoto logged off, then back on. The balance remained the same. 'Evans-san must be very rich.'

'I believe so.'

'That explains everything.'

Akira raised his eyebrows. 'How so?'

'Why Kim has kidnapped his woman.'

'Kim? Basho Kim?'

'Yes. Kim, perhaps. I will know for sure soon.'

'But Kim is a big man, surely not a criminal.'

'A big man, yes,' said Yamamoto, 'but very deep in debt. He owes trillions of yen more than he can repay.' He sat down heavily in a chair that was normally on the other side of his desk. He frowned and appeared to fall asleep. His eyes flickered open. 'His name may be on much of the Tokyo skyline but he has run out of the means to maintain his repayments.' He laughed in a single burst of a low toned syllable. 'It is a trap in which many of us are caught and one he has worked very hard to become ensnared by.' He exhaled in a growl. 'He is the lowest of the low. If I would kill anyone it would be him.'

'Kim-san a kidnapper?'

'And worse.' Yamamoto stared up at the ceiling. 'So much worse. I suppose I must tell you a story.' He let out a long snort.

'When I was still young I used to enjoy chasing the ladies. Life was good. I had money.' He smiled a little. 'The world was so fresh and finally it was being good to me. Life can be so good. I had a sweetheart, who lived in the Ginza, and I was very much in love.' He paused to recall. 'To a rough guy like me, she was a princess, a sweet little bird who sang for me. She lived in this tiny apartment and I made sure she was all right and could pay her rent. Ginza is such an expensive district, as you know. She always made me laugh. I still smile at the thought of her...' He fell into a reverie.

Akira watched him remembering.

'Then one day she vanished. Gone like a picked flower.' His face was twisted in anger. 'I traced her family, what there was of it, but no one had any word of her. She had not given up her lease. She did not use her bank account. There were fresh groceries in the kitchen the day she went away. Ah, Akira, I was heartbroken. I had not realised how deeply I loved her. She was my happiness.'

Yamamoto glanced at Jim, who was listening in the way people do when they cannot understand what is being said. He turned back to Akira. 'I became crazy. I hunted high and low. I hired detectives, two or three at a time. I fired them and hired more. I spent all the money I could to try and find her. Then one day the answer came. She had most likely been kidnapped and taken to North Korea. I was horrified and filled with uncontrollable rage. How could this happen?'

Jim had given up trying to understand and had returned to the trading screen. Gold looked about to take a dive. He wanted to jump on it. It was a screaming short. A few clicks and he could be on for the ride. He sat back and shook his head. He was like an alcoholic who had fallen off the wagon and bought a nice big bottle of whisky.

'Then I went looking,' growled Yamamoto. 'I wanted to find

out how people could be kidnapped like that. Korean visitors could not just show up to pick people off, like plums from a tree. It took organisation, money, skill. I would use my contacts and track these people down. Then I would make my play.' He grunted in disgust. 'While I was doing this, devoting my time to the search, I was making money like never before or since. My property portfolio was growing and its value was shooting up. This was the beginning of the bubble years. It was a deep irony to me.' He frowned as if a great sadness had filled him.

'So then one day the secret opened itself to me. A friend of a friend who stole the tax on ships came to me and asked a favour. I told him my puzzle and promised to solve his problems if he solved my riddle. He went pale. I saw this and he knew I saw it and he told me. Basho Kim-san.'

'What did you do?' asked Akira.

'I reverted to the old way.' He looked pleased with himself. 'I sent him a letter with her name on it and the letter was charred. Then I burnt down one of his buildings. I repeated this action every moon and sure enough, after a few months, my sweetheart was returned.'

'Was she all right?'

'No. She was a broken woman.' Yamamoto rose. 'I still look after her.' He looked across the city. 'She's down there somewhere – she has a husband and children. It's a happy ending.' He turned to Akira. 'That is my story, one of many in my strange life.' He pushed back his tidy grey hair. It made to puff up in a ghost of a quiff. 'And now the story continues.'

'When do you think you will know for sure?' asked Akira.

'I know for sure. It is a matter of where, not who. I guess it will become a matter of how to get her back.'

Jim's mobile was buzzing in his pocket. 'Yes?' he said.

'Jim Evans?'

'Yes.'

'Your lady is very sick. We need the objects in twenty four hours or we cannot be sure she will survive.'

'Prove to me she's alive.'

'Of course.'

'Who are you?' said Jane, her voice echoing in a hard space. 'Are you talking to me?'

'We will organise an exchange.' The phone went dead.

Jim looked at Akira and Yamamoto. 'We're running out of time.'

54

His room in the Grand Hyatt was lovely and the bed was perfectly comfortable, but he was finding it very hard to sleep. It was daytime in London and his body knew it. He lay awake, his mind racing. He had called Stafford three times and all was quiet on the home front. It wasn't like him not to be able to sleep. Then at five a.m. the inevitable happened: he passed out.

The phone at his bedside woke him. It was seven a.m. Akira was on the other end.

'Evans-san, Yamamoto-san has news. When will you be ready?'

'Give me a few minutes. I'll come straight down.' He jumped out of bed and ran into the shower. The water shocked him with a cold blast. 'Fuck,' he muttered, adjusting the temperature. He was out again in two minutes, drying himself.

Akira met him in the lobby. He looked rough, as if, like Jim, he hadn't had much sleep or time to shave. 'Yamamoto's car is waiting.'

They walked swiftly outside to a black Toyota Crown. It was an old car but it shone like new. They got into the back. Yamamoto was in the front passenger seat. 'I think I have found her. Let's go.'

The chauffeur set off. Jim noticed he was a very old man, who drove as carefully as if the car was stuffed with nitro-glycerine. The roads were busy but the traffic flowed. 'Where are we going?' he asked.

'Where are we going?' repeated Akira in Japanese.

'You'll see,' said Yamamoto.

Jim got out of the Crown and looked at the polished grey granite building. Across the broad entrance it said 'Yamamoto Towers' in English, then probably the same in Japanese characters.

Yamamoto was striding towards the entrance and Jim jogged to catch up. The Japanese businessman bustled through the revolving doors to where a reception committee stood.

Everyone bowed. The welcoming party saw them to the lifts and bowed at them as the doors closed. The lift was saying something to them and Jim wondered what it was. He hadn't been in a talking lift before. They were heading for the roof.

When it stopped, Yamamoto strode out, and around the roof garden to the far side. Jim gazed at the rocks and gravel, all perfectly placed, and thought how bizarre it was that anyone would want a rockery on the top of an office block. A telescope was set up at the far end with a young guy of about Jim's age beside it.

Yamamoto squinted through the eyepiece and smiled at his employee. He said something that sounded to Jim like 'Well done.' Then he indicated that Jim should look through the eyepiece. Jim crossed to the telescope and found he was focused on another giant tower. The floor in the centre had some kind of garden in it – with what looked like an aviary. If you're going to build a rock garden on top of a building, he thought, why not a greenhouse?

Yamamoto was talking to Akira.

'So, so, so,' said Akira. 'Evans-san, your lady is being kept in the zoo you can see before you.'

He stood up. 'That's a zoo? Whose zoo?'

'Kimcorp Zoo.'

Jim was scanning the floor for a glimpse of Jane, but all he could see was vegetation and birds. 'Are you sure?'

'Yes.'

'What the fuck is Kimcorp?'

'Huge property company,' said Akira, 'one of the top five.'

'Can't we just get the police to bust in?'

'I'm afraid Kim would be the first to know. By the time a raid happened, your lady would be gone.'

Jim took a deep breath and blew it out, frustrated. He looked back through the telescope. 'Can we see the other side of the building?'

Akira asked Yamamoto.

'Yes,' said Yamamoto. 'We should have helicopter photographs very soon.'

The animals went silent and, moments later, the lift door opened. She stood up and held the plate by her side. She had sharpened it in the small hours and hoped they might not have noticed. She had tried to be subtle about it, but if they'd been awake… As she could hear only one set of footsteps, she guessed she had got lucky.

Kim stood in front of the cage, well back. She watched him closely. Only a small section of the plate's rim was now blade sharp. If she hurled it through the bars at him she'd pray for a miracle.

'Who are you?' said the man.

'Who are you?' she replied.

He reached into his pocket. 'It doesn't matter,' he said, pulling out the dart gun. He pointed it at her loosely. 'I don't need to know your name.' He fired.

It took him a moment to register the clank.

Jane picked up the dart from the floor. It had discharged most of its load with the blow. She didn't think. She just did. Thinking made the barely possible impossible. She had to be in the moment, in the zone. Accuracy came from the deep subconscious, the

236

brainstem, the hypothalamus. She lanced the dart through the bars at Kim. He flinched as it stuck in his neck.

He squeaked in shock and reeled back. He pulled the dart from his flesh, dropping it to the ground.

Jane was smiling. A very satisfactory shot. The tranquilliser was in a puddle at her feet and she guessed the round was spent, but her victory had a kind of small perfection.

Kim tottered forwards and staggered, then careered headlong into the bars of the cage.

'Thank you, Jesus,' she said, and ran to the bars. Clearly the round had had some sting left. She knelt down, grabbed his arm and pulled it through the cage bars. He didn't have a watch or a band on his wrist. He must have a tag under his skin. She took the plate. She couldn't lift him to the door latch, so she'd have to cut his arm off. In the circumstances it wasn't such an unpleasant prospect. She pushed up his jacket and shirt sleeves. She went to undo his cufflink.

'Bingo,' she muttered. The cufflink was the key. She took it out of his cuff and stood up. Red lights around the room started flashing. 'Damn it,' she muttered. She pushed her arms through the bars to the control surface.

Nothing happened. She already knew the problem. She went back to Kim and pulled his other arm through. It was the other cufflink. When they were both in range the system operated; when they were further apart than the length of his arms, they set off an alarm and ceased to function. She tried the lock again and the door clicked open. She leapt out. She opened the gorilla's door. 'Come with me,' she said, but the gorilla just looked at her.

She didn't wait. The lift was going down to the floor below. She called it, then looked into the camera. Its little red light was lit. If she could deal with the people in the lift she could get free. She could go back and use the man as a shield, but she wouldn't be able to carry him with her. No matter. Attack was always the best way.

Jim looked at the photos. An indistinct figure sat in a cage. Was it Jane? It was hard to tell. He felt sick and his face bunched up in disgust.

'I'm so sorry,' said Akira. 'This is horrible.'

'Don't be sorry,' he said. 'At least, if that's her, she's alive.'

Yamamoto was slumped in a chair, apparently fast asleep. 'Pay the ransom,' he said.

'What did he say?' asked Jim.

'Pay Kim.' Akira told him.

'That's not going to work, is it?' said Jim.

'Why?'

'For one thing I owe you an object, and for another, if we give them to him, he can't leave any witnesses behind, can he? Not me, not you, least of all Jane. We can't take the easy way out.' Jim sat up a bit. 'I've got something for you,' he said, smiling ironically at Akira. He reached under his shirt and pulled out the Yasakani no Magatama. He lifted it over his head and handed it to Akira.

Akira held up his short hand in shock.

'Take it,' said Jim.

Yamamoto had woken up.

'No,' said Akira, 'not yet. We are not sure if it is Jane-san. Nor do I wish it returned until I have secured the sword Kusanagi and Yata no Kagami.'

Yamamoto was suddenly wide awake.

'That doesn't make any sense,' said Jim.

'I trust you to continue to bear Yasakani no Magatama with honour.'

Yamamoto was staring at Jim. 'Kusanagi? Yata no Kagami? Yasakani no Magatama?'

'I'm sorry, old friend,' said Akira, 'but I have lured you into a legend.'

James Dean Yamamoto was sweating profusely again. He watched Jim put on the green glowing necklace and cover it with his shirt. Then he began to laugh uproariously. Sweat and tears were trickling down his face and he clasped his legs.

'What's so funny?' asked Jim.

Akira shrugged.

'This will surely kill us all,' wheezed Yamamoto.

Akira translated.

55

The lift door opened to reveal four men with stun guns. They'd have to be dweebs not to get the better of her. There was no time to let them surround her. They were fanning out. The guy to the left jabbed at her and she kicked him in the chest. He fell. She grabbed the guy to the right as he lunged – but the charge from the guard in front shot through her. She flipped backwards, then cried out as another shot pulsed through her.

When she woke up, she hurt like hell. They'd done a good job of tenderising her. The gorilla was looking through the bars. She lay there for a few moments, then hoisted herself up. At least they hadn't stripped her. 'You should have come and given me a hand,' she said, sitting down by the beast. It put a hand on her head and stroked her hair.

Jane was wondering whether she was going to get another chance. She looked around the cage. The plate was gone. She checked her pocket. Not unsurprisingly the cufflinks were gone too.

The necklace felt hot around Jim's neck, the ends of the jade teeth pressing into his flesh – like fingers. He adjusted it. Then he jumped to his feet. 'Fuck me,' he said. 'Kimcorp! Is that like a listed company?'

Akira looked up from the photos. 'Yes, Evans-san, on the TSE main market.'

'Main market listed?'

'Yes.'

Jim sat down again with a bump. 'Well, well, well.' He clutched the necklace under his shirt. 'You know what? I think I might have a bit of an idea brewing.'

Jane stood in front of the gorilla. She put her right hand on a bar and the gorilla did the same. She gripped a bar about a foot away with her left hand and the gorilla copied her. She stood on the two middle bars, then pulled with her hands and pushed with her feet, trying to wrench the bars from their moorings. They didn't move – but the gorilla might have the strength to bend them and shatter the welding.

The gorilla watched her curiously, seeming amused by her antics.

Jane dropped down from her braced position. 'You don't get it, do you?' she said, laughing a little. She scratched the back of her head.

The gorilla scratched its head too, then offered a hand to Jane. She took it. 'Got to get out of here,' she said, 'before it's too late.'

She let go of the gorilla and walked to the middle of the cage. She sat down, legs crossed, and put her hands into her lap. She closed her eyes. She was going to clear her mind. Then she was going to send herself out of her body, float around the cage and imagine it afresh. There was always an answer to any puzzle; it was just a matter of working it out. Once you had the answer, it seemed obvious, but before you had it, it could stare you in the face and you wouldn't see it. Calm was the platform of survival. It didn't matter how desperate you were or how close to death, calm was a prerequisite for rescue.

As she stilled herself she imagined she was like the gorilla: sentient but not quite smart enough to work out a way to escape. If she could double her IQ, she could waltz out of there, but instead she had to strain for the insight that would set her free.

In trying to fly beyond the boundaries of her mind, she hoped to release herself from her preconceptions and assumptions. Her mental bonds trapped her as effectively as the bars. That was why the mad were especially dangerous. Their thoughts were untrammelled, their solutions often unimaginable to the normal mind. Without the limitations of the sane, they could find the doorway to another level. This was the doorway she sought.

'Do the obvious,' she told herself.

She stood up and walked to the ledge where the tiger had lain. She had hidden the chopsticks there. She had put them on the other side of the bars where the cage frame met the floor and was shielded by the ledge. She squatted down, pushed her hand along the cold edge of the metal cage, and fished out a chopstick.

She smiled. They'd missed it.

She climbed onto the ledge and put the chopstick between her teeth. The bars of the cage were about six foot above, but the tiled shelf had a ridge to grip about three feet above her reach. She scrambled up the wall to it and hoisted herself onto the bars. She balanced, adjusted her grip, then swung from bar to bar. She turned, rotating ninety degrees to hang between the horizontal bars. She had become so strong over the years that the stress of holding her own weight by her hands was of no account. Finally, all those years of swinging on frames were actually proving useful.

Jane swung her legs up between the bars and wrapped them around one so that her weight was braced by her feet. She slid along it until she was comfortably below the CCTV camera. She took the chopstick out of her mouth and stretched out to the CCTV with the point. The extra six inches of wood gave her the necessary reach to stab it.

The camera wasn't designed to take abuse and, after a couple of minutes, the plastic eyeball fell out of its housing and hung on its wires. Jane put the chopstick back between her teeth, reached up as far as she could and took the camera in her fingers. She tore it out and dropped it onto the floor.

That's better, she thought. A little privacy.

She unlocked her legs and hung from the bar, six feet off the ground. She looked out of the window into the blue sky of the Tokyo afternoon. Hanging felt good: it was like stretching. About half a mile away a chopper was hovering parallel to the window. She focused on it. It was at the same level as her window and in line with it. She dropped to the floor, ran to the window and waved frantically. The aircraft's nose dropped and it headed away.

Had it come for her? Was it her people, the DIA? Was it just another pervy moment from the creeps holding her in the cage? Was a tourist having a look at the zoo on the sixty seventh floor?

She sat down and went back to clearing her mind.

'Evans-san,' called Akira, 'we have confirmation. Please come and see.'

Jim walked to Yamamoto's desk and looked over Akira's shoulder. There was a picture of Jane hanging behind the bars of a cage. 'Oh, bloody hell,' moaned Jim.

Akira flicked onto the next image. Jane was on the ground, waving at them. 'Thank goodness for that,' sighed Jim, 'I thought she was strung up.'

'No, Evans-san,' said Akira. 'She looks to be all right.' He flicked through the images uploaded from the chopper.

'I hope they haven't spotted the helicopter,' said Jim.

Akira didn't reply directly. 'There is no building that overlooks this side of Kim's head office. It was the only way to be sure.'

Jim nodded. 'I know,' he said. 'Now we've got to get in there and bust her out.' He picked up his satellite phone. 'Here goes. If this doesn't work, I'm just going to go in there on my own.'

'I will be with you,' said Akira, clenching the fist on his short arm.

For the DIA man it was two a.m., but when his phone rang he answered. 'Hi,' he said, his voice gravelly and slow.

'Will, it's Jim.'

Will sat up in bed. 'What's up?'

'I've found Jane.'

'Go ahead.'

'I need your help to get her to safety.'

'Where is she?'

'Tokyo.'

'Leave it to us.'

'No,' said Jim. 'She'll be dead as soon as you make a call to the authorities.'

'What's going on?'

'North Koreans connected at the highest level in Japan. I can rescue her if you'll help me, but it has to be fast and it has to be now.'

'I'm listening.'

'OK, this is what I need.'

56

Kim was sneering at the doctor.

'I'm afraid, Kim-san, that your heart is weak. You need more rest before you can resume work.'

He didn't reply, just held the oxygen mask to his face. The tranquilliser had laid him so low that he had nearly died. He knew he was unfit, and he had not made his health a priority, but he had been shocked to discover just how weak he had become. Now he lay disconsolate in his bed, confused, his whole body aching to sleep again.

He hated the doctor for the news and despised the nurses who tended him. He was nauseated by the thought that they should see him in such a pathetic and vulnerable state. When he regained his strength he would go up to the zoo and shoot the woman. She was a demonic banshee and had to be liquidated at all costs. He didn't have the strength to imagine what else he would do with her, but it would come to him. Then he would know he was strong enough to get up.

Jim was downloading his trading software onto James Dean Yamamoto's computer. He was praying it would work. Software was almost guaranteed not to work first time. Whatever could go wrong would go wrong.

The installation ended with a prompt for his login and password. 'Ah,' he said, mildly surprised that it was working. He typed in his ID and his password: jelliedeel. He offered a prayer to the gods of binary.

'Yes!' he exclaimed, as the desktop booted up. There was an

hour and twenty minutes before the close of trading in Tokyo. He pulled up Kimcorp's stock chart. It looked OK – but he smiled when it dawned on him that the chart looked as if it was going to crash. 'You betcha it is! And I'm going to crash it.'

He called his friend at the bank, Sebastian Fuch-Smith.

'Jim?' came the startled reply at the other end. 'You've caught me heading to work.'

'You want to make some money?'

'Me, mate?' said Sebastian, every syllable honed at Eton. 'I'm never unhappy to make a little extra cash, old chap.'

'Kimcorp on the Tokyo exchange. It's about to go down like a duchess.'

'When?'

'Any time now – count to a hundred if you like. Tell the floor.' Jim hung up.

Akira pulled up a chair next to him. 'May I watch?' he said.

'Sure,' said Jim, as he laid out the chart of the stock in the right-hand corner of the screen. He placed the order window – the interface where he entered buy and sell instructions to pick up or let go of shares he was trading – to the left. He had all kinds of orders he could place and robots to slice and dice them before they were sent to the market. For Jim it was like a textual version of a computer game where armies were massed and sent against the troops of other players. In this game there were only buy and sell orders and whether, when you called a move in the market, you were right or wrong.

Traders would stare at charts, hoping to guess the next few seconds and thereby glean an advantage over the other players, but with hundreds, sometimes thousands, of people buying and selling, the outcome of every following moment was strictly random, or so it seemed and so they said.

Yet for Jim what happened next was obvious. He was supremely rich because he could see what would happen while others had simply no idea.

'What are you going to do?' asked Akira.

Jim grinned. 'I'm going to crash the Kimcorp stock price.'

'I know Evans-san, but how?'

'Do you buy shares, Akira?'

'Not really.'

'Is that no or yes?'

'Occasionally.'

'OK.' Jim was watching pressure increase as Fuch-Smith and the London bank started to sell. 'When a stock is falling do you want to buy?'

'No.'

'When a share is rising do you want to buy?'

'Most likely.'

'So you have some shares and the share price suddenly starts falling heavily. What do you want to do?'

'I want to cry,' Akira said, as if he had actually experienced such a moment.

'Well, apart from that, do you feel more like selling?'

'Yes.'

'Well, that's what I'm going to do. I'm going to make people want to sell. First, though, I'm going to own the market.'

'Own the market?'

'I'm going to buy from all the sellers and I'm going to sell to all the buyers, and when they're all satisfied and gone, I'm going to fill up all the places for buyers and sellers with my orders and I'm going to control the price. Then I'm going to walk the price down.'

'Walk the price down?'

'I'm going to sell when the buying is weak and make the price fall even further. Then I'll let it settle, maybe buy some back. Then I'm going to do it again and sell it down. The price will fall and fall and at some point panic selling will set in.

Then, when the market collapses and pukes, I'll buy back again and I might even make a profit. I'm going to do it again and again and again. By the time I've finished Kimcorp's share price will be a smoking crater.'

'Is that legal?'

Jim smiled at him. 'You are the one with the *carte blanche*, so you tell me.'

'Yes,' agreed Akira, 'you are correct and I think this is a good use of our permission to do what is required to be done.'

Kimcorp's share price was already falling gently.

'Right,' said Jim. 'Let's get going.' He filled the input screen with a series of orders. 'Bombs away.'

In the hour and a quarter to close, Kimcorp dropped 32 per cent. The news wires buzzed with speculation. Had Kim-san died? Was Kimcorp mired in scandal? Was Kimcorp in breach of its banking covenants and therefore on the brink of bankruptcy?

James Dean Yamamoto walked behind Jim and bent down to the screen. He exclaimed in Japanese. Jim grinned up at him.

Akira said, 'Yamamoto-san says you are a very frightening person.'

'I wish my nan was alive to hear you say that,' he said. 'She might have been impressed.'

Jane smashed the camera casing on the floor. It cracked open like a walnut. She examined the pieces. There was a lens, a circuit board and a small aluminium frame bent for the assembly to nestle in. She broke out the components and spread them in front of her. She picked up the metal housing and bent out one side. It would make a blade of sorts. Blades were good. It might be what she was searching for.

Much later Jane looked out into the night. A set of lights far in the distance hovered in the sky. She waved.

'She's seen us,' said Jim.

Akira translated.

'Oooh!' said Yamamoto. 'Time to leave then. If she has seen us, others might.' He piloted the helicopter away.

Whoever you are, thought Jane, I hope you're friendly. And if you are, get on over here fast.'

Kim lay in bed, dozing, the morning light illuminating the room with a bluish tint. His apartment took up the floor below the zoo. It was modern and minimal. The whole floor was more of a facility than a home. He didn't like decoration unless it was a priceless antique. Then it was just another asset and, like all his assets, hocked to the banks.

Sometimes, like now, lethargy overcame him and he would lie there for two or three days, exhausted. Great pleasure was usually succeeded by something like despair; after victory came disappointment.

This time the exhaustion was unbounded. Although he was physically recovered the malaise had overtaken him. The tranquilliser had triggered it.

His assistant came into his room. 'The finance director must see you now. He assures you it is of vital importance.'

Kim sat up.

Toyoda entered respectfully and bowed. 'Our share price has collapsed.' He opened a folder and handed Kim a sheet of paper with Kimcorp's stock chart on it.

'What has caused this?'

'I do not know. This morning our share price is falling again. The banks are bound to start calling soon. Soon we will be in breach of our debt conditions.'

Kim's stasis was replaced by anger and fear. 'When?'

'In theory we are in breach if the market falls another twenty-five per cent.'

'I will be in my office in twenty minutes. Leave me.'

Jim was hammering Kimcorp. He owned the market in the stock. Kimcorp and other stocks traded via a system called an order book. It collected all buying and selling into one place and, via the coming and goings of buyers and sellers, settled the price. It was like a rolling auction that matched up the people trading the share. Jim had muscled in and overwhelmed the other players. Kimcorp would normally trade fifty million dollars of stock a day and move a percentage point or so. Now Jim had waded in, he had taken control of the price and was driving it down. He was cornering the market.

Market corners, as they were called, were as old as markets themselves. Cornering the market in a commodity or stock was an old game and always ended badly. The market was always right in the end and you couldn't fix the price of anything for long. At some point the market would bite back and hurt the manipulator. Whether it was the silver corner, by Bunker Hunt the Texan billionaire, Enron cornering electricity, or the oil corner of 2008, sooner or later it had imploded and prices went back to normal. Corners were usually about making a price go abnormally high, but in this case Jim was forcing a price down. He was crashing the stock by bullying the market.

And, of course, he had an advantage: he could see what was going to happen next an hour or two at a time and could accentuate the moves he wanted. By making money from them, he ploughed the profit into forcing the price the way he wanted it to go.

Fundamentally Kimcorp was bust and he could see it in the company's stock chart. He was just accelerating the inescapable gravitation forces of financial reality. With the picture of Jane hanging from the bars beside his keyboard, he was trading Kimcorp into the ground.

57

Kim looked at the chart of his stock. It was being destroyed. The stock price line tried to rise but it was as if a hammer was smashing down on it every time it raised its head. There had been a call from a big US investment bank. This must be something to do with them. He looked up the name of the individual attached to the number. It was one of the bank's top board members. Something was going on, something outside his knowledge and skills. Japanese bankers had been easy meat when he had lured them into lending him billions. They would give him all the money he wanted if it was backed by property. When they were in deep, they had no other option but to lend him more.

Americans were different: they lent you money, then destroyed you and took what you had created. They were predators like him. Predators needed to concentrate on feeding off the meek rather than turning on each other, he thought, but Americans didn't understand this.

He called.

Wolfsberg would do Jim any favour he asked. Jim was a phenomenon, the very thing that PhDs and Nobel Prize winners said couldn't exist. He was the guy who conclusively proved the markets weren't random. He was the kind of person you wanted to be indebted to you. The kid had worked for him once. Jim had made his name at his bank, then gone off and done some crazy shit even Wolfsberg couldn't quite believe.

Wolfsberg hoped he could entice Jim to buy the bank one day. Then the sky would surely be the limit for him and the organisation. With Jim, the bank really could become the all-powerful global engine the conspiracy theorists thought it was, rather than a crazy gambler, bullying and cheating its way along. With Jim, they really would be able to call the shots. Using his foresight, they could go from 'doomed to fail' to the world's power pivot.

'Mr Kim, I'm so glad you called.'

'Mr Wolfsberg, I have read a lot about you,' he lied.

'I'm flattered. Thanks for calling me back.'

'What can I do for you?'

'Well, we've been watching your recent difficulties, so I thought I'd give you a call and see if we could be of any help.'

'Thank you, but what do you have in mind?'

'Our analysts reckon you could use a debt restructuring and maybe some new equity.'

'I do not think that is necessary.'

'You're probably right, but you know how it is. Perhaps you should have a back stop. We don't know what your debt covenants look like but we're thinking you might be in breach soon enough. You know how that can set off a meltdown, however unfair that might be.'

'Our covenants are not linked to our stock price.'

'That's great,' said Wolfsberg. 'When can you take a meeting with a team of ours? I think we can help you with your stock price.'

Kim knew they were probably driving his price down to get their claws into him. It was a kind of extortion racket. He understood that well enough. His stock price had just gone vertically down. 'You can come tomorrow?'

'Tomorrow,' said Wolfsberg, hitting 'return' on his keyboard. 'Ten?'

Jim's Skype said, 'Show them some love?' It was Wolfsberg.

Jim started buying. Kimcorp stock spiked three per cent.

Kim saw his stock shoot up. He grimaced and gripped the phone. 'Very well.'

'We look forward to doing business.'

'Goodbye.'

Jim sat back, smiling. 'We're in.'

Kim stood up from his desk and pulled open the second drawer on the right of his desk. He took out the pistol and headed to the lift. He would kill the woman and go into the cage. He touched the cufflinks on his shirt. Then his bad luck would end.

Yamamoto led them to the board room and they followed him. 'Wow,' said Danny, on seeing Jim.

The four Americans stood up and began shaking hands.

'Reece.'

'Jim.'

'Brandon.'

'Jim.'

'Casey.'

'Jim.'

'Major, right?' said Casey.

Jim laughed. 'For about three hours once.'

Akira looked at Jim strangely. 'Army major?'

'It's a long story, Professor,' said Jim.

'And I'm Danny. This is turning into an epic,' said Danny.

'Sit down, guys,' said Jim. 'First off, thanks for coming.'

Reece smiled up one side of his face, 'No problem.' They hadn't had a choice. 'Nice to be out of the dog house. What's the plan?'

Jim took the blueprint from James Dean Yamamoto and

rolled it out on the table. Yamamoto pinned it down with four paperweights. 'Colonel Jane Brown is held on the sixtieth floor of Kimcorp Tower.'

Akira put some photos down the side of the blueprint.

'Is that like Major General Brown?' said Danny.

'Yes,' said Jim.

'Wow,' said Danny. 'Like *the* Major General Brown, now Colonel?'

'Probably,' said Jim.

'Danny's her biggest fan,' said Brandon, shrugging.

'Hell, yes,' said Danny. He smirked at Jim.

'I take it we're busting her out,' said Casey.

'Hell, yes,' said Danny again.

'Yes,' said Jim.

'How quiet has this got to be?' said Reece.

'Don't let that worry you,' said Jim.

'Chopper onto the roof, in through the windows,' suggested Casey.

'Roof's covered in aerials. There's no good landing spot,' said Reece, studying the blueprints. 'We could rappel down, then off the sides and go in through the windows.'

'She's in a cage," said Jim. "We have to be able to get into that. We've got a different plan. We're going in through the front door.'

'We have an appointment with Kim,' said Akira. 'We will take him, then he will release her and we will leave the way we came.'

'Sounds good,' said Reece. 'What do you need us for?'

'In case it gets nasty,' said Jim.

'I guess you think that's likely,' said Reece.

Jim nodded.

Reece grinned. 'That's cool. It's been a while since we've had some real action.'

'We've got to get you boys suited up,' said Jim. 'Can't play investment bankers in jeans.'

'Hey, hey,' said Danny.

'Better be loose,' said Casey. 'We're going to be packing a lot of iron.' He lifted his holdall onto the table and pulled out a machine pistol.

'We'll buy you briefcases,' said Jim.

'Big briefcases,' said Danny. 'Giant ones.'

'Yamamoto-san will organise the pick-up outside Kimcorp and we end up back here,' said Jim. 'All the floor plans for the top five floors are there. It's either a simple in-and-out performance or we're going to get completely fucked.'

'Oh, yeah,' said Casey, looking up from the plans. 'That's how it always goes.'

Kim walked out of the lift, gun in hand. The woman was some kind of witch. As soon as she died the curse of bad luck would be lifted from him. His heels clicked on the tile flooring. He took the pistol off safety and squeezed the butt. A pistol had only one purpose: killing people. It was good at it. A life was ended with little more than a gesture.

A pointing movement, followed by a slight twitch of the index finger was all it took to destroy someone. A complex, amazing creature could be shattered beyond repair in a fraction of a second on his slight whim, a moment of beautiful poignancy. Without power someone was worthless and with power they were like a god. A pistol made anyone a god and right now, like a god, he was going to extinguish a life with a clap of thunder. But first he would torture and humiliate.

The gorilla looked up at him as he passed. A fine animal, he thought. When he found a bigger, better one, he would kill this one and put the new one in its place.

He scanned the tiger cage for the woman. Where was she? He

walked quicker to be able to see the entire cage. It was empty. There were wires hanging over the lock mechanism, with what looked like a camera attached to them.

He swivelled around, holding out the gun, expecting the woman to jump at him. There was nowhere for her to hide. He spun back to the cage. It was still empty.

He shrieked in anger. How was it possible? He went to the wires. They were jammed between the door frame and the lock mechanism. How had she opened the lock with that? The cage door was on a spring so it would have closed once she had escaped, but what contraption had opened it?

He wrenched it out and stuffed it into his pocket. She must be hiding on the floor somewhere. There was no way out, apart from the lift. Maybe someone had rescued her while he slept – perhaps one of his men had stolen her for someone else.

He paced around the zoo, the animals shrieking. She must be there somewhere. She would not have been able to operate the lift without help.

His phone rang. It was his finance director. 'Tokyo bank request an urgent meeting.'

'When?'

'Now.'

'Tell them no.'

'They are in the lobby waiting to see you and so are Kyoto Maritime Bank.'

'*Soooooo.*' He put the pistol onto safety and shoved it into his pocket. 'I will see them on the hour.'

Who had betrayed him and released the woman? It must have been someone very close, someone very close indeed. He would work out who and he would cut them to pieces from their toes upwards and from their fingers in.

58

Apart from the occasional click of the mouse, the room was silent. James Dean Yamamoto had taken the SEALs out to buy investment-bank outfits. Getting to a store that fitted outsized Americans needed the sort of local knowledge they didn't have. Yamamoto was in love with the American GIs – it was like reliving a dream from childhood. He was actually living an old Hollywood movie. He was sure this was a moment of fate, the final chapter of his life where destiny would enjoy the joke of a puppet dancing to its own ironic song. He was being honoured. He would jump into the abyss with abandon.

'Got a minute, Professor?' Jim was getting up from Yamamoto's desk.

'Yes, Evans-san,' said Akira, looking up from a magazine.

Jim lifted the Yasakani no Magatama from under his shirt. It always felt a little colder when he took it off. He handed it to Akira. 'Time to get this back where it belongs. We don't want Kim to get his hands on it.'

Akira took it. 'You cannot go without me,' he said, his eyes narrowing. 'I will take this and be back in one hour, but you must promise to not leave without me.'

'You'll probably just get in the way.'

'And you?'

'Yeah, me too, but I've got more reason than you to get in the line of fire.'

'How so?' said Akira, slipping the necklace into his pocket.

Jim shrugged. 'You know, love and all that.'

'Honour is as powerful as love,' said Akira.

There was a knock at the door. It opened and a tall, beautiful girl walked into the room with a plastic tray. '*Mashi*,' she said, bowed and left.

Akira picked up a box. 'So,' he said, 'I have the correct calling card and therefore I must come.' He smiled. 'You have not promised me yet.'

'OK, I promise not to leave without you.'

'I will be back at one thirty.'

Akira jumped out of the cab and walked quickly up the pristine alleyway. Freshly watered bowls of flowers hung from braces, and window boxes were filled with multicoloured pansies. The alleyway was a tidy confusion of personal things carefully left out. He stepped up to his parents' door and let himself in. 'It's me, Akira,' he called.

'Son,' called his father, 'I'm here.' He was standing up. 'I have tried to reach you for days. I was worried.'

Akira hugged him, something he had not done since he was a small child. 'Where is Mother?'

'Visiting her sisters.'

Akira took a step back. 'Father, I have a favour to ask and a great burden for you to bear.'

'What is it?'

Akira took the necklace from his pocket. 'This is Yasakani no Magatama. It has been lost for several hundred years but I have recovered it.' He passed it to his father.

The old man looked down at the necklace, glowing green and gold in his hand. It felt hot in his palm like a bowl of miso soup. 'What must I do?' he said.

'You must return it to the Emperor and only to him. If it is known you have it, you will most likely be killed. You must take it immediately.'

'Son, you bring glory to your family and to your father.'

Akira bowed. 'I must leave immediately, Father.'

His father bowed. As he stood up he felt as if his bent back had straightened a little. He saw his son clearly. 'Goodbye, Akira.'

Jim was flat-lining Kimcorp's stock, holding it in a range limit to the upside. Every time the stock rose and hit a certain price he sold it on at that price. The share hit this ceiling, and fell back.

Pretty soon the buyers would give up hope and sell out, and he would buy the shares back on the fall. He could sense traders coming and going, throwing their money at the stock in the hope that it had hit its bottom. He could tell by the size and speed of the orders how much they had to play with and he could swat them like flies.

Kimcorp had been worth five billion dollars when his campaign had started and it was now worth eight hundred million. For all the bucking of the market, he was only losing fifty million dollars and hardly short of Kimcorp stock at all. If he had been playing the game for money he would have given the stock one last terrifying downdraught and filled his boots with it on the final 'puke' as major shareholders baled out in a last panic. Then he would have left the stock alone and it would have risen again to its correct price, netting him a very fat profit indeed. But this wasn't for money: he would blow all his billions if that would get Jane out. The trading was just a means to an end.

'Hey, Major, put this on.' Something clumped onto the desk. It was a pistol holster.

Jim looked up to see Danny beside him. 'You look good in a five-thousand-dollar suit,' he said.

'No way, man,' said Danny. 'This is a five-hundred-dollar suit – I just look like five thousand in it.'

Jim struggled with the holster, trying to keep his eye on the charts. Danny adjusted it roughly on his shoulder and pulled the strap up to tighten it.

'Got to get my trading bots all lined up while we're gone. As soon as I take my boot off this wanker's neck, his stock price is going to pop up.' He glanced at the holster under his arm. It looked flash.

'Time to go,' said Casey, walking in carrying a briefcase.

Jim stood. 'Let's rock.'

Danny grinned knowingly at Casey. 'Don't forget your attaché case.'

Jim picked it up. 'Don't expect me to use this shit properly,' he said.

'Just don't bleed on us if we have to carry you out.'

'It's blue blood, mate,' said Jim. 'You won't notice it on your jackets.'

Kim had sat and watched the meeting. He had not been called upon to say anything. His minions had done the talking and the banks the listening. Toyoda presented well. He had all the figures to hand and in his head, and when he was questioned, he could slice and dice them all ways, so that however they rebuilt the numbers, they totalled up correctly and agreed.

The figures were, however, all lies, accounting fictions like intangibles, amortisations, depreciations and accruals making a mockery of the real picture. He was almost out of cash to pay the bills and they would lend him more cash to pay them the very interest he was about to be unable to afford. They did this on the basis of numbers that had no meaning in the real world and no connection with cash. It would be funny if it were not so vital.

If he gave his finance director all of his company's intangible assets, Toyoda could no more buy a bowl of rice than a homeless man living in a cardboard box by Tokyo station. Yet Kimcorp would borrow hundreds of millions against those empty assets. Without the lies of legitimate accountancy, his business would not have been built, but without the lies of illegitimate accountancy, it would not be standing.

Toyoda was so accomplished, he reflected. Could he be the traitor in his midst? He listened to the accountant bat back the questions from the banks. With Kim gone, Toyoda would surely be the boss of Kimcorp. Could Kim operate without him as CFO? He would think carefully about Toyoda. Once the situation had stabilised he would have a better idea of who the traitor was.

59

The old man marched swiftly up the ramp to the palace gatehouse. The immaculate guard stepped out of his cubicle. 'How can I help you, sir?' he said, addressing the distinguished gentleman in his grey raincoat.

'I am Captain Nakabashi of the Imperial Bodyguard, retired. I have an urgent matter for the head of the household.'

'Do you have an appointment, sir?'

'No,' said Nakabashi, offering him his papers, 'I do not, but it is an emergency of the highest importance.'

The guard looked at the documents. Sure enough, they were those of an Imperial bodyguard retired ten years before. 'I will call my captain to advise,' he said.

'Very good,' said Nakabashi. He put his hand inside his outer suit pocket. The necklace seemed to absorb his body heat and reflect it back to him. His whole side felt warmed by it. Perhaps it was the magic of legend.

A captain was trotting down the slope towards them. He was bowing. 'Captain Nakabashi, it is an honour,' he said. 'How may I help you?'

'I must see the head of the household as I must have audience with the Emperor. It is of national importance.'

'This way, sir,' said the captain. 'I am already ordered to admit you.'

'Very good,' said the old man, bowing with the seniority of age. He felt a wave of relief sweep over him. He might just be able to achieve the impossible and deliver the treasure to the Emperor.

He walked quickly through the halls he had known so well. They had been newly built when he had first worked there and remained seemingly unchanged since he had departed a decade ago. He walked flanked by the Imperial guard to Private Audience Room Four.

Two guards were standing behind the Emperor and his detail of two men stood close by. Two advisers Nakabashi did not recognise flanked him on either side.

Nakabashi bowed as low as he could. 'Your Imperial Majesty, I must speak with you alone.'

The Emperor nodded and the room emptied.

The door clicked closed. 'Yoshi,' said the Emperor, beaming now. 'It has been so long. How are you, old friend?'

'I am very well, Your Imperial Majesty. I have come to return the Yasakani no Magatama to you.' He put his right hand into his jacket pocket and lifted out the necklace. He took a step forwards and bowed, offering the jewel to the Emperor in his cupped hands.

The Emperor stepped forward and took it, a wide smile crossing his face. 'So your son is winning the day.'

Captain Nakabashi stood up. 'I fear he is in great peril.'

The Emperor nodded gravely. 'So are we all.' He put on the necklace. 'At least now I can say I am truly crowned. That much danger is now passed.' He clapped his hands and the doors opened. 'Let us take tea together, for this is surely a moment for celebration.'

The guards' and the advisers' eyes were wide with amazement. The Emperor was wearing the Yasakani no Magatama, a treasure no one other than priests had seen for more than half a millennium. It glowed like wet seaweed.

Danny looked at Akira and at Jim. 'Are we really taking Yoda with us?'

'Yes,' said Jim, 'unless you can suddenly speak Japanese and just happen to be carrying permission to blow up Tokyo.'

'OK,' said Danny, grinning manically.

Yamamoto was pushing something into Akira's hand. It was an old pistol. 'Take this, kid. It won't let you down if you need it.'

Akira passed it to his short arm and tried it for size. 'Thank you.' He smiled. 'I remember this,' he said, gripping the rubber handle of the snub revolver. 'It used to be much bigger.'

'Let's go, guys,' said Reece.

Two black Toyota Crowns were waiting in the office block driveway, three storeys underground. Jim got in with Reece. They slammed the limo doors.

'Hey there,' said Reece, 'do you mind if I smoke?'

The driver looked around worriedly. 'No Engrish, no Engrish,' he said apologetically.

'Good,' said Reece, not apparently about to smoke. 'We can probably talk. What the hell was in that gold box we found?' he asked, as the car pulled away towards a ramp heading up to the road above.

'The Japanese Crown Jewels.'

'Oh,' said Reece. 'Is that right?'

'I'm afraid so.'

'And that's what this is all about?'

'Oh, yes,' said Jim.

'That's kind of crazy.'

'You can say that again.'

'And the Colonel is your girlfriend, right?'

'Right.'

'That's what Danny thought. He's kind of disappointed.'

'He's brighter than he looks,' said Jim.

'And where does Godzilla come into the picture?'

'Do you mean literally or do you mean Kim?'

'No, it was kind of a joke.'

'Got it,' said Jim, with a sinking feeling in his gut. They emerged into the bright Tokyo sunlight. 'I hate this bit.'

'You mean the going into action?' said Reece.

'That's the one.'

'It's not as bad as getting hit,' said Reece.

'I'm not sure,' said Jim. 'I can't remember those bits clearly.'

'You've been hit before?'

Jim pulled the hair on the crown of his head to one side. 'That was just a week or so ago.'

Reece could see a thin red scar. 'It's healed pretty well.'

Jim nodded. 'How about you?'

'Not once,' said Reece. 'All I get is abrasions.'

'That must be skill,' said Jim.

'I'd hope so,' said Reece. 'I like to think that, but you kind of know it's luck.'

'Luck is good.'

'I got a question for you.'

'OK.'

'How do investment bankers act? I want to walk in there and look credible.'

'That's easy,' said Jim. 'Just swagger in like you think you're some death dealing Navy SEAL killing machine in an expensive suit. That's pretty much average investment banker behaviour. If you can come across like an obnoxious jerk at the same time, you'll be completely credible.'

'I can do that.' He grinned.

'I hope you didn't mind me calling you Yoda,' said Danny, now remorseful for dissing the professor.

'No,' said Akira. 'I took it as a compliment.'

'That's good,' said Danny, 'because it was meant to be one.'

'I think it was meant as an insult,' said Akira, 'but I chose to take it as a compliment.'

'Right,' said Danny. 'I'm sorry about that and I hope we're cool, Professor. Are we?'

Akira scanned him with his inscrutable gaze. 'We are cool,' he said finally, a smile flickering across his face.

Brandon watched central Tokyo pass his window. A lot of the adverts had American stars promoting booze, cigarettes and mobile phones. They were photographed in such a way it was hard to recognise them. In some cases their eyes appeared to have been touched up and made to look Japanese. 'My urban warfare skills are pretty shaky,' he said finally to Casey.

'Mine too,' said Casey. 'This is going to be real sketchy.'

60

Jim felt like a terrorist. They entered the office building armed to the teeth, surrounded by innocent unarmed people utterly unprepared for what might happen. They were passing through their normal world set on a course that would probably erupt into extreme violence. Keep walking, he said silently to the people who passed him. Don't look back.

Reece, Brandon, Danny and Casey did look like investment bankers. The sort who went running at five a.m. for an hour before getting to work at seven. Unlike the boozy often corpulent British bankers, there was always a cadre of young American bankers who used their looks and arrogance to navigate around the world of finance. To the casual eye the SEALs perfectly fitted the mould. Only their faces gave them away. Their features hinted at a level of fitness even the most diehard gym patron could never attain. Only people constantly on the move had hard, muscled faces like theirs.

If Jim's heart hadn't been pounding so hard he would have laughed. He could have taken the SEAL team to any investment bank and walked them into million dollar jobs: they were perfect.

Kim had never dealt with an American bank before. He had avoided it. They had a bad reputation. They relied on contracts and pulling tricks. They were paid too much to be easily swayed by favours, like women and booze. They thought that because you did not say no you had said yes. They thought a deal could be done by flying in, making a couple of presentations and emailing over a contract. He wanted nothing to do with such business practices. He relied on the Japanese system of relationships built over years, unwritten and unspoken deals made over dinner, whisky and cigarettes. That was a long, subtle game he was good at, and at which he won. Business was war for the Americans and they never respected an ally, let alone an enemy.

Now he had no choice.

He didn't like the look of the room. The bankers looked like nightclub bouncers and the junior American seemed angry. The translator didn't feel right either. His shrivelled arm repulsed Kim – it made him feel queasy.

'So, gentlemen, down to business. How can you help me?'

Reece had taken the senior spot and knew it was his role to speak. 'Well, to kick off, I'd like to bring in my analyst here to give us an overview of the situation. Go ahead, Jimmy.'

Jim's nose flared. His lips pursed and drew back into a rictus smile. 'Thank you, Reece,' he said, his British accent surprising Kim. 'The situation is this.' He pulled his pistol. He didn't raise his voice: 'You've got my girl upstairs in your fucking zoo.' Kim rocked back in his chair and held his hands up. 'And you're taking us up there right now or I'm going to blow your fucking brains out.'

'Very good,' said Reece, grinning. He grabbed Kim's shoulder, his other hand on his briefcase of weaponry. 'Let's go.'

'No tricks,' said Brandon, quietly, in Kim's ear, 'or I'll snap your neck.'

Kim said nothing. He had turned the stone on his cufflink and was now regretting it. 'There is no woman in my zoo,' he said, resetting the stone and switching off the alarm: if his guards intervened now, he would be shot. 'Who do you think I am?'

'Just do as you're told,' said Jim, 'and you might get out of this alive.'

Kim could see they knew where they were going. 'Open the lift, please,' said Casey, looking at Kim as though a negative response would mean instant death.

Kim placed a cufflink over the call panel, which lit up. In a moment there was a *ding* and the door opened. His secretaries watched them enter the lift, bowing. There was only one floor on the panel and Kim pressed the button, then swiped his cuff over the control. The doors closed and the lift rose.

Down in the control room they watched the screens. Kim had set the alarm, then switched it off. They didn't know what to do. Wherever he went the cameras were strangely blurred and the scene was hard to decipher.

Kim fingered the cufflink. He would set the alarm as soon as the Americans started to leave. His men would intercept them at the lift on his office suite floor and he would have a chance to escape. Before then, he might convince them they had made a big mistake. Thank the gods the woman was gone.

The lift doors opened.

'Wow,' said Danny, trying not to gawp at the zoo.

'This way,' said Jim, looking down the aisle.

'You have made a mistake,' pleaded Kim. 'Why would you think I keep anything but animals here?'

The animals were making a spectacular din.

Brandon's attention was on the gorilla standing by the bars, staring soulfully at him.

'Right there,' said Jim. But the cage was empty. 'Oh, shit. She's gone.'

'Not gone,' said Kim. 'Never here.'

'Where have you taken her?' Jim pulled the gun from his pocket and pressed it against Kim's forehead. 'Tell me or you have seconds to live.'

In desperation Kim rotated the stone in the cufflink.

The cameras came on in the zoo. Through the distortion the operators could make out that something bad was happening. They hit the security alarm.

'I don't know what you mean,' cried Kim. 'I don't know who you are talking about. I don't know where your girlfriend is.' He was sobbing.

'I'm here,' came a muffled voice. Jim looked into the cage – the voice was coming from the far corner.

Kim made a lunge for Jim's pistol but Danny socked him in the side of the head and knocked him to the ground. 'Stay there,' he ordered Kim.

A board slid out from between the shelf and the cage bars and a head poked up awkwardly from the gap. 'This is a freakin' hard manoeuvre,' said Jane, her hands appearing next. She began to squeeze her body through the small space. 'This is way tight,' she complained. 'That's better,' she reported, as she worked her butt out. 'The cage key is in the guy's cufflinks. Take them off and wave them over the lock.'

Jim bent down and took them out of Kim's shirt sleeves. He ran to the cage and waved the cufflinks over the lock. There was a clank. Jane pushed the door open. 'Didn't expect to see you,' she said, smiling.

'Thanks,' said Jim.

Jane took a cufflink and walked over to Kim. She pulled him to his feet. 'Come with me,' she said, dragging him to the gorilla cage.

'We might need him,' said Jim.

'No deal,' said Jane, Kim staggering behind.

The monkeys in the cage beyond were screeching at the tops of their voices and the birds further back were hooting and squawking in alarm.

'Please don't,' he begged.

She unlocked the gorilla cage and slung Kim in. He cried out as he hit the floor. 'No,' he screamed, scrambling up as the cage slammed shut. The gorilla ambled over to him on its knuckles, took him by the arm and pulled him into its lap. It wrapped its arms around him, crushing him. Kim cried out as he felt a rib crack under the pressure of the embrace.

'Sorry I can't take you with me,' said Jane, pouting at the gorilla. She turned to Jim and the SEALs. 'Let's get out of here.'

Reece threw Jane his pistol and took out the compact machine gun from his case. 'Hi, Professor,' she said, as they trotted to the lift.

'Hi, Jane-san,' said Akira.

Jim swiped the cufflinks on the lift call panel and the doors opened. The cries of the animals were deafening. The lift descended.

When the doors opened again, men with stun batons were waiting for them. The security guards reeled back at the sight of a lift full of heavily-armed men, machine guns pointing at them. They backed away.

The SEALs exited the lift in tight formation.

The main lift bank was across the atrium. A man with a pistol stepped out of a doorway and aimed. Brandon cut him down with a burst of fire. The men with batons turned to run. Jane was paying one particular attention. She jumped forwards and tripped him as he turned to escape, then wrenched the stun gun from his hand. 'I remember you,' she said.

She stuck the baton between his legs and pressed the switch. He let out a howl and spun around onto his back. She didn't know whether he was looking at her consciously or was out cold, but she pressed the button again anyway. A spasm twisted and shook his body. She straightened. 'Let's go.'

Reece was already heading for the main lift.

'Was that necessary?' asked Jim, as he passed her.

'No,' she said, 'but it felt good.'

A lift door opened and they bundled in. A secretary tumbled out, screaming.

They took up a fire formation in the lift as they waited for the door to close. The SEALs didn't press the door close button because it never worked in the US. Akira pressed it and the doors shut immediately.

The express lift would take them down fifty eight floors in two minutes. Then all they had to do was make a fifty-metre dash outside to freedom.

The lift was slowing. It was stopping at the fifty second floor.

They braced to open fire.

The doors opened and they saw a group of men with their backs to them, bowing. Another group of men and women were bowing to them in farewell. They turned to the lift and the men with machine guns. They leapt back and stared agog, frozen to the spot. The lift door closed.

'Bloody hell,' muttered Jim. It was stopping at the fiftieth floor. They braced themselves. The secretaries outside the lift shrieked and one threw her Starbucks into the air, showering the others with latte. They fled.

'Stay focused,' said Reece, as the lift slowed to the fortieth floor. As the door opened Brandon, who was crouching, fired through the gap. The other SEALs opened up as the doors slid open. They burst out into the corridor over the two felled armed guards. Reece and Casey took the hallway beyond. 'Clear,' they shouted, turning and running back.

The doors closed again.

The lift was picking up speed. 'Maybe this time it'll go the whole way down,' said Brandon.

Jim looked at the TV screen above the doors. It was showing the financial news. The yen was rallying.

The lift started to slow. 'Here we go,' said Reece.

Jim kissed Jane.

The doors started to open. Brandon was straining to see any movement and as soon as the gap was wide enough he rolled through it. They piled out, scanning around them.

'Clear,' shouted Reece. They ran in formation for the escalator that would take them down to the main lobby and entrance.

Two security guards were looking up at them. They were armed but made no attempt to pull their guns.

The team raced down the escalators. Then it was only twenty metres to the main doors. Brandon and Danny took position at the bottom of the moving stairway and immediately there was a burst of gunfire from behind. The plate-glass window near the entrance shattered and glass showered to the floor.

The SEALs opened up against the pistol fire with a crackle of machine gun. The fat old security guards threw themselves down and held out their arms in blind surrender to whoever was firing. Reece and Jane shot out more windows directly ahead, opening up an escape route only metres away.

'Go!' shouted Casey. They ran as he and Danny fired into the space behind the escalators where the attack had originated. There was no returning fire. Casey and Danny were running backwards, covering the rest of the team.

'Where is Yamamoto?' shouted Jim, hurdling through a shattered window and skidding down a polished granite sill.

'There!' yelled Akira.

Jim looked across the plaza. Six off-road bikes were parked behind a black Harley, all with helmeted riders, engines running.

They sprinted to the bikers who were revving their engines. Jim jumped onto the pillion of a bike and grabbed the rider around the waist. It was a woman. Fuck me, he had just enough time to think, as the bike lunged forwards from the kerb. She had a red and yellow tattoo on her neck, partly covered with strands of hair that had fallen out of her helmet. He closed his eyes in terror as the bike hurtled recklessly through the traffic. Whose idea was it to hire these maniacs to get them away?

Jane jumped on the back of the Harley. She wondered who the old guy in the half helmet was. 'Nice bike,' she said.

'*Domo.*' He coaxed the bike into roaring off sedately.

'You again,' said Stafford, as he opened the door to Smith.

'I'm afraid so.'

'Do come in. Are you planning to become a permanent fixture?'

'That's not a bad idea,' said Smith. 'Certainly beats my little pad in Brixton.'

'Very good,' said Stafford. 'And what delights are we to expect tonight?'

'The usual,' said Smith. 'A Triad raid, perhaps, or maybe a North Korean blitzkrieg – possibly, even, another ninja onslaught.'

'Jolly good.' Stafford closed the door. 'And will you be dining?'

'I've eaten,' said Smith, 'though a plate of baked beans on toast won't come amiss later.'

'I'm sure we can stretch to that.'

'I'll help with the washing up,' said Smith.

'That won't be necessary. Do you have laundry?'

'I've got that covered, Bertie.'

'I really do wish you wouldn't call me that.'

'Sorry, Stafford, I keep forgetting.'

'That's much better.'

61

Jim felt uncomfortably powerless on the back of the bike as it wove in and out of the traffic. It was as if the riders had entered their own private race and were cutting through the traffic to win a bet. There didn't seem to be anyone in pursuit.

What was the point of attracting attention to yourself once you had got a certain distance away? Holding on to the rider with one hand while clutching a heavy briefcase with the other was tough physical exercise, which he was finding hard to manage. He thought about jumping off at a red light but it was never clear whether a red light was going to be obeyed or not.

Jim had no idea where they were or where they were going but he was hoping devoutly that the trip would end soon.

The biker's jacket said 'Happy Foxes' and sported a cheeky babyish face of a *manga* fox grinning mischievously. The bike reared up on its forks and he gripped the girl's midriff with all his might. If he came off the back his brains would splatter over the pristine Tokyo tarmac.

Jane was admiring the Tokyo landscape as it floated by. The friendly old guy had given her a half helmet. She sat back in the seat, her feet up on the fold out rests, one hand on the grip. It was good to be free. The other bikes were long gone.

She hadn't expected to see Jim with a bunch of SEALs or, for that matter, the professor. It felt strange to be rescued. She considered herself as always out on her own. It didn't matter if she was part of a team, or even an army: she was no one's responsibility but her own.

Jim was the guy with everything and he was stupid to stick his neck out for her. If anyone was going to spring themselves from a fix like that, it was her. Jim could have easily got them all killed. She realised it was dumb for her to be angry with him. He hadn't complained when she had fished him out of the Congo jungle, so why should she be angry with him for getting her out of trouble? Yet she was and that was that.

They were riding beside the moat of the palace. It was an enormous entrenchment and she marvelled at it as they rolled by. She grinned to herself as the wind blew on her face. The sky was blue: it was a perfect day in Japan.

Yamamoto read the sign as they passed it: 'One person killed on the road today in Tokyo.' He wondered how many people would be born in Tokyo that day, how many boys would kiss a girl for the first time, how many would fall in love. They should build a sign that told everyone that too.

Jim jumped off the bike the moment it screeched to a halt at the underground entrance to Yamamoto Towers. His body was trembling and his feet were happy to be on the ground. The rider pulled off her helmet. She was a tall, beautiful woman, whose long black hair fell onto her delicate leather padded shoulders. 'Couldn't you have gone any faster?' he exclaimed. He put the briefcase down and forced a smile. 'You scared the shit out of me.'

The girl laughed. 'You're funny,' she said, and looked away from him as the other bikes drew up.

The last of the Happy Foxes came down the ramp with Danny. 'Woo hoo,' he yelled.

Brandon's biker had somehow got onto his shoulders. She was waving her arms around and shouting.

Where the fuck is Yamamoto? Jim wondered.

Akira closed his eyes and opened them again. His rider was still looking at him through her visor. She took her helmet off. She had red hair, big eyes and a long, thin face. She was a beauty. 'Fox with five tails,' she said, cocking her head. 'Your hair is turning white.'

'Turning white?'

She touched his head with her slender fingers and ruffled his hair. 'Yes, the roots of your hair have turned white as snow.' She pointed at her wing mirrors. 'See?' He bent down to peer at himself. Sure enough, the first millimetre of his jet black hair was white. The stress had turned him into an old man.

He straightened as he heard the engine of the Harley fill the underground space. 'Quickly,' he said. 'You must take me to my father.'

'Jump on, Kitsune.'

'Kitsune?' he asked. 'Me?' He clambered on.

'Never hurt me,' she said, peeping at him over her shoulder.

'I will never hurt you,' he said. 'Never go away.'

She set off with a jump and a high toned clatter.

'Thank fuck for that,' exclaimed, Jim striding over to the SEALs and their riders, who whooped and hollered as Yamamoto and Jane drove down the ramp. The engine of the Harley filled the cavern with its roar. 'Where the hell is the professor going?' shouted Jim, waving his arms at the bike as it passed.

Jane had jumped off the Harley and was high fiving the SEALs.

'I was wondering where you'd got to,' he said to her as she clapped with Reece.

'Traffic.' She offered Jim her palm.

Jim fancied a kiss, but he high fived her clumsily and everyone clapped.

She turned back to the SEALs. 'Guys, we've got to get straight to the embassy.'

'What?' protested Jim.

'Jim, we've just been in a first class diplomatic incident. We've got to get onto US soil right away.'

He took her by the waist and kissed her. She didn't resist, but neither did she reciprocate much. He let her go. 'Later,' she said giving him a look. 'American Embassy,' she told her rider.

Jim's biker had obviously understood the conversation because she shouted something to them all. They saddled up and, in a deafening storm of engine noise, took off.

The sound of the engines died away, leaving behind nothing but the ambient hum of the equipment that pulsed and rattled in the depths of the building. His rider was standing by her bike, sucking a mint. 'What's your name?' he asked her.

'Kuda.'

'Hi, Kuda,' he said. 'Seems we're the only ones left.'

'Want to play?' she said.

Jim looked twice at the willowy girl in metal encrusted knee high boots with black and red leathers. She was holding a Sony PSP in her hand. He realised his pistol was not on safety. He took it from his pocket, flipped the catch and put it back.

Kuda didn't blink.

'Let's go inside.' He smiled at her. 'What games you got?'

'Final Fantasy XX, Bubble Trouble Extreme Five.'

'Great!'

'We could go to Akiharbara and shoot zombies.' She held up her helmet as if to put it on.

'Got one of those for me?'

'Yes.'

'Let's go, then.'

The last of the creatures were coming at them. Kuda was wielding her pump action shotgun with precision and expertise. Jim had caught on slowly and finally got up to speed in the time it had taken to pump ten thousand yen into the machine.

The robot dragon human combo super-baddie was suddenly on the game screen. He was saying something in Japanese that was clearly a final challenge. He was carrying some limp girl in his gigantic talons. 'Shoot at his middle eye when it opens,' said Kuda, blasting at the floating lightning bolts that cascaded towards them.

The eye opened. Jim shot and missed. Kuda shot and the monster shook backwards. A small amount of energy left its power bar.

Jim's phone rang. 'Bugger,' he muttered, putting the red plastic shotgun into its holster. He fed the machine some more hundred yen coins.

'I've got this,' said Kuda, blasting away.

Jim answered the sat phone.

'Are you OK, Evans-san?' said a worried Akira.

He must be able to hear the gunfire down the phone, Jim thought. 'Yeah,' he said.

'The guns?'

'Just zombies. I'm in an arcade.'

'Yamamoto-san and I were concerned. Are you returning?'

'Yes,' said Jim, 'just keeping myself busy.'

'So, so, so,' said Akira, 'when?'

'As soon as I've killed the superboss.'

'*Gambatte*, Kudasi.'

'Thanks,' said Jim, wondering what it meant. He hung up and picked up his gun. The eye of the superboss opened. He shot. He missed.

The restaurant's wooden door slid open. Jim stood outside as Yamamoto, Akira and the Happy Foxes filed in. Kuda stayed with him. There was a chorus of shouting from within as the staff greeted the party in a ritualistic way.

'We're leaving in the morning, Stafford,' said Jim. 'Everything's fine here. You?'

'Pacific.'

Jim thought for a moment. 'Is that a code word?'

'Calm,' said Stafford.

'Right,' said Jim. 'It's not been calm here but we're cool now.'

'What is the plan?'

'Can't say on the phone,' said Jim. 'But there is one and it's short and sweet.'

'Good,' said Stafford. 'Because Smith seems intent on camping here until he gets an explanation.' He threw a glance at Smith, who was grinning laconically at him. 'The blasted man has installed a television in the lounge.'

'Say hi to him from me,' said Jim, smiling, one finger in his other ear to cut out the noise coming from the restaurant. 'Any messages?'

'No, sir,' said Stafford.

'Nothing from Jane?'

'I can check your email again if you wish.'

Jim sighed. 'No, that's OK.'

62

Jim had drunk quite a lot of cold sake out of the square wooden box in front of him. He had also eaten quite a few odd things that the professor had explained to him. The chefs sat on a raised dais with charcoal fires, meat and vegetables in front of them. The diners sat around them like an audience and picked out things to eat from the display.

Yamamoto and Akira were choosing the dishes and the waiters were constantly shouting orders to punctuate the proceedings. It was an enjoyable if rather confusing spectacle.

Jim had started off with a sheet of roasted baby fish and a couple of oddly-shaped mushrooms. That was followed by a red fish on a skewer that, even dead, looked pretty surprised. Next up was a plate of weird tasting grilled pine nuts, which had the distinct but not unpleasant flavour of floor polish. They went down great with the sake.

The professor and his Happy Fox seemed to have hit it off rather well.

'Where did you disappear off to?' Jim asked Akira, as the chef handed them a selection of what looked like potatoes on the end of a long wooden paddle.

'I went to see if my father had successfully returned the Yasakani no Magatama.'

'And?'

'He had handed it to the Emperor himself.'

'Great,' said Jim. 'I bet you're relieved.'

'Very.'

'I've got a question for you,' he said, sipping more of the

delicious sake. 'Who are the Happy Foxes?'

'Very famous,' he said. 'They are celebrity bodyguards. They give protection to pop stars at events and nightclubs. Japanese fans are famously obsessive.'

'I could have told you that,' whispered Kuda, in his ear.

He turned to her. 'I'm sorry, I suppose you could have,' he said. 'So you're a bodyguard to the stars?'

'It's just showbiz,' she said,. 'It's not enough to be good at your job. You have to look good too.' She smiled. 'So what is your story, Englishman?'

'The standard one. Boy meets girl, boy loses girl.'

'I know that story well. I like the beginning part very much.'

Jim wondered where Jane was. She was probably forty thousand feet up in the air on her way back to Virginia, or in a bar somewhere with one of the SEALs, laughing about blowing stuff up.

'What about the boy loses girl part?' he said.

'That bit can be fun too.'

Jim picked up a roasted giant sea snail. It tasted like a grilled action figure but he could kind of imagine it might be really tasty to a starving person. 'So what did you think about today's bit of action?'

She seemed to consider a couple of different replies. 'If we don't get thrown in jail, we will definitely be able to put our fees up.' She swished her hair. Jim wondered what the tattoos appearing from under her outfit did below the line.

He took out his sat phone. There was still no message from Jane. He switched it off.

The professor was talking animatedly to his Happy Fox. They seemed very close.

Kuda threw him a talk to me look.

'So you don't mind unhappy endings?' he said.

'The end of one story is the beginning of another,' she said.

The waiter was topping up Jim's box of sake. He wondered why Jane couldn't at least ping him an SMS. The simplest explanation was that she didn't give a damn. 'Do you believe that the simplest answer to a tricky question is the right one?' he asked Kuda.

She batted her beautiful eyes at him. 'No,' she said.

'That's good,' he said, switching the phone back on in the hope that when it synched up a delayed message might suddenly beam down to him. The phone was running on its 3G circuit, or so it told him, so it was acting like a normal phone. The signal bars pulsed.

Nothing.

'You're sad,' she said, taking his hand.

'Jetlag.'

'Let's go for a drink after dinner,' said Kuda. 'My favourite bar is at the top of the Park Hyatt.'

'I'm staying there.'

'Wow,' she said. 'That is very convenient.'

A huddle of wealthy young Tokyoites were waiting to be seated at the bar's reception desk and a long line snaked back to the elevators. Kuda, with Jim in tow, waltzed past it and they were ushered straight to a table. The bar was a giant glasshouse suspended in the clouds, an uplit cavernous space with interesting shadows. Jim liked the sciencefiction film-set atmosphere. Rain ran down the panes, sparkling like diamonds rolling over a mirror.

They were assailed by a bevy of waiters who fawned on her and, by reflection, him. She took off her tiny jacket, revealing a crazy sleeve tattoo of psychedelic undergrowth on her right arm. It was beautifully drawn, not the clumsy scribbling of the normal tattooist.

A bottle of Dom Pérignon Enotica appeared and was poured. She leant forwards so that her long soft hair touched the side of his face. 'So what do you do when you are not having shoot-outs in Tokyo?'

'I save the world.' He smiled cheekily. 'You know the kind of thing.'

'To saving the world!' She raised her glass. '*Campai!*'

There was still light in the love-hotel bedroom. Akira's eyes were accustoming fast and he could see more than her shape. They had stopped kissing and now she was taking his shirt off. He stood frozen. She would see his stunted arm in its awful naked state, the full horror of a hand reaching out where an arm ought to be. The dream would end. With every move she made to undress him he felt as if his skin was being flayed.

As she pulled the shirt off him she was kissing his neck. He was rigid with tension as he waited for the inevitable signal of revulsion. His shirt was on the ground. She was kissing the fingers of his short hand. A shiver streamed through his whole body. No one had ever kissed it before, and from her lips he experienced hot shocks of pain and pleasure.

He took her around the waist and lowered her onto the bed. He was enveloped in sensation and his reason had left him. All he could feel was her; all he could hear was her breath.

'No,' said Jim, swaying down the corridor. 'You can't come in. I've got to be up in four hours and heading for Narita.'

Kuda didn't reply, just giggled in the way Japanese women did to please their men. She stopped him and they kissed. 'I won't stay long,' she said.

She felt so good in his arms. Her perfume lured him; her lips made love to his. She was pressing herself against him, and he could feel himself heading quickly to the point at which he would be unable to resist. 'Look,' he said, 'that's my room down the hall and I'm very sad to say I'm going in there on my own. I have my reasons and you can probably guess them.' He smiled sheepishly. 'They don't make much sense to me right now, but I have to do the right thing. You understand?'

She flicked his nose. 'OK,' she said. 'Your loss.'

'Yes,' he said. 'I'm sure of that.' He made for the door, hoping for a clean getaway. He was having trouble finding his room key. When he looked back, she was gone.

Idiot, he thought. We were thirty seconds away from a mind-blowing fuck.

His fingers registered the old-style metal key. He slotted it into the lock. There was a click. He pushed in against the strong door spring, struggling to extract the key.

The lights were on. No doubt the bed was turned back and a little chocolate was waiting for him on his pillow.

He started.

Jane was in the bed, reading a book. She looked up. 'What kept you?'

Jim took a moment to collect his thoughts. He suddenly felt a bit too drunk to think straight. 'I was drowning my sorrows.'

'What sorrows?'

'My baby left me high and dry.'

'Too bad,' she said.

'What are you doing here?'

'I'm not here – I'm at the embassy. Coming here would be a dumb-ass thing to do.'

'Right.' He focused. 'I'm having a shower.'

'Good idea.'

63

Jim saw the professor waiting outside Virgin check-in on the concourse. He looked unusually relaxed and happy.

'Good morning, Evans-san.' He smiled boyishly. 'Now to finish our historic quest.'

'That's a hell of a long cab ride to the airport,' said Jim.

'You look very cheerful today, Evans-san.'

'Really? I don't know why – I've only had about an hour's sleep.'

Narita airport was a paragon of efficiency, and in a few minutes, they were going through the formalities of leaving Japan.

There was a parade of luxury stores inside the airport but he knew buying anything for Jane was pointless. For one thing he had no idea when he was going to see her again. His head was throbbing. He found himself in a shop selling strange candies. 'These are very famous,' said Akira. 'Rice cakes.'

Jim squinted at the boxes and their exotic contents. 'Rice cakes?'

'Very delicious,' said Akira.

'Let's buy some for Stafford,' said Jim, and wondered what his butler would make of them.

'He will enjoy them, I'm sure.'

The Virgin lounge at Narita continued the Austin Powers theme that had started in London and seemed to complement Jim's mild hangover. He was eating a sausage butty and the professor was regarding his sushi as if he had to show it a little respect before he consumed it.

'So,' said Jim, swallowing a mouthful, 'we get in first thing in the morning, go straight home, pick up the items and take them straight to your embassy on Piccadilly.'

'It opens at ten but they will not be expecting us. I can't trust anyone but you with the plan.' Akira sipped his green tea.

'I have no idea where Stafford's stashed them,' said Jim, 'but they must be relatively handy. The sooner we get hold of them the better. They know you at the embassy, right?'

'I will show them my letter if there is any delay,' said Akira. 'Once we are through the front door I think we are safe.'

'I disagree,' said Jim. 'Once we've handed it over properly, we're home and dry, but on the wrong side of the counter we may as well be out on the street.'

Kim sat at the back of the small HS-125 jet. They were refuelling. Damascus had stayed open for him and military fuel was being pumped into the tanks. His masters had friends, and their friends were only too happy to oblige him.

He had refused pain relief from his doctors in Tokyo. He didn't want anything dulling his mind, and the pain in his ribs would spur him on. The nurse sat forwards in the galley and awaited his command, but no man had ever died from bruised ribs.

The mirror and the sword had not yet been returned. He would smash his enemies into a pulp and take Kusanagi and the Yata no Kagami.

The banks were calling his office incessantly as his stock price had failed to recover from its collapse. Rumours of the incident at his office had spread like wildfire, and the gossip was as bad as any front page headline. To some extent, he had managed to hush it but... The mirage of his invincibility had vanished. He had to get the remaining pieces of regalia or he was finished. Even one item would be enough to buy him out of his dire financial situation. If he could get both, his riches and power would multiply.

It was a desperate gambit, but it had to work. Otherwise his life was over. His best men awaited him in London.

Jane was reviewing her email on the floor of the transport plane. She would have preferred a seat, but the floor would do. She had enjoyed the first hour or two but now her butt needed something less Spartan. When she'd had enough of the hard floor, she would go for a walk and talk to the pilots. These days, some of them knew her by reputation and that was a buzz.

The trouble was, a question kept popping up in her mind, and no matter how she thought about it or responded to it, it wouldn't go away. It was like a furious itch that wouldn't be banished by scratching.

The conundrum lay somewhere between: What the hell am I going to do with Jim? and What the hell am I meant to do with Jim?

Ranking officers had husbands and wives and they lived the army life. It was a comfortable, normal American existence in happy, well kept communities. They went to church and followed college sports. They had barbecues and drank beer. They did charity work, and held garage sales. They wore T-shirts, shorts and flip flops.

Normal expectations didn't intersect with the Jim-world. She was having the kind of does-not-compute moments that guys had with her.

Going any further down the road with him would rip her world apart. He wouldn't turn into some dim, gentle, shrugging guy taking care of business while she shot off around the world blowing shit up. He wouldn't be sweating the money and the kids' education. How was she going to be in charge with him, Mr freakin' Billionaire, successor-designate to the legendary Max Davas, the US Treasury's own financial market manipulator?

If she committed to Jim she'd end up heading straight at a hell she had spent her whole adult life avoiding: the idea of a family being a guy and his little wife.

She knew what her mom would say – she could even hear her voice in her head: 'Don't be a fool! What are you waiting for? You love him, so what's the issue?'

She knew what her dad would say too: 'Duh! I mean, you don't want him? That strikes me as not the smartest thought you've ever had.'

When she had saved Jim's skin in the Congo, she had felt much closer to him. Now he had done the same for her in Tokyo, she felt out of control.

She was staring at her email stack, her eyes unfocused. She blinked, then scanned the plane's no-nonsense skeletal interior. Stripped down was good. Complicated was bad. Her thing with Jim was complicated. *Ergo…*

She wished she had a stick of gum to chew. It would help her think.

Maybe the next time they were together the whole thing would resolve itself. She closed the Apple Airbook, got up and walked towards the flight deck.

Stafford came into the lounge where Smith was watching the television. 'It would appear from this cryptic message that Jim will be back in the morning.'

'Really?' said Smith. 'Can I see?'

'If you must.'

'"Get the tea on,"' he read out. 'Very cryptic.'

'I thought so,' said Stafford.

'Do you think he got Jane out?'

'I would imagine so,' said Stafford, 'or his message would not have been so flippant.'

'I could find out – what do you think?'

'Can we wait to hear it from Jim himself?'

'I'm expecting full disclosure, you know,' said Smith, as if it was a punishment.

'I remember.'

'And London is still crawling with Far Eastern miscreants,' Smith goaded.

'I don't doubt you,' said Stafford.

'I hope your explanations are going to live up to my expectations.'

Stafford closed his eyes. 'I can't possibly guess.'

Smith made an exasperated grumbling noise, then perked up. 'You wouldn't have a beer hidden away somewhere would you, Bert– Stafford?'

'I'm sure I can find one.'

Akira appeared at the end of Jim's Upper Class cubicle. Jim pushed the monitor to one side.

'Evans-san, can I speak with you?'

'Sure,' said Jim, taking his foot off the little seat at the end of his plastic and leather clad capsule.

Akira sat down. 'I want to ask you something.' He pulled out his mobile. He opened it and started hitting buttons with his thumb. He registered something and smiled. He turned the phone around and showed it to Jim. It was the Happy Fox he had been chatting with all night at the restaurant. 'Is she not very beautiful?'

'Very,' said Jim.

'Her name is Mitso.'

'Nice.'

'I'm not a man of the world like you, Evans-san. I am an

academic and a cripple.'

The word 'cripple' rang harshly in Jim's ear.

'Do you think she and I can be together?' said Akira.

'I don't know,' said Jim. 'Does she like you?'

'Yes,' he said. 'More than I could have hoped for.'

Jim was struggling to put the right question. Eventually he came up with 'Was she still liking you this morning?'

'Yes.'

'Well,' said Jim, 'that's OK, then. If she likes you that much, there's no reason she won't carry on liking you.'

Akira took the phone back and pressed a button with his thumb. 'The Happy Foxes are very famous celebrity outlaws,' he said, showing Jim a glimpse of another picture, this time with Mitso posing by a large custom bike.

'Does that mean trouble?' asked Jim, as Akira showed him another image of Mitso pulled from the Internet.

'For me, yes. For her, no.' Akira flipped to another picture.

Mitso wasn't wearing much in the glamour shot Akira showed him next.

'Don't expect me to be any help,' said Jim. 'My love life's a disaster.'

'But Jane-san is your wonderful sweetheart,' said Akira, suddenly concerned.

'Yes,' said Jim.

'And you heroically rescued her from the evil man Kim.'

Jim sighed, 'Well, that's all well and *manga*, but the reality is, Professor, that I'm here and she isn't.'

Akira nodded. 'I feel that loss for the first time myself.' He clutched his chest. 'It is a heavy sensation.'

Jim took the phone from Akira and looked at the next picture he had selected. Mitso was skimpily clad in leather pants with a tight T-shirt and was again draped over some alien motorbike. The professor clearly had no clue what he was getting himself into. 'Nice motorbike,' he said.

'Would you like to see more?'

Jim stifled a sigh. 'Sure – how many have you got?'

'Many.'

64

Kim looked at the plans with the captain, who was also called Kim. Captain Kim was far too old to be an army captain any more. He had been working in the organisation for fifteen years and was the key man in Europe. He was responsible for kidnapping in Britain, Holland, Germany and France, and his success and skill had reflected on his clan's prosperity in the deep countryside of North Korea. His sons were in China as a result of his boss's patronage. He had sold his life and those of the people he took for the sake of his children. He believed any man in his place would have done the same. One day the impossible might happen and he might escape, but while his family and village depended on his absolute obedience that was just a tantalising dream.

His boss perused the plans. 'I don't understand this man. It is not a normal house, it is a fortress.'

'It is the house of a very rich man,' said Captain Kim.

'But so young,' he shook his head, 'too young.'

Captain Kim didn't reply. He waited for the boss to finish his inspection of the plans.

'Can you not just break the front wall down with a truck?'

Captain Kim waited for a respectful moment. 'That might work but these are very solid walls and we would need to push away any parked cars in front before the ramming assault. If the truck did not breach the frontage, the attack would be over and thwarted.'

'An explosion will bring attention quickly.'

Captain Kim nodded. 'Yes. We have six minutes to execute

the operation.'

Kim stood slightly stooped – his ribs were aching. He looked gravely at the captain. The banks were demanding meetings and Toyoda had reported that they were beginning to threaten foreclosure. He had no alternative but to risk it all on a desperate plan. 'You must bring them to me alive.'

The captain took a deep breath. If what he said turned out to be wrong it could prove disastrous. If he was right, it might save the whole risky endeavour. 'Sir, I believe the items you seek are in the house.'

Kim whirled round to face him, pain shooting through his torso. 'How so?'

'We have observed, and we believe the old servant brought the items to the house from their hiding place at a moneylender's. Our watcher had no opportunity to strike.'

'Are you sure of this?'

'No, sir, but I believe it to be highly likely.'

Kim scowled. 'This changes everything. You must do all you can to recover the items. Beyond this, the people inside have no value.' He looked at Captain Kim, his face implacable. 'I cannot instruct you further. You must and will succeed.'

The captain nodded.

'If you succeed,' said Kim, 'it will be a happy day for all of us.'

The captain knew there would be a terrible punishment for failure, but so many provisional death warrants hung over his head that the threat meant nothing. He wondered for the thousandth time whether killing his master might be the real solution to his living hell.

65

It was five and the sun was about to rise. It was dark in the cavernous warehouse. Strip lights illuminated the space, throwing long shadows. Kim stood in front of his men. He could see the fear in their eyes. They were unnerved by what they had to do. They were going to the lion's den a second time and they had no choice.

Not only did he hold their lives in his hands but also the lives of their families in North Korea. They had heard how relatives disappeared when Kim was displeased. They knew, too, why their families had survived the famines and dire conditions of their country. Their families fed while others didn't. Their wives receive Party rations because they were Kim's soldiers. Every three years when they returned home on leave, they brought back money and things that made them heroes in their villages. They were heroes of their nation – so long as they did whatever Kim asked.

Kim knew they feared him more than death. He made sure of it. He knew they understood that what they did was terrible and he knew they did it for their own survival. Now his own survival hung in the balance. Many times in the past there had been moments when failure would have destroyed him. Those moments had often been followed by long periods of success.

'Men, today you will attack the house again and bring back what I require. You will not fail and I will reward you well. You will not fail and your loved ones will bless your name. You will not fail and your country will praise you. You will not fail.'

'We will not fail,' shouted the captain.

'We will not fail,' echoed the men.

The troop saluted.

Smith heard the doorbell, grabbed the machine pistol and rolled off the bed fully clothed. He didn't mind sleeping dressed – it was better than having to fight barefoot and naked. He had taken the mickey out of Stafford – fancy waiting for a blitzkrieg in dressing-gown and pyjamas! – but the old spy wasn't having any of his teasing. He seemed prepared to die a gentleman in his PJs rather than lie down to sleep in his day clothes.

Stafford must already have been up because he was at the door surveying the scene outside on his iPhone. 'Is everything clear?' said Stafford, into the intercom.

'Yeah, no problem,' came Jim's voice.

Stafford seemed to weigh his new pistol in his grip for a second, then opened the door. Smith was aiming his machine pistol into the space that would be filled by a sudden rush of attackers.

Jim and Akira walked in, lugging their bags.

Stafford hurried them along and closed the door smartly.

Jim patted Stafford on the back, then caught sight of Smith. 'John, what are you doing here?'

'Playing Davy Crockett at the Alamo. What about Jane?'

'We got her back.'

'Excellent,' said Stafford, spontaneously.

'Well done,' said Smith. He came forwards and took Akira's heavy bag. 'Now I'm expecting some explanations.'

'I've got the Japanese Crown Jewels,' said Jim. 'They've been lost for a few hundred years and we've got to get them back to the Emperor.'

Smith looked at him sourly, 'For fuck's sake, Jim, when are you going to let me in? This is no joke.'

Jim pushed past him, grinning.

Stafford flexed his right eyebrow sardonically.

'The situation is still very dangerous,' said Akira.

Smith's face showed that he was having difficulty in accepting this. Akira stared blankly at him.

Smith turned and followed Jim into the lounge. 'You're not serious, are you?'

Jim sat down in front of his computer and fired up his email. 'They aren't some bunch of rocks and gold stuck with fur,' he said, opening a window to look at Kimcorp's share price. 'They're like the embodiment of the spirit of Japan. One is like King Arthur's Excalibur, and another is a mirror the sun goddess thought was so beautiful she came out of a sulk for it. They would have paid me a trillion dollars for them if I'd asked.' He clicked his mouse. He had made money closing his Kimcorp short position and the price was still in the toilet. 'But we've got to give them back. They're toxic.' He turned to Stafford. 'Where are they?'

'Here.'

'Here?' said Jim.

'Yes.'

Akira looked excited.

'And there is a reason for that?'

'Yes.'

'OK,' said Jim. 'And the reason is?'

'I felt that putting them into someone else's safe keeping might not, in the end, prove sensible. I thought they might be expropriated.'

'Right,' said Jim. 'I have no idea what you're talking about.'

'I thought about lodging them at the Bank of England,' continues Stafford, 'but as the regalia are worth many times our gold reserve I thought better of it. Lodging them in a pawn shop also seemed rather too basic a solution. I have no wish to see the regalia nationalised, purloined or seized.'

'Where are they?'

'Under my bed.'

Jim shook his jetlagged head. 'Whatever. Can you bring them down? When the clock hits nine we're going to make a run for the Japanese Embassy.'

'A trillion dollars?' said Smith.

'Excuse me,' said Akira, 'but you asked for a hundred billion dollars."

'Would you have paid more?'

'It's difficult to know,' replied Akira.

'I think that's a yes,' said Jim.

'Possibly,' shrugged Akira.

'So,' continued Jim, 'this Korean property guy, who must have been tipped off, kidnapped Jane to swap her with me for the jewels.'

'Why didn't you tell me?' said Smith.

'Wait,' said Jim. 'Forget the jewels. Think of the money. A hundred billion dollars, five hundred billion, a trillion. Do you think your life or my life or ten thousand other lives wouldn't be sacrificed for that? If someone else had got hold of the regalia we would have never got Jane back. It wouldn't matter if it was the Japanese mob, your bosses, the CIA or Stafford's lot. Jane would have been dead by now and probably all of us too.'

Smith didn't seem very happy.

'If I'd told you and you'd reported back, we'd be swarming with yet more killers wanting to get their hands on a trillion dollars.' He fixed Smith with a stare. 'John, just think. We're dealing with hundreds of billions of pounds and they're ready for the taking by whoever is prepared to go no holds barred.'

'I don't believe any of it,' said Smith.

Stafford came in carrying the sword and a bag containing the mirror.

Smith scowled. 'A hundred billion?' he said.

'A trillion.'

Smith took the bag, opened it and looked inside. 'You must think I'm stupid,' he said, taking out the sword and passing the bag to Stafford.

'Don't worry, mate,' said Jim. 'It's all going to be sorted today.'

'It'd better be,' said Smith, 'and when it's all over if you don't tell me the real story I'm going to arrest all of you under our delightful anti-terrorist laws and keep you locked up till you explain in triplicate every last detail of what's been going on. Even then I might not let you out.'

'I take it I'm excused that,' said Stafford.

'Don't be too sure.'

Jim looked at his gold Rolex Cosmonaut. It was seven a.m. Japan's stock market closed. 'Boom.' He was looking at the crashing share chart. Kimcorp's had sagged further in the closing minutes.

Stafford was looking at his iPhone. 'Oh dear,' he said.

66

There was a terrific explosion outside and the lounge door blew open. A blast wave compressed the room and Jim and Akira were hurled to the ground. Jim struggled to his feet and Smith thrust the sword into his hand. Stafford was already at the door. Akira scrambled up, clasping the mirror that Stafford had handed him.

There was a thud at their feet as Smith threw two pistols to them from a holdall. He dragged the bag to the door as they heard a burst of fire in the hallway.

There was a whirr of servos and Jim turned to the window. The new bulletproof installation was lowering.

'Stafford thinks we should go this way – out the back and along the shoreline,' said Jim.

Akira's head flicked from side to side to the noise of gunfire.

There was more firing in the hall.

Jim ran to the window. The exposed foreshore was empty.

He guessed Stafford thought it was better for them to run for it rather than be penned inside. Had he had time to check the CCTV?

The window wasn't lowering fast enough, so Jim jumped up on its thick rim and vaulted over. He took the pouch from Akira, turned on the ledge and jumped the eight feet down to the shingle below. He landed lightly, stayed in his crouch and looked upstream to where a stone staircase led up to an alley that in turn led to the road that ran past the front of the house.

Gunfire cracked to his left.

Akira jumped down with a grunt and scrabbled upright.

'You OK?' asked Jim.

'Enough.'

'When are your people coming?' shouted Stafford to Smith.

'Forget it.'

'Forget it?' shouted Stafford, as he fired at a flicker of movement.

'No one's going to wade into a full-scale war zone,' Smith shouted. 'They'll hold back and cordon everything off.'

'Get behind the stairs. There's a door there. Then cover me,' shouted Stafford, taking a pot shot. He took a mini-gun and fired in bursts as Smith dashed down the hall dragging the holdall.

Stafford took out his phone. The screen was smashed. 'Damn,' he muttered, dropping it. He ran up the hall after Smith, firing randomly behind him as he went. 'Open the door,' he ordered Smith. 'It leads to the garage. When I get to the bottom, follow me, then hold your position. Once the car's running, get in.' Stafford ducked through the open doorway and staggered down the narrow staircase as fast as he could.

Smith opened fire down the corridor to suppress any attempt to charge it. As soon as Stafford had cleared the stairs, he swung the bag down with a crash and jumped after it, slamming the door behind him.

He found Stafford climbing into the Maybach. Smith waited for him to start the engine, then ran with the bag and jumped into the back seat. The limo doors locked. He poured the weaponry into the back footwell, then slid through the gap between the seats into the front.

'I do hope Jim and the professor took my advice to go out

the back,' said Stafford, watching the garage doors shiver into action. 'And I really do hope the makers of this car did a proper job.'

'Amen,' said Smith, putting on his seat belt.

Stafford turned off the airbags and waited for the doors to lift, his right eye particularly engaged. 'Off we go,' he said, pressing hard on the accelerator.

Jim froze in the dark shadows of the alley. He could hear his garage doors opening. He snatched a glance around the corner. A dozen men, dressed in black, were running around outside and crouched to fire at whatever came out of the basement car park.

Was Stafford coming for him or making a break for it? He ducked back. Akira was looking out of the darkness in the other direction at a large white truck. Jim could hear its engine running. He felt a tug under his arm. Akira had pulled Kusanagi out of its scabbard. 'What are you doing?' said Jim, as the professor marched out into the street.

There was a screech of tyres coming out of the garage and Jim ran after Akira.

The Maybach surged onto the road under a hail of bullets and ploughed straight into three crouching men. The rest scattered as the car reversed back and around, smashing another to the ground.

Smith glimpsed Jim and Akira running at the truck. 'Jim needs a diversion,' he shouted.

Stafford put the car into drive and accelerated at three more men who were firing frantically into the limousine. The bulletproof windscreen was covered with divots, cracks and crazing. 'Getting hard to see,' he muttered, swerving to hit a figure in black. There was a series of thumps and crunches as bullets rattled down the side of the car.

Akira jumped up to the cab's open window and drove Kusanagi through the gap, impaling the unsuspecting driver's head, like a toothpick penetrating an olive. He pulled the door open and the quivering body of the driver fell out. Akira jumped in and Jim followed.

'You drive,' said Akira. 'I never learnt.' He slid the sword back into its scabbard.

Jim was sitting in a puddle of blood. He slammed the cab door, put the truck into gear and dropped the handbrake. He was going to have to flatten the remaining cordon of men and somehow miss the Maybach, which was swerving back and forth like a dodgem car.

'Get down,' he told Akira, who didn't seem to hear. He pulled away from the kerb and floored the accelerator.

'Jim's in the lorry!' shouted Smith. 'For fuck's sake, don't crash into it.'

'Right,' snapped Stafford, reversing. He started up the road towards the truck, which was setting off towards them. The remaining black-clad men were running, some towards the truck, some into the house, others away down the road.

Two armed men were making straight for Jim. They seemed oblivious as to who was driving the truck and waved him down. He saw horror in their eyes as they registered his face. There was a bang as he ran them down, then the hideous thumping of objects being crushed beneath the wheels.

Akira looked up from the GPS. 'There is only one saved location on the navigation computer,' he said calmly, 'and we are going there to end this.' He set the course.

'No,' said Jim. 'Let's hole up somewhere and get to the

embassy when it opens.'

'We must kill Kim, or the cloud of death will always hang on our horizons.'

'How do we even know he's there?'

'I know he is there,' said Akira, clutching the sword. 'I can smell him.'

Jim gripped the wheel of the truck and pushed himself down into the padded seat. 'Buckle up, then,' he said.

His mobile was ringing. When he glanced at the screen he recognised Smith's number. When he answered, Stafford's voice spoke: 'Where are you?'

'Heading for Dagenham,' said Jim.

'Turn around,' said Stafford.

He looked at Akira, holding Kusanagi in his short hand. His face bore an expression of grim determination.

'No,' said Jim. 'We're going on. Akira seems to think he knows where Kim is. You get safe.'

'Where are you going in Dagenham?'

Akira read out the address.

Smith was trying to enter their new destination into the inbuilt console of the Maybach.

'Exactly where is this police cordon?' snapped Stafford.

'How the fuck should I know?' Smith was still struggling.

'Allow me,' said Stafford, taking the console controller.

Something came loose under the car and there was a banging noise as it bounced away. Smith looked in the wing mirror and saw a severed arm lying in the road.

He turned round to peer through the cracked, splintered windscreen. 'Can you see where you're going, Bertie?'

'Just about.'

Jim entered the East London link tunnel just as three police cars, lights flashing and sirens blaring, steamed out of the tunnel in the other direction. A minute later they raced past the Maybach.

'Exactly how many shot-to-pieces limousines do your lot see in a day?' said Stafford.

Smith shook his head sourly.

'What a complete shower,' added Stafford.

'Convenient in the circumstances, though,' retorted Smith.

Jim's phone rang and he picked it up from the seat, covered with blood. It was Jane – she sounded sleepy.

'Jane, what time is it there?'

'About three. I was just thinking… What's that noise?'

'I'm in a lorry.'

'Lorry? Right. Anyway, I was thinking, thinking a lot… Maybe we shouldn't – You're in a truck?' Her voice was suddenly awake. 'Are you OK?'

'What were you going to say?'

'Nothing.'

'Were you going to blow me out?'

There was a silence.

'At eight o'clock in the morning after I just saved your life?'

'Are you OK?'

'Apart from sitting in a pool of someone else's blood, just having had my house blown up, I'm absolutely peachy.'

Akira was looking at him intently.

'I love you,' she said.

'That's better – much better. And don't say "but". I love you too.' He hung up.

'Seven minutes,' said Akira, reading the time to destination from the GPS. '*Banzai*,' he said.

'Seven minutes to Banzai,' said Jim. He laughed, a note of insanity in his mirth.

'Evans-san, will you tell my father?' said Akira.

'Tell him what?'

'Tell him of our adventure if I cannot myself.'

'Yes,' said Jim, suddenly sober again. 'Remember, as my nan used to say, that there is no challenge too big or problem too large that you can't turn on your heels and run away like a rabbit.'

'No, Evans-san. We must go on.'

'This better have a happy ending,' said Smith, putting his phone away. 'Half of London's being closed down because of it.'

'Happy ending?' snorted Stafford. 'I think that's highly unlikely.'

Smith was fetching guns and ammunition from the rear footwells and stuffing his pocket with clips. 'This is for you,' he said, putting magazines into the armrest cup-holders.

'Thank you,' said Stafford, sticking two magazines in his breast pocket. 'Could you reload this?' He passed Smith his machine pistol.

Smith changed the magazine and gave it back. 'All set.'

The GPS said three minutes to destination.

Fifty yards ahead at the end of the cul-de-sac there was a red-brick warehouse. Its top half was constructed of corrugated iron and so was its slanting roof. Two dirty windows above a wide grey shutter gave the building a primitive face. It scowled down at them, its cheeks tattooed with graffiti.

'You going to ring the doorbell?' Jim asked Akira.

'*Banzai!*' yelled Akira, brandishing the sword.

Jim knew what he meant. '*Banzai!*' he roared. He stamped on the accelerator and the lorry jolted forwards. Thirty miles an hour should do it, he thought. He didn't want to hit the shutter too hard. It loomed large as they hit twenty-five and

Jim braced himself at the wheel. The cab shook violently as it struck the entrance, ripping the roll-up and its frame from the brickwork. He trod hard on the brakes and the shutter crashed to the ground.

He looked into the warehouse through the cracked windscreen, his eyes accustoming to the gloom. There was another shutter fifty feet ahead. He stamped on the accelerator and set off to ram it.

Kim jumped up from his chair. He was alone, and if he stayed in the office above the warehouse he would be trapped. There was a truck downstairs – he would use it to escape. He ran for the metal staircase and tore down it as fast as the shooting pains in his chest would let him. He was gasping for breath as he sprinted across the dusty concrete towards the vehicle.

There was a crash at the inner door – he glanced over his shoulder. It was stoved in. From the other side he could hear the roaring of a large vehicle manoeuvring.

He was finding it hard to see, but still he ran with all his strength. There was another crash behind him.

'Fuck, fuck, fuck,' shouted Jim, reversing again. '*Banzai!*' he bellowed, flooring the accelerator once more.

This time the lorry burst into the main warehouse in a shower of broken metal.

'Kim!' shouted Akira, pointing.

Jim saw the man make the final feet to the lorry fifty yards away.

'Get out,' said Akira. 'Get out, Evans-san. I will finish this.'

'But you can't drive.'

'I can drive enough for this. Go now.'

Jim grabbed the mirror and jumped out of the cab.

Akira was in the driving seat, one hand on the wheel and

Kusanagi drawn in the other.

Kim's lorry jerked forwards, and Jim stepped back as Akira set off.

Kim stared at the truck in front of him. It was his men's but Evans had got out and was running for the stairs to the mezzanine level. Kim's pistol was between his legs on the seat.

His men's smashed-up truck was coming straight at him. They were on a collision course.

Jim was racing up the metal staircase. He was suddenly very exposed. If Akira didn't manage to crash into Kim he'd get mown down himself. On top of that there might be people in the offices above.

'Oh, shit!' he exclaimed. Kim was heading his way. If he avoided Akira, he was going to plough straight into the stairway. He took the stairs three at a time.

Akira's mouth was open in horror. The truck wasn't responding to his swerve. It felt as if something was stuck, stopping it turning fully. The ramming had damaged the steering and as he yanked down on the wheel it failed to veer far enough to the left. Kim's cab passed his.

Kim crashed into the staircase just as Jim reached the top, the whole gantry shaking and twisting with the blow. Jim cried out as he lost his footing and fell, rolling backwards like a ball down the shattered stairs and onto the roof of Kim's truck.

He opened his eyes and gazed up at the ceiling, spreadeagled. His phone was ringing. It stopped. He rolled onto his side. A truck was heading straight for him. The truck below him shifted and the jolt forced him onto his back again. He felt the impact of the collision, which threw him across the roof of the truck. He was hanging off the side now, dazed and bleeding.

His mind was operating automatically. He was hanging in a tight space between the side of a truck and a wall. If the vehicle set off again, it could easily squash him against the brickwork and crush the life out of him. He heaved himself back onto the roof with a grunt.

Kim tried to reverse but the trucks were locked together. He grabbed his pistol and jumped out of the cab as Akira leapt down, the sword in his short hand. 'Cripple! You brought a sword to a gun fight,' he sneered.

Akira was screaming as he ran at him.

Kim aimed and pulled the trigger. He had forgotten to take the safety off. He felt a sharp blow on his wrist, followed by a burning sensation that flowed like an electric shock up his arm. His hand fell to the ground, the pistol in it. He bent down to it and saw a flash of white light like a magnesium flare that dazzled him. He knew something had happened but couldn't think what.

He felt himself falling, the world spinning as he fell. A rush of despair and desolation filled his soul. He felt pain as his head hit the concrete but he couldn't feel his body. He tried to move, and felt nothing but the quiver of his tongue and a wet trail of saliva slide from his mouth.

He saw Akira's shoes and the tip of the sword Kusanagi. A dusty fleck of cardboard blew past his eyes as they blinked one last time.

Akira turned as the Maybach screeched into the warehouse.

Jim stumbled across the roof of Kim's truck and lowered himself down at the far end. His body was burning as if he had been skinned and covered with salt. He dropped the two feet to the ground and crumpled, but forced himself upright and limped to the rear of the other truck.

Stafford was aiming at him. 'Jim!' he exclaimed. 'Thank God.'

Akira turned to him, the sword Kusanagi in hand. 'Where is the Yata no Kagami?'

'Fuck knows,' gasped Jim. He looked about wildly. 'Up there – on the gangway.'

'I'll get it,' said Smith. He vaulted onto the cab of the truck, scrambled up the mangled metal staircase, picked up the mirror and deftly climbed down.

Jim looked at the decapitated body of Kim. It was a truly ugly sight. Then he looked at Akira who was wiping the blade of Kusanagi with a brown wool cloth. 'Let's get going,' he said, as a wave of dizziness passed through him.

Akira took the scabbard from the cab and slid the sword into it.

Jim hobbled to the Maybach and got in. There was ammunition all over the place. He sat down and closed the door. Akira got in, followed by Stafford and Smith.

'How are we going to get to the Japanese Embassy?' said Jim.

'May I look at that sword?' asked Smith.

Akira passed it to him.

Smith pulled it a little from its scabbard. There was a glint in his eye. He pushed it back and handed it to Akira. 'I'm sure I can arrange an escort even with half of London under siege.'

'Great,' said Jim, slowly getting his wind back.

'No thanks to any of you, of course,' added Smith. 'I have one condition, however.'

'What?'

'My superiors get the biggest thank-you note in the history of East–West relations, because otherwise my career is well and truly over.'

'Yes,' said Akira, as the car pulled away. 'You have my word.'

Smith took out his phone and dialled.

The outrider cavalcade picked them up on the A13 and ferried them through central London as if no one else was meant to be on the streets. Jim was impressed by how little explanation Smith had been called upon to give. His conversations were limited to 'I'm sorry, that's classified.'

Jim SMSed Jane: **Everyone's fine. Will call later.** He wondered if he had been a bit premature.

At last they were outside the Japanese Embassy in Piccadilly. Akira got out, ran around the rear of the bullet-riddled car, then up the stairs and into the building. Armed policemen ringed the door.

'I'll be in touch,' said Smith, getting out.

'Where to now?' said Jim.

'The Dorchester,' said Stafford, pulling away with the escort. 'I've booked suites.'

'I could do with a drink,' said Jim.

'Perhaps I might take you to lunch at my club in Herbert Crescent. The walk will do you good.'

67

Bowing, Akira held out the sword to the Emperor, who passed the mirror to his private secretary. He was smiling broadly. His eyes were sparkling as he took Kusanagi. 'This is a moment of destiny,' he said, drawing the sword. The small crowd gasped and applauded.

The Emperor examined the blade. 'So, the sacred grass cutter is returned and with it our fate is changed.' He slid the sword back into its scabbard and handed it, too, to his private secretary, who laid it on a cushion on a low table.

The Emperor's special adviser stepped forwards.

'Professor Nakabashi, Japan thanks you for your heroic recovery of our national treasures. We cannot thank you or your helpers enough.'

Akira felt there was something ominous about this statement.

'Please pass our gratitude on to them,' continued the adviser.

'Certain important niceties are required to avoid embarrassment,' said Akira.

'Of course, but we cannot risk difficulties,' said the adviser, smiling pleasantly.

'Professor Nakabashi and his English friend must be given what they deserve,' said the Emperor.

'Evans-san is a connoisseur of antiquities, is he not?' said the adviser.

'*Hi*,' said Akira.

'Then we should make exquisite copies of the regalia so that he can enjoy a memento of his part in this great story.'

'*Hi*,' said Akira, and bowed with a smile. 'I will arrange it.'

The adviser glanced at the sword Kusanagi. He looked excited and, in a strange way, hungry.

68

The priest unwrapped the parcel slowly, making sure not to crack or split the ancient paper. He laid it out and opened the inner box. He cut the string holding the gold bar and took it out. He put the sword into the box and closed it, then wrapped the paper round it again. His old gnarled fingers were shaking as he fastened the package with a faded silk ribbon.

The return of the Sword of the Gathering Clouds of Heaven was an awesome event. Japan's warrior spirit was set to return. Gone would be the days of pacifism and peace. He could not help shedding a tear, whether in happiness or sadness he did not know.

He took out his phone from his robes and read the *haiku* from the chief priest at the Meji temple.

The lost reflections
Returned from far away
Show us all once more

The old priest considered sending him a scroll of calligraphy in reply.

69

Stafford was regarding the construction work with mute concentration. In his right hand he held the tightly rolled blueprints. 'It would be much quicker if you didn't want such a complicated facility in the basement.'

'The submarine dock?'

'Yes,' replied Stafford.

Jim's eyes glazed: he imagined navigating one of the personal subs he'd been reading about out of the old warehouse and into the river at high tide. The epic silliness of it made a wide grin spread slowly across his face. 'Whatever it costs I'll give ten times as much to Africa,' he said.

'Yes, sir, I know,' said Stafford.

'Maybe we could buy next door and knock it through.'

'I suppose after the recent incident they might take an offer.'

'Then I could have both mini-subs.'

Stafford looked doubtful.

Jim pulled out his Smartphone and checked for texts. Weeks had passed without a word from Jane. From the moment she had made sure he was out of trouble she had vanished off the radar. She was gone for good this time, he was sure of it. He stared at the blank screen for a few more seconds, then switched it off and returned it to his pocket.

Stafford was watching two men in hard hats walk along the highest gantry.

'Well,' said Jim, his reverie at an end, 'it'll be brilliant when it's finished.'

'Yes,' said Stafford. 'Quite a lair.'

70

It was a cool autumn day, the white fluffy clouds blown across the blue sky by a constant fresh wind.

Jenny, the chief archaeologist, was wearing a green Barbour as she scraped at the earth with her trowel. In front of her stood a great seventeenth-century mansion, its fancy red brick fascia and its black mullion windows basking in the warm light of the afternoon. The leaves on the mature trees in the grounds were starting to turn. She was daydreaming about the coming weekend when a little flash of gold grabbed her attention. She sat back on her kneepads. 'Got something.' She called again, louder this time, so that the others would hear: 'Got something.' Maybe whatever it was would keep their patron happy for a bit.

Well, Jimmy,' she said, chewing her Nicorette gum. 'It's over to you.'

Jim took the little teaspoon she offered him and knelt in the earth. He stared at the little blob of gold poking through the rich dark brown earth of the Elizabethan apothecary garden.

The sound of a distant car grinding up the long gravel drive broke his attention. He focused and flicked away some grains of earth. He dug a little more, and then a little more. He couldn't make out any design on the gold surface. Was it a coin? He sighed and sat back. He lifted up an old milk bottle top.

'Never mind,' said the archaeologist, 'maybe next time.'

A black Mercedes rolled past and stopped outside the main entrance.

Jim scrambled to his feet just as Akira got out with a case.

'Professor!' he shouted, waving. He trotted towards Akira. 'How are you?' He noticed that Akira's hair had turned completely white.

'I'm well,' he said. 'I bring you gifts from the Emperor.'

'Brilliant,' said Jim. 'What do you think of the new place?'

'Very nice,' said Akira, turning to admire the huge red-brick house and its ornamental parkland.

'I thought I should buy historic houses and dig them up,' said Jim. 'You know, turn them into my own archaeological digs.'

'Interesting,' said Akira. 'What have you found?'

'Bugger all,' said Jim, 'but it's early days yet. Come on in.'

His office was a huge book-lined room with a giant walnut desk in a bay window. 'I won't take too much of your valuable time,' said Akira, opening his bag. 'Can you help me with this?'

Jim helped him lift a gold box onto the desk. The golden sun rose over a golden coast. It felt heavier than he remembered. 'It's not, is it?' he said.

'No,' said Akira. 'It's a very beautiful reproduction. Sadly we have not been able to reproduce the mechanism as that would have added many months to the process. The top is released by a latch on the side.' He pressed a hidden button and lifted the lid.

He passed the necklace to Jim. It was as lovely as he remembered it. He put it on. It didn't feel the same – it lacked the almost imperceptible sensation of warmth. He took it off and laid it on the table. Akira passed him the mirror. The carving didn't seem so incredibly refined and the mirrored surface was perfect, clear and undistorted. Jim's chin wasn't nearly so rugged. He laughed. 'Thanks,' he said, smiling. 'It's a beaut. You shouldn't have gone to so much trouble.' He laid it down, tilted up on its lotus bud handle.

Akira gave him the sword. The sun was streaming in through the window and lit the room with a white light. He pulled it from its scabbard and held it up. He smiled, his heart suddenly pounding. The blade flashed, and outside a breath of wind blew through the trees. 'You didn't?' he said, his mouth falling open. The iridescent blade seemed to pulsate. 'You haven't, have you?'

'I was told by the Emperor to give you what you deserved,' said Akira.

'Bloody hell,' said Jim.

'The Emperor needs all the health and wisdom the heavens can offer.' He frowned. 'But does Japan need any more courage or valour? Does it need more warriors? Does it need war?'

'What am I meant to do with it?' said Jim, looking down at the shimmering blade.

'Hang it on your wall,' said Akira, 'and hope that you never need to take it down.'

Clem Chambers is CEO of ADVFN (www.advfn.com), Europe and South America's leading financial market website. Established in the last quarter of 1999, Chambers floated the company in 2000. The ADVFN website now has over 2,000,000 registered users who generate in excess of 300 million page impressions a month. ADVFN is the number one destination for UK private investors, who log on to view global market data and use the site's leading edge trading tools.

A broadcast and print media regular, Clem Chambers is a familiar face and frequent co-presenter on *CNBC* and *CNBC Europe*. He is a seasoned guest and market commentator on BBC News 24, Newsnight, *BBC 1, CNN, SKY News, TF1,* China's *Phoenix TV,* Canada's *Business News Network* and numerous US radio stations. He is renowned for calling the markets and predicted the end of the bull market back in January 2007 and the following crash. He has appeared on ITV's *News at Ten* and *Evening News* discussing failures in the banking system and featured prominently in the *Money Programme's Credit Crash Britain: HBOS — Breaking the Bank* and on the BBC's *City Uncovered: When Markets Go Mad.*

Clem Chambers has written investment columns for *Wired Magazine, The Daily Telegraph, The Daily Mail* and *The Daily Express* and currently writes for *The Scotsman* and *Forbes.* He was *The Alchemist* – stock tipster - in *The Business* for over three years and has been published in titles including: *CityAM, Investors Chronicle, Traders Magazine, Stocks and Commodities, the Channel 4 website, SFO* and *Accountancy Age.* He is a regular market commentator across the UK Press.

He has written two previous novels which can be purchased as ebooks or print books from all good bookshops/online retailers or from the publishers: www.noexit.co.uk/clemchambers

clemcham@advfn.com

http://twitter.com/clemchambers

http://en.wikipedia.org/wiki/Clem_Chambers

http://en.wikipedia.org/wiki/The_Twain_Maxim